Heart Trouble is an in-depth look at one woman's path through the landmine-infested quest to love.

With the title of *Heart Trouble* I should have expected the difficulties experienced by 27-year-old Jackie. I was expecting a romance, and instead was treated to the astounding journey Jackie experiences as she traverses her way through life. The book spans several years from Jackie being on her own when she moves away from home and her partner of four years. She has been on her own for three years when the book begins, and we live her life for the next year (1999) very closely with her. The bulk of the story takes place in that year.

I don't want to give any of the twists and turns this author brings to the novel except to say that the last few chapters is a rollercoaster I should have seen coming, but didn't.

The excellent humor in this book is what I have come to expect from this author. The writing and editing provide the reader with a novel that reads very fluidly.

~E. B. Mulligan, Amazon.com, August 27, 2006

"I love to see new names writing in the lesbian fiction genre, especially when they're as promising as this one. *Picture Perfect* by Jane Vollbrecht is pure formula, but she really makes the formula work. Vollbrecht does a masterful job of dealing with two seemingly incompatible plot issues—a parent with a debilitating illness and a romance between a driven, move-through-the ranks accountant and a laid-back (and drop-dead gorgeous) gardener, who wants nothing more than to live in the mountains and tend to her aging parents. The author delivers surprisingly mature, well-developed characters with depth and dimensionality, including such issues as a dead lover, guilt over being closeted at work, surviving in a 'good old boy' establishment, and much more. I thoroughly enjoyed this book and hope the author delivers an encore soon."

~K. Johnson, Amazon.com, October , 2005

How the romance (between Kate and Casey) develops and how problems are solved is the meat of *Picture Perfect*. If you enjoy reading romances about real people with real problems, this is the book for you.
~R. Lynn Watson, *Mega Scene*, June 3, 2005

In her first published novel, Jane Vollbrecht shows that with love and the will, there is a way to overcome adversity and even find romance when life events block the path. What should be a distressing look at how Alzheimer's type dementia wreaks havoc on a family is, in fact, a life-affirming account of how two brave women deal with a dreadful disease that afflicts their fathers. *Picture Perfect*, a worthy finalist for a 2005 GCLS Literary Award, has earned its place among books of substance. Vollbrecht is an author to watch, as she is getting off to an impressive start.

Picture Perfect is touching, sweet, believable, vivid, and has plenty of humor to keep it from being completely depressing. After all, Alzheimer's disease isn't a picnic. Vollbrecht does a fine job of tapping into the human condition and the emotions that accompany it in a well-written novel equipped with romance between memorable characters and well-plotted action. Dealing with ill parents is never easy for the children who end up switching roles with their elders, but Casey does an admirable job of taking on the arduous task with amazing strength and valor. Having Kate's help is the one thing Casey comes to count on, but can their love survive Kate's professional ambitions?

While *Picture Perfect* is a truly satisfying romance, it is not simply a glorified lesbian love story. By showing how love helps conquer all, or at least how it makes life's adversities more tolerable, Vollbrecht provides the reader with just the right mix of pathos, information, and narrative to bring the reader into the story.

With love scenes that don't need to be graphic to convey the intense love and lust between these two women, characters you'll become invested in, and a story with a moral that reminds us what's important in life, *Picture Perfect* proves that Jane Vollbrecht is an author who has already left her mark on lesbian fiction. I am looking forward to additional offerings by this talented and prolific author.
~Cheri Rosenberg, Midwest Book Review

In Broad Daylight

Jane Vollbrecht

Regal Crest

Nederland, Texas

ISBN 978-1-932300-76-5

First Printing 2007

9 8 7 6 5 4 3 2 1

Cover design by Katherine Smith

Published by:

Regal Crest Enterprises, LLC
4700 Highway 365, Suite A, PMB 210
Port Arthur, Texas 77642-8025

Find us on the World Wide Web at
http://www.regalcrest.biz

Printed in the United States of America

Acknowledgments

Lori L. Lake, an extraordinary editor and a fabulous friend, has my profound gratitude for her immeasurable assistance with this book. I treasure her for her insights, her wisdom, and for her boundless heart.

Katherine Smith of Byte Size Media once again produced an outstanding cover and also gave me the benefit of her suggestions for ways to revamp my early drafts of the manuscript. I am in her debt.

Cathy LeNoir, Publisher, Regal Crest Enterprises, granted me the creative freedom necessary to write this book. For that, and for all she does in giving my books a home, she has my sincere thanks.

As always, I would have been lost without the support and inspiration of my sister, Kathy, and my brothers, Paul and Tony. They say you can't pick your family, but I'd happily have picked all of them.

For Kelsey,
who gives me hope and so much more.

Some there be that shadows kiss;
Such have but a shadow's bliss.

William Shakespeare
The Merchant of Venice, Act II, Scene IX

Chapter One

Columbus, Georgia
March, 2005

"SEX SELLS, COLLEEN."

"I understand that, but all the sex scenes in the world won't save a lousy story."

"And for the audience that reads Triple S books," Elizabeth Albright said, "even the most engaging story won't sell a dozen copies without enough sex between the covers."

"Bed covers or book covers?" Colleen McCrady asked. A nervous twitch tugged at corners of her mouth as she eased back in her chair and looked at the owner and managing editor of Standing in Sappho's Shadow Publishing—or Triple S, as it was known around the industry—across the cluttered desk top.

"Both. In my experience, novels with some well placed love scenes sell far better than those without them." Elizabeth relaxed her shoulders and unclasped her hands.

"But I've always felt that subtle was better than explicit. I've been in a lot of writing classes, and the instructors always cautioned us to leave the bedroom scenes to the readers' imaginations."

"Those instructors probably didn't have much exposure to the world of lesbian fiction, did they?"

"No, I suppose not," Colleen said, "and I sure wasn't about to ask them. I know none of the course descriptions said anything about workshops on how to compose a sure-fire sex scene between two women."

"I'm not saying every book has to be an endless lust fest. In fact, for any Triple S book, I draw the line well before anything that I consider to be pornographic, but romance novels need—well—romance." Elizabeth studied Colleen's face and saw the doubts lingering there. "I've been publishing lesbian fiction for almost fifteen years. You've got to trust me on this. I know what's made this publishing house successful."

"Is that why you asked me to come in today? To tell me that I won't ever be a Sappho's Shadow author?"

"No, not exactly. I don't usually discuss manuscripts with prospective authors, but I've made an exception in your case."

Colleen blushed. Elizabeth did her best to ignore it. "Since you live right up the road in LaGrange, I thought it might work well for you to meet with me here at Triple S's office so we could talk about your work."

"Your office manager called on Monday and asked if I could make a ten o'clock appointment with you today, but she didn't tell me much more than that."

"You've sent us three manuscripts—"

Colleen interrupted. "Actually, it's four." Then she blushed again.

"Okay, four manuscripts." Elizabeth pulled a single sheet of paper from a stack by her elbow and skimmed it. "My first-read reviewers have told me about your books. Your writing is technically perfect. Your style is professional without being dramatic or contrived. Your story lines grab and hold the readers' attention. Your characters are engaging and believable. But every time they finish one of your manuscripts, they have the same deal-breaker reaction. You don't include enough amorous exchanges between the leading ladies for them to recommend it for publication."

"I'm sorry, but I'm still not sure exactly what you're trying to tell me." Colleen leaned forward in her chair and fixed her gaze on Elizabeth.

Inexplicably, Elizabeth caught herself thinking of leprechauns— kind, generous, inscrutable leprechauns. The green of Colleen's eyes was reminiscent of the hue from a shamrock that's fading a bit—a soft green, with gold around the edges. Elizabeth had to remind herself she was in a serious business conversation and forced herself to look away from those rich, inviting eyes. She stared at the sheet of paper again while she brought her wandering thoughts under control.

"The usual order of events here is that if my staff readers think a book should be put under contract, they forward it to me. I review it to see if I agree, and then I make the final decision. If they don't like a submission, they send the manuscript back to the author with a standard rejection letter."

"I could probably recite that letter word for word." Colleen laughed self-deprecatingly.

Elizabeth used her most reassuring tone. "After my readers finished your most recent submission last week, they broke one of my standing rules by sending it to me, even though they weren't recommending that Triple S make you an offer."

"Why did they do that?"

"Because they think I'm missing out on the chance to publish someone who could become a very successful author."

This time, Colleen blushed so deeply that Elizabeth couldn't let it pass without remarking on it. "Don't be embarrassed, Colleen. If my staff is willing to risk a blast of what I'm told is my 'notorious Albright ire' by urging me to take a look at your rejected book, it must be pretty special." Elizabeth opened the bottom drawer of her desk and pulled out a thick bundle. "My assistant arranged your meeting with me so I can give you suggestions on how to take this book—which would have earned you your fourth rejection notice—and with a few fairly simple changes, make it something that carries the Triple S logo and earns you the title of published author."

Colleen could hardly believe her ears. "I don't know what to say. I mean, if you don't usually talk to writers..."

"Oh, I talk to writers all the time, but for the most part, it's authors I have contracts with. If I gave feedback or commentary on every book we opt to kick to the curb, I wouldn't have time for anything else. But when I read this one," Elizabeth laid the palm of her hand on the manuscript she'd taken from her desk, "I felt like it was worth the investment."

"Gosh, Ms. Albright—"

Elizabeth lifted her hand from the book and held it toward Colleen. "No, please, call me Elizabeth. 'Ms. Albright' makes me sound like some suburban housewife with two kids and a mini van."

"Okay, Elizabeth, then. I take it that means you liked my book." Elizabeth saw the look on Colleen's face which, loosely translated, said she wished she had some way to control what was beginning to feel like a lifelong crimson hue on her cheeks.

Elizabeth resisted the images of leprechauns that once again sprang to mind. Colleen's look of open, honest eagerness gave Elizabeth the sense of satisfaction that came whenever she remembered why she wanted to open a lesbian publishing house in the first place.

"Yes, I like this book." Elizabeth laid the cover page aside. "Your title, *Scrapbook*, is right on the mark, given the way you use newspaper articles about the protagonist's mother for your flashback scenes. I'm always pleased to see a writer write about slightly more mature women—women who have some significant life experiences and who have come to understand that 'free lunch' is only a marketing ploy. You managed to take a difficult subject and use it as a medium to build a touching love story. When I read the opening section, I wondered how this could possibly turn out to be about two women falling in love, but you did it. I was impressed with the way you used the mother's situation—a moderately famous dancer who was now forced to use a wheelchair after a skiing accident—as the catalyst for your protagonists' involvement." She stole a glance at Colleen, who was beaming. "I was glad that neither of your primary characters was crazy or needy or incapable of functioning on her own. They were strong women who got stronger from loving each other. But—"

"But they didn't hit the sack and talk dirty."

Elizabeth laughed brightly. "I was going to say but I had to rely on your telling me that they loved each other instead of having you show me by what they did and what they said."

"Same idea, different words."

"Yes and no." Elizabeth flipped forward to a sticky note she had left protruding some thirty pages into the manuscript. "Look at this situation...." She rotated the manuscript around so Colleen could see what she was referring to. "No, wait, then I can't see it. Bring your chair around here so we can look at this together."

Colleen scooted around and sat side by side with Elizabeth.

"Here." Elizabeth pointed to a sentence. "*And Caitlin knew the broken clock in her heart could finally start marking the passage of time again.*" Elizabeth glanced at Colleen's profile. Colleen met Elizabeth's gaze. "It's a great line—it conveys lots of emotion and it makes me want to keep reading, but when I turn the page, you've jumped to a scene about the mother's anger at being in the wheelchair. I feel cheated out of what happened between Caitlin and LuAnn. If the clock in Caitlin's heart is keeping time again, I know they did something—I can feel it—but they went off stage and whispered sweet nothings to one another, and I didn't get to witness it. This is a perfect place for an intimate interaction between your heroines."

"I don't think they should have sex yet," Colleen said as she folded her arms across her chest.

"So don't have them do 'the big it' yet, but they could have a nice date, a romantic dinner, a long, meaningful conversation at home on the sofa while sharing a bottle of wine. They could go for a walk or give each other backrubs. Something—anything—to keep your readers on board with you about the relationship between these two probable lovers. They want Caitlin and LuAnn to be a couple. Give them a taste of what's to come."

Colleen uncrossed her arms and reached for a pencil on the desk. "Can I make some notes while we talk?"

"Sure."

Colleen wrote in the margin, "Warm this part up. Concert in the park? Home-cooked meal? SHOW the budding romance."

Elizabeth saw what Colleen had written. *She gets it! She understands what she needs to do.*

Elizabeth spent the next two hours working through the

manuscript page by page. Colleen scribbled reminders to herself at every place Elizabeth pointed out a problem or plot hole.

"And you did a great job working the word 'scrapbook' into this last bit of dialogue. It gives a sense of completion to the story," Elizabeth said as she flipped the final page onto the stack. "This could be a real barnburner of a book."

Colleen hung her tongue out of her mouth in mock exhaustion. "Whew. I've got a lot of work to do."

"I don't want to scare you off, but this is only the first phase. If I offer you a contract on *Scrapbook* after your rewrite, then you'll still have to go through the whole editing process before it will be ready to send to the printer." Elizabeth gathered the pages together into a neat stack and slipped a large rubber band around it.

"I don't dare think about that yet. I've got too much to do just from what you've shown me today."

Elizabeth slid the manuscript toward Colleen. Colleen rose from her chair, picked up the manuscript, and held it against her chest. "I truly appreciate all the help you've given me, Elizabeth. I'm going to get started on this as soon as I get home. "

"You're welcome." Elizabeth pushed back from the desk and reached out for a handshake. "But remember, I run a publishing company. Books are my bread and butter, so I have ulterior motives."

ELIZABETH LOVED HER work. She spent every day surrounded by lesbians in love. Sure, they were lesbians on the pages of assorted works of fiction, but still, what a way to make a living. In the seventies and eighties, Elizabeth worked as an editor for one of the pioneer alternative life style presses. The books she reviewed were solid lesbian romances—and in her opinion, a little too predictable and formulaic. Every time she approached the managing editor about breaking out of the mold with some edgier offerings, she was reminded that her job was to sharpen her blue pencil and refrain from rocking the boat. Then in 1989, Elizabeth came into a tidy inheritance when her parents died. She was the only child of a stock broker and his Daughters of the Confederacy wife from a sixth-generation Atlanta family.

"Now you can finally start your own independent press," her lover, Alana Montaigne, had said to her, "and I won't have to listen to you carp about the lackluster options coming out of the lesbian fiction houses."

Why not? Elizabeth had almost twenty years of experience in the business and bucks in the bank to back the venture, so she and Alana started Standing in Sappho's Shadow Publishing on a dream and a dare.

Alana wasn't merely the woman who encouraged Elizabeth to open her business; she was also the only woman Elizabeth had ever loved. They had been together seventeen years when they launched Sappho's Shadow. Elizabeth was sure that they'd be partners, business and personal, for all their lives, but four years into their endeavor as publishers, Alana discovered that the artist who designed their book covers was as good a lay as she was at layouts, and Elizabeth and Alana's partnership hit the shoals and sank. Even though Alana hadn't contributed much to the company financially, she convinced Elizabeth that a handsome buy-out—to the tune of fifty thousand dollars—was the shortest route to a quick and easy dissolution of their entanglements.

It was only money.

Elizabeth would have gladly paid double that if it would have eased the anguish of Alana's betrayal. Elizabeth's father had always told her it's impossible to hang a price tag on a necessary life lesson. She usually regarded her father's view as unassailable, but thanks to Alana Montaigne, for tuition of fifty thousand dollars, Elizabeth learned that her business life and her personal life must always be kept totally separate and that no woman would ever be worth putting herself or her business at risk for that kind of punishment— fiscal and emotional—again. Nope, never again.

For the past decade, Elizabeth's only mistress, lover, and passion had been Triple S Publishing. She would gladly have it continue that way for decades to come.

ELIZABETH HEARD A knock at her door and looked up.

Toni, Elizabeth's office manager, stepped into the office and asked, "How was your meeting with Colleen McCrady?"

"Good, but you know I ought to chew you a new one for pulling that end-around maneuver on me. By the time you told me you'd asked her to come in to meet with me, it was too late for me to overrule you on it." She wagged her index finger at Toni. "You know you're my best first-read reviewer. I count on you to play by the rules."

"Three hundred sixty-four-and-a-half days a year, I do, boss," Toni said, amicably. "Admit it. She writes some kick-ass stuff, doesn't she?"

"Definitely better than average."

"So I guess I won't need to find a good proctologist to stitch up my new butt hole."

"Not this time, but don't think you can get away with yanking my chain any time you feel like it."

"I wouldn't dream of it, your highness."

Elizabeth rolled her eyes. "Was there something else you wanted or were you merely checking on whether you should be expecting your severance pay with this week's salary?"

"I've got four new manuscripts I think you should see. Alex, Joanie and I all think they deserve the Elizabeth Albright stamp of approval."

"Haul 'em on in here." Elizabeth looked at the clock above the open doorway. "I should be able to knock off at least one of them before I leave today."

Toni returned shortly, her arms loaded with manuscripts. "When are we gonna do these reviews electronically online? We kill a tree a day with all the paper we use around here." She dropped the collection on Elizabeth's desk.

"It's in the works, kiddo. Rome wasn't built in a day."

"You would know. Weren't you there for the ribbon cutting?"

"I'm not nearly as ancient as you make me out to be."

"Maybe, but the dry cleaner called to tell you your togas are ready."

"If you're thinking of making stand-up comedy your career, I'd advise against giving up your day job for a while yet."

"They say losing your sense of humor is one of the first signs of old age."

"One more wise crack about the number of candles on my birthday cake, and I'm going to reconsider my decision not to chew you a new opening."

Toni took a step toward the door. "I'll go back to my duty of making the world safe for lesbian readers." Toni gestured to the heap she'd deposited in front of Elizabeth. "Enjoy."

"I'm sure I will."

Elizabeth tugged the top book from the stack. *Delicious Indiscretions* by Lenore Quisling she read on the cover. Elizabeth hastened through the first two chapters. Chapter three detailed a steamy tryst in a trailer at a rodeo. Lenore did a good job describing the physical characteristics of the two women and their various gymnastics while doing the wild thing on a lumpy mattress. Neither of the characters had green eyes, an Irish name, nor any resemblance whatsoever to leprechauns.

So why the deuce was Colleen McCrady the only woman she could picture?

SHE LIKES MY book, she likes my book, she likes my book, she likes my book. Colleen repeated the words—sang the words, chanted the words, prayed the words, shouted the words, whispered the words— as she drove from Columbus to LaGrange.

She could hear Elizabeth Albright's voice giving her pointers on specific rewrites for fixing *Scrapbook*. Her mind was racing with the possibilities. *I could be a published author under the Triple S logo.* She thumped her fist on the steering wheel as soaring hope raced through her. By the time she pulled into the driveway of her house on Orchard Hill Lane, she already had several sections tentatively reworked in her head.

Once inside, the first order of business was to call the administrative offices of the local school system. She was a substitute teacher. She could work almost every day if she chose to, but she usually accepted just enough days to stay in the good graces of the principal. Now that she was hot on the task of fine tuning *Scrapbook,* the heck with molding young minds; she had a book to write.

Through the wonder of telecommuting, Colleen also freelanced articles for the alternative culture publications in the Atlanta gay and lesbian community. She sent e-mails to the editors at "Creative Loafing" and "Southern Voice" and asked to be taken off the call list for ad hoc articles until further notice.

In 1994, Colleen had inherited a number of assets from her family. Through what she labeled nothing more than dumb luck, she had invested the proceeds in several stocks that paid very nice returns. She also had steady payments from a rental property back in the Midwest, so making an income from selling her novels wasn't Colleen's first priority. She loved the feel of creating stories and having characters grow into themselves. She always said she would write books even if they never made a dime for her. What drove Colleen was the journey—the craft of putting words together in the perfect combination—and not the destination of a royalty check.

Buster and Muggins, the mixed breed strays that she had adopted at the Troup County animal shelter four years earlier, barked at the back door. They had been outside in the fenced yard enjoying the early spring sunshine since Colleen's departure for Columbus at eight-thirty. Now that she was home, though, they wanted to come inside and lounge with their person.

"All right, you two. C'mon." Colleen stepped aside as they charged in side by side. Their frantic movements all but caused them to wedge themselves in the doorway. "If you took turns coming through the door, you wouldn't always have bruised ribs, you know."

Muggins, a smallish black and white wire-haired terrier and who-knew-what-all-else dog, scampered around her feet doing what Colleen called his happy feet dance. He barely kept one foot on the floor while he gyrated and wiggled.

Buster—Buster Brown, when he had done something bad and Colleen called him by his full name—had gone directly to his food bowl beside the refrigerator on the off chance he'd missed a bite of kibble at breakfast or that Colleen had put his evening puppy chow down several hours early. The look of disappointment on his face as he looked from his empty bowl to his heartless owner made Colleen laugh. The square, boxer-like head perched on his long, hound-dog body with its slightly bulging belly always caused Colleen to describe him as a study in geometric contrast.

She dropped down on the kitchen floor and leaned her back against the cupboard. Both dogs hustled over to flop down beside her, one on either side. "Listen up, boys. You're going to have to entertain each other for the next couple of weeks. I've got a big writing project that's going to keep me tied to my computer for a while. If everything goes all right, when it's all done, I'll buy you each an extra big rawhide treat and a new squeaky toy, okay?" She tugged on Buster's ears and scratched Muggins on his back, right where his tail joined his body.

Family time didn't last long. *Scrapbook* called to her like a siren, and she was powerless to resist. Ten minutes later, she was in her sweat clothes sitting in front of the monitor on the desk in the second bedroom, cutting and pasting her manuscript for all she was worth. She had one goal, and one goal only: prove to Elizabeth Albright that she could turn *Scrapbook* into a release they would both be proud of.

Funny how the prospect of hearing Elizabeth tell her, "Good job, Colleen," made her knees go rubbery and her stomach flip.

Chapter
Two

"THANKS FOR MAKING the drive, Colleen. It's nice to see you again." Elizabeth was standing beside her desk at Triple S Publishing.

"It's nice to see you, too. It's an easy trip from LaGrange, so no problem."

"Sit down, won't you?" Elizabeth walked behind her desk and sat as well.

"I was very surprised when you called this morning and asked if I could come down." Colleen looked at the charcoal drawings depicting the covers of three of May Sarton's books on the wall behind Elizabeth, buying time while she summoned her courage. "I screwed up my rewrite of *Scrapbook,* didn't I?"

Elizabeth lifted her chin toward the ceiling and laughed out loud. "Hardly. If that were the case, would I be making you an offer to publish it?"

"What?" Colleen jumped up from her chair with a look on her face that said she was ten years old and had just won a pony at the county fair.

"I don't seem to do a very good job of sticking to my own policies when it comes to your books. What typically happens is I send an e-mail to the author with the terms of the contract. We work out any differences through cyberspace or on the telephone, and I drop the finalized document in the mail for signature."

Colleen returned to her chair and perched on the edge. "But this time—"

"But this time I thought it would be nice to have a civilized conversation with a woman I hope becomes one of Triple S's most popular writers. Congratulations, Colleen, and welcome to the group that stands in Sappho's shadow." Elizabeth reached across her desk and offered the contract printed on letterhead paper. "Of course, you'll want some time to look it over. We can iron out any details after you've had a chance to review the terms I've outlined."

"Oh, I'm sure it will be fine, Elizabeth."

"No, I insist you read every word of it and push back at me on anything that doesn't make sense or seem fair."

"All right. Do you need this back today?" Colleen riffled through the eight-page document.

"Of course not. Take it home. Read it, then read it again. Sleep on it. Let me know if you have questions or counterproposals."

"Okay. I will." Colleen was still radiant, her checks flushed and glowing. "Thank you. Thank you so much. I wish I had words to tell you what this means to me." Somehow, her smile grew even bigger. She stood and took a step toward the door.

"If you don't have to get back to LaGrange right away, I hoped you might let me take you out for a celebratory drink."

Colleen stopped in her tracks. "Sure. That would be great."

"I suppose I should tell you—"

"Wait, let me guess." Colleen lowered her head as if to tell a secret. "You don't usually do this with your authors."

With a smile to match Colleen's, Elizabeth joined Triple S's newest addition and walked out into the warm summer sun.

THE CONGRATULATORY DRINK lasted a little longer than either of them expected.

They left Elizabeth's office at four o'clock Friday afternoon and went to the bar at the Cork and Cleaver. Elizabeth toasted Colleen's prowess as a writer; Colleen returned the favor and toasted Elizabeth's success as a publisher. Two loquacious bibliophiles didn't need much encouragement to get into a long discussion about the current state of literature in America. When Elizabeth proposed dinner—after all, they were already at a restaurant—Colleen accepted. She calculated that Buster and Muggins would be fine 'til at least nine, and her watch read only five-thirty.

She and Elizabeth were deep in debate over *The Secret Life of Bees* when Colleen next noticed the time. "I hate to do this, but I need to go. It's an hour's drive back to LaGrange, and my dogs are counting on me to get there before the whites of their eyes turn yellow." Colleen dug in her hip pocket for her credit card.

"This is my treat, remember? And I'm sorry you feel you need to leave." Elizabeth laid her hand on Colleen's as she reached for the check. Colleen lifted her eyes and locked them on Elizabeth's face. Elizabeth suddenly felt as flustered as a virgin at a pornography convention. She fumbled for something coherent to say. "Besides, I wanted to hear your assessment about Sue Monk Kidd's treatment of the implied romance between the black boy and the main character."

"We could talk about it some more back at my place, but it's a bit of a drive." Colleen's voice was so soft Elizabeth could barely make out the words.

"Could I follow you?"

"WHEN YOU TOLD me sex sells, is this the sort of thing you had in mind?" Colleen murmured into Elizabeth's damp, tangled mane of hair.

"Don't you dare sell it or auction it or barter it or give it away—not to anyone but me."

Back at the house in LaGrange, Colleen had shooed Buster and Muggins to the back yard. Elizabeth had waited in the living room for Colleen to return from her dog mom duties. In less than two minutes, shoes, socks, blouses, slacks, glasses, were lying wherever they had landed as they yielded to the consuming attraction for each other. Both were completely naked by the time they made their way to the bedroom. What felt like only two heartbeats later, they were lying together as though they had done so for years.

"Is this your usual way of welcoming a new author?" Colleen asked, trying to sound sincere.

Elizabeth stifled a chortle. "Not by a damn sight." For a moment, she was shocked at what had happened. *At least I wrote the contract before I invited her to dinner, and I didn't let the fact that she's the most gorgeous woman in the world sway me into accepting her book for publication.*

Colleen eased up along Elizabeth's torso so that they were lying side by side. "I'll have to remember that gambit about starting a discussion of a book and then suggesting it be continued at the unsuspecting lady's home when the hour draws too late."

"I'm not quick enough on my feet to have planned this. Besides, I'm afraid books are going the way of the dinosaurs. Another decade—two at most—and bookstores will be as extinct as record albums. Everybody wants everything in instantaneous sound bites these days."

"Plato complained about the decay of society way back when, but we've managed to endure. Who knows what will happen even ten minutes from now let alone in the next ten years?" Colleen thought that they might be on the verge of a deep, philosophical discussion, but Elizabeth's next comment made her forget she'd ever so much as heard of the ancient postulators.

"I know something that I'd like to have happen in the next ten minutes." Elizabeth ever so gently rocked her pelvis against Colleen's upper thigh. Colleen picked up the rhythm and joined in the horizontal dance.

"You know," Colleen said, "old broads like us ought to be mindful of arthritic joints and fragile bones." Colleen was losing the battle of keeping her yearnings in check.

"Old broads? Broads, maybe, but hardly old," Elizabeth scoffed. "I'm forty-eight and you're—how old are you?"

"Fifty-three."

"See? We've got another thirty years before I'm willing to own that label." She moved her hand from the back of Colleen's head and raked her fingers back and forth along the base of Colleen's neck. Spontaneously, every cell in Colleen's body—or so it seemed to Elizabeth—quivered with arousal.

"Let me do you first this time, love," Colleen begged, an edge of supplication in her voice.

"I'm so slow to get to the finish line," Elizabeth hedged.

"No, I adore every minute. It will give me that much more time to enjoy you." Colleen gently pushed her fingertips into the inviting lips between Elizabeth's legs.

Elizabeth abandoned any further arguments as Colleen amazed her with her skills as a lover. Elizabeth drifted away as the magician beside her on the bed conjured up responses and reactions from her that she had thought were lost to her forever. Her stomach somersaulted in excitement as Colleen tenderly pulled her nipples into her warm, alluring mouth.

"You could be a poster child for Aer Lingus," Elizabeth mused.

Colleen paused only long enough to reply. "Welcome aboard. I can't wait to see how high we can take you."

Elizabeth went on with her inventory of her lover's attributes. Colleen's skin was milky white, almost translucent. A dusting of delicate freckles was scattered across her face. Her hair was beyond strawberry blonde, but not quite red, with highlights and undertones that made it look like it was lit from every possible direction. She kept her hair close-cropped in hopes of keeping some of the curls at bay. And those eyes—those magnificent green eyes—kind and innocent and intriguing. If she stretched real tall, she might be five foot five. Elizabeth was surprised that someone who looked so delicate and fine-boned could be so powerful. When she was wrapped in Colleen's arms, she felt like she was protected by an invincible shield.

Elizabeth's reverie in savoring Colleen's beauty was interrupted. She said, "Oh, sweetest, that feels so good." Colleen slid down Elizabeth's body and snuggled between her legs.

"Soon, my darling, soon." Elizabeth labored to utter the words. And then—an explosion that left Elizabeth wondering where it had come from and how the house could still be standing around her. Unbidden, tears eased down her face as Colleen raised herself up and dropped down, weightless as a breath of air, on top of her chest.

"Why the tears, love?" Colleen brushed a drop from Elizabeth's cheek.

"Because some things are simply too far beyond words." She squeezed Colleen tightly to her.

Colleen kissed the edge of Elizabeth's collar bone. "Good thing neither of us tries to make a living as a wordsmith then."

The humor was right for the moment. They lay contentedly wrapped around one another, listening to the sounds of each other's breathing.

"I think it's your turn now," Elizabeth whispered.

"I was hoping you might make that offer." Colleen raised Elizabeth's upper leg slightly so that it fit between her own and leaned in hard against it. "Sorry I'm such a one-trick pony," she moaned as the pressure brought her near orgasm.

"I'm only along for the ride, darling," Elizabeth assured her. "Let it happen whenever you want to."

Colleen told herself she'd hold back, postpone the gratification, savor the sensation, but the point of no return was upon her, and she felt the release flooding through her. How could this woman she barely knew elicit such a reaction—exhilaration so new, yet so familiar? She crashed over the top and folded against Elizabeth's body, limp but euphoric.

The spent lovers soon slipped into a motionless slumber. Elizabeth awakened first, Colleen still half atop her as she had been when they finished their lovemaking.

"What time is it?" Colleen asked as she stirred.

"Too late for me to go back to Columbus."

"Good. I'd rather have you here with me."

"HOW CAN THE weekend be almost over already?' Colleen lay as tightly against Elizabeth as the laws of physics allowed.

"I know what you mean. Seems like only a minute ago it was mid-afternoon Friday and I was asking you if you stay and have a drink with me to celebrate your first contract. Now, it's almost seven o'clock Sunday evening."

"I suppose not leaving this bedroom in the past forty-eight hours for more than ten minutes at a pop might have something to do with the telescoping of time." Colleen traced each bone in Elizabeth's ribcage.

"I used to think I was ticklish, but when you do that, it feels like angel kisses." A small shudder escaped as Elizabeth spoke. "I wish I could stay here with you like this forever."

"I'm not kicking you out."

"Glad to hear that, but Triple S won't run itself."

"How did you start your company anyway?" Colleen felt Elizabeth tense slightly. "I'm sorry. I guess I'm being presumptuous to ask."

"No, it's okay, Colleen. I guess for the past two days I've sort of forgotten that I'm a publisher and you're one of my authors."

"Do you regret the offer?"

"To publish your book or to buy you a drink?"

Colleen couldn't place what she was hearing in Elizabeth's voice. At a minimum, she sensed Elizabeth was trying a little too hard to be flippant. "We both can see what came of the invitation to lift a glass. Maybe you'd better tell me how you feel about putting *Scrapbook* under contract."

"I tell you what." Elizabeth pulled away from Colleen's embrace. "Let's make a pact. We won't discuss business unless we're both wearing clothes and in an upright position."

"Which probably also means you don't want us making love on top of your desk in Columbus."

Elizabeth's eyes flew open wide at the mere mention of such a thing.

"Seriously, I would like to know the history of Standing in Sappho's Shadow—not as a nosy new author there, but as your—your..."

"As my infinitely sweet lover, perhaps?"

"Yes, that's one way to put it." Colleen knew she was red from the base of her neck to the tops of her ears. "Maybe we could get dressed and sit in the living room and talk for a while before you go back to Columbus."

"All right." Elizabeth stood and grabbed her blouse. Colleen watched as Elizabeth slipped into her clothes. Elizabeth carried herself like a jock, shoulders squared to the world. Some might call the way Elizabeth walked a strut, but Colleen saw it as a purposeful stride. From the tone in her muscles, Colleen surmised that Elizabeth probably had been quite an athlete in years gone by, but because she spent most of her time behind a desk these days, her once rock-solid muscles were now less "rock" and more "rock and roll." Colleen liked the look.

Elizabeth was something of a gentle Butch, strong but not overpowering. Her dark brown hair showed a silver streak here and there, but Elizabeth didn't seem the type to rush to the Lady Clairol aisle. A few tiny crow's feet—laugh lines—edged the corners of her eyes and mouth. Colleen saw them as endearing and thought they suited her. Elizabeth's eyes were such a light brown that Colleen had looked at them many times over the past couple of days to decide if "brown" was actually an appropriate description.

She liked the fact that Elizabeth was taller than she was, nearly five-eight. Both times she had seen Elizabeth at work, she was wearing the sleeves of her blouses rolled up a turn or two. The style showed off Elizabeth's hands and forearms, and now that Colleen knew all marvelous things Elizabeth could do with those hands, she decided that was the only way Elizabeth should wear her sleeves.

"Something on your mind?" Elizabeth's question brought Colleen back from her reverie.

"No, merely enjoying the view."

"I think mine is better." Elizabeth cast an appreciative glance at Colleen's still-naked body.

"Guess I'd better get dressed, too, if I want to have that discussion about the genesis of Standing in Sappho's Shadow."

Elizabeth worked her feet into her loafers. "Do you want me to put the dogs out?"

"That would be great. Thanks. And if you don't mind, scoop some dry food into their bowls. I'll pull my clothes on and meet you in the living room in a few minutes."

ELIZABETH FELT AN involuntary seizing in her gut as she walked to the kitchen to deal with Buster and Muggins. How could everything be both so simple and so complicated? Fact: She was falling head over heels for Colleen McCrady. Fact: She had offered Colleen McCrady a contract with Triple S Publishing. Fact: Triple S's other authors might well take a dim view of the owner and editor-in-chief sharing pillows with one of her authors. Fact: She and Colleen had transgressed some major business boundaries. Bigger fact: If she rescinded her contract with Colleen to allow her to take her books to another publishing house, she could lose the most promising new author she's encountered in years. Biggest fact of all: she was on the verge of doing the one thing she had promised herself she would never do again — let her business life and her personal life within a hundred miles of one another. And how about the fact that she knew next to nothing about Colleen McCrady in the first place? Oh, sure, she had written some entrancing novels, and in the bedroom, she could make Elizabeth's body react like she was a hot jock in college again, but was that any reason to put her heart — and her company — out on the auction block?

Triple S Publishing could certainly benefit from having a new, talented author. And Elizabeth Albright could certainly benefit from having a living, breathing lover instead of accounting ledgers and marketing strategies to cuddle up with night after lonely night. Problem was Colleen McCrady could easily satisfy either of those needs. *Damn it all to blazes, Elizabeth, don't set yourself up for the sure disaster of expecting Colleen to fill both roles.*

But how would she decide which option to pursue? Colleen the lover or Colleen the author? And what if the cost of the one she picked proved to be too high?

Worse yet, what if Colleen wanted what Elizabeth couldn't permit — to be both lover and author?

As she filled the dogs' food bowls, she acknowledged she had been premature in congratulating herself on offering Colleen the book contract before acting on her attraction to her. Now she didn't know if what she might have with Colleen was fish or fowl. Their relationship was already beginning to feel suspiciously like a herring with wings or an eagle with gills.

COLLEEN CLAIMED A seat on the sofa next to Elizabeth. "Okay, now tell me all about how Elizabeth Albright, the person, became Standing in Sappho's Shadow, the publishing company."

"It's a tale of riches to riches."

"How so?"

"Both of my parents came from established Atlanta families. My dad died in 1988 and my mom the year after that. As the legal documents say, I was their only issue. I had a plump bank account and a dream about broadening the horizons of lesbian fiction."

"So all on your own, you set up a new publishing house?"

"No, I had a partner."

"Oh?"

"Her name was Alana Montaigne." Elizabeth paused a bit too long.

"Not only your business partner, I take it?"

Elizabeth looked away before answering. "Guilty as charged. But it's been over for a long time. We parted ways over ten years ago."

"I see." Colleen struggled to overcome the jealousy that suddenly swelled in her. "Tell me more about what you wanted to do about — what was the expression you used? — broadening the horizons of lesbian fiction."

"I used to work for Brazen Girls Press."

"The mother ship of alternative books."

"Right. After I graduated from Brown with my English degree, I tried working at some of the mainstream houses in New York, but both the city and the books made me nuts. For an eighty percent cut in salary, I hooked up with Brazen Girls in North Carolina and edited there for fifteen years."

"Brazen Girls is still going strong. They must put out thirty books a year. Not that they had any use for mine, you understand —

and I've got the rejection slips to prove it. But I still don't understand what you wanted to accomplish."

"I'm not knocking Brazen Girls. They've got a loyal reader base, and they're a well run company, but they want all their books to be plain vanilla. Any time something came in with the littlest bit of potentially controversial content, they wanted it edited out."

"Like what?" Colleen leaned forward so she could scratch Muggins who was trying to convince her to play tug-o-war with the old knotted up sock he'd brought her.

"No interracial couples, no serious illnesses, nothing that dealt with complicated, untidy life issues like sick parents or incest."

"Sunshine, lollipops, and rainbows, huh?"

"That about sums it up."

"That gives me a much better idea about why they turned down all my submissions."

"I'm sure. From what I've seen of your books, your characters have too many quirks and flaws to fit Brazen Girls' mold."

"But you still want the books you publish to have steamy sex escapades in them sufficient to melt the crotches out of the leather underwear in every lesbian's wardrobe."

"I've found that it helps to have that be one facet of the books I publish. But first and foremost, I want books with lesbian heroines who triumph over tragedy and prevail in spite of devastating loss. I look for women who know life isn't always peaches and cream. I think Triple S's readers draw strength and inspiration from characters who pick themselves up and keep going even when it would be easier to give up."

"And then fall into bed and live happily ever after, in the updated lesbian version of Snow White meets Cinderella." Colleen tossed Muggins's sock across the room and nuzzled in close to Elizabeth again.

"Doesn't seem like a bad idea, does it?" Elizabeth returned Colleen's embrace.

"No. What seems like a bad idea is you going back to Columbus and leaving me here with two attention-starved dogs." Colleen offered a kiss that Elizabeth hungrily accepted.

"If we're done talking about business for a while..."

"Your desk is seventy miles away, so there's no danger of us being caught *in flagrante delicto* on top of it."

"You know, I could spend the night here and drive back to Columbus tomorrow morning in the daylight."

"Come with me, Snow White." Colleen stood, then pulled Elizabeth to her feet.

"Right behind you, Cinderella."

"GOOD MORNING, COLLIE."

"I don't usually let anyone call me that, but it sounds nice coming from you." Colleen lay atop Elizabeth for the third morning in a row. "And good morning, yourself. Does everyone always call you 'Elizabeth,' or do you go by something else sometimes?"

"I hate 'Betty,' and I'm not all that fond of 'Liz,' either."

"How about 'Liza'?"

"I don't remember anyone ever addressing me that way."

"What's your middle name?"

"Jane. Why?"

"Elizabeth is a good name for you—it suits you. But when we're all wrapped up in each other, I'd like to call you something that sounds a little less formal, so I'm trying to come up with something you'll like." Colleen traced Elizabeth's jaw line. "I know. How about LJ?"

"LJ?"

"Uh, huh. For Liza Jane."

"That's sweet. No one has ever wanted me to have a nickname before." She tugged gently on Colleen's earlobe. "And now that we have my secret bedroom identity established, I absolutely have to hit the road soon."

"I know. So far, our drink to celebrate my contract has lasted a little over sixty hours. I'd keep you here another sixty, and sixty more after that, if I could. I'd like to get some more practice calling you 'LJ.'"

"I'd stay if it were possible." Elizabeth luxuriated in the sensation of Colleen's body in full frontal contact with hers. "You realize, of course, that not only have you given me a new name, you also know almost every detail of my life, but I know absolutely nothing about yours."

Colleen rolled off Elizabeth and plumped up her pillows. "A lackluster tale, I assure you."

"Let me be the judge of that. I'm in the publishing business, you know." Elizabeth turned on her side and looped her arm over Colleen's midsection.

"I've heard rumors to that effect."

"So what's the Colleen McCrady story?"

"That's too broad a topic. Narrow your search criteria."

Now that's unusual. Give most people that opening and they'll gnaw your ears off with details from kindergarten to two seconds ago.

"Okay. Where are your parents?"

"In the cemetery of the First Presbyterian Church in my home town. Mom died in seventy-eight and dad in eighty-three."

"So you're an orphan like me." Elizabeth gave Colleen a quick hug. "Siblings?"

"Just me."

"Another thing we have in common."

"Uh huh."

"Where did you grow up?"

"We had a farm in central Minnesota."

Sheesh. This is like pulling chicken's teeth. "Education?"

"I went to college in Moorhead, Minnesota. I've got a B.S. in history and English."

"How did you end up in LaGrange, Georgia?"

Colleen laced her fingers with Elizabeth's. "After college, I decided I was sick of the crappy winters up there, and I lucked up and got a teaching job in Atlanta. But Atlanta in the mid-seventies was a much more bearable place. About five years ago, I'd had as much of life as I could stand in the fastest growing city in the South and moved down here. I can still get there if I need to, but I try not to need to very often."

"That makes something else we have in common. When I was setting up my company, I left Atlanta and moved to Columbus for the same reason." Elizabeth stifled a yawn. "Sorry. I'm used to getting more than twenty minutes of sleep a night."

"I didn't hear you complaining the last three nights, Ms. LJ Albright." Colleen poked Elizabeth gently in the ribs.

"I'm not complaining now, merely stating a fact. Did you always know you wanted to write books?"

"It's cheaper than therapy."

"Meaning?"

"Meaning if I don't get up and let the dogs out, I'll have to spend the entire morning mopping up puddles in my kitchen."

Hardly an answer to my question. Elizabeth watched as Colleen left the bedroom, both dogs impeding her progress as they clambered around her legs. *Oh, well. I need to get to the office anyway. We can talk about this next time.*

Elizabeth hit the mute button on the little voice in her head that was demanding to know exactly what "next time" meant.

Chapter
Three

LaGrange, Georgia
September, 2005

THE SUN WAS about to slip out of sight.

"I'm sorry that you're always the one who has to make the drive here, LJ. You know I'm happy to see you when you can get away to spend the weekend with me, but it doesn't seem fair that you should have to load up and come to LaGrange all the time. You've made the drive almost every Friday for the past three months." Colleen yanked Elizabeth's overnight bag out of the backseat of her Lexus. "Not that I'm complaining, you understand. I love it when you come here." She gave Elizabeth a knowing glance. "But I could get one of the neighbors to keep an eye on the dogs for me so that we could spend some weekends at your place."

Elizabeth grabbed her briefcase and shoulder bag off the passenger seat, opened the driver's door, and stepped out of the car to join Colleen in the driveway at Colleen's house on Orchard Hill Lane. "No, I think it works better for me to come down here. No sense disrupting the dogs' routines. Besides, it forces me to actually take a break from work. If we were in Columbus, I'm sure I'd go by the office five times a day. I know I put in at least eighteen hours there last weekend. When I come down here, we actually have some time together." Elizabeth closed the car door and used her free hand to grab one handle of the overnight bag that Colleen was holding. "Here, let me help with that. I brought my laptop and a couple of new manuscripts along. That thing must weigh a ton."

"I knew it had to be more than underwear and a toothbrush."

They walked into the house and carried their loads to Colleen's bedroom at the rear of the house. As soon as their hands were free, they were wrapped in one another's arms.

"Missed you," Elizabeth said as she kissed Colleen's neck.

"Missed you more," Colleen replied as she rolled her head back so that Elizabeth could kiss the hollow between her collar bones. "Mmm. The feel of your lips right there always makes my skeleton turn to Pla-Doh."

"What does this do?" Elizabeth asked as she laid a heartfelt kiss on Colleen's lips.

"Makes my buttons fall off and my zippers split."

"You are so easy." Elizabeth's laugh from deep in her throat left no doubt in Colleen's mind that she'd been paid a compliment.

"I prefer to think of it as your fault for being so very, very arousing."

"Will the dogs be okay in the backyard for a while?"

Colleen heard the urgency in Elizabeth's voice. "What dogs? What backyard?" She kicked her shoes off and began working her way out of her tight jeans.

Moments later, they had shed every stitch of clothing and were under the covers on the bed. Colleen trailed her fingers down the side of Elizabeth's ribcage and used the palm of her hand to caress Elizabeth's thigh. "Do you have an opening for an aspiring author?" she asked.

"On my publishing schedule or on my person?"

"An hour from now, I'll want to talk to you about your schedule, but right now, the only thing I care about is the opening that I've been dreaming about since you left here." Colleen eased two fingers between the enticingly damp lips between Elizabeth's legs.

"What a coincidence," Elizabeth said after a sharp intake of air. "I've been dreaming about you filling that opening for about the same length of time."

"Let me make that dream come true." Colleen plunged her fingers home and positioned her thumb in exactly the place she knew Elizabeth needed it. The next moments hung in suspended animation until Elizabeth stiffened, gave a long cry of ecstasy, then relaxed so completely that Colleen pictured a rag doll—a rag doll with a big, half-moon shining happily on her face.

Elizabeth sighed deeply. "Every time, I swear I'm going to do you first and stop acting like such a selfish glutton." She pulled Colleen into a snug embrace. "And every time, you play me like a music box and make me forget every promise I made to myself."

Colleen stroked Elizabeth's cheek. "I love the tunes that come out of that box, and I love that you're so open and so responsive."

"But you always have to wait. Why should you always be Tonto to my Lone Ranger?"

"You never make me feel like a sidekick or an afterthought, sweetheart. Instead of Tonto and the Lone Ranger, I see it as more like Ferrante and Teicher playing a duet. Both parts individually are nice, but the two of them together is what makes for the incredibly beautiful music." Colleen shifted so that she could pull Elizabeth's leg between her own. "Besides, feeling you come is always so exciting for me. It makes me want it all the more."

"Ready to have your ivories tickled?" Elizabeth ran all ten fingers up and down on Colleen's shoulders as though she were practicing scales. "I'd love to hear your version of the Lover's Concerto."

"Past ready." Colleen rocked with increasing frequency against Elizabeth's leg. "Almost," she whispered. "Almost."

"Now or next year. I'm here for as long as you'll have me. Let it go whenever you want to."

Colleen gasped. Yet again, Elizabeth had proven that all she needed to do was tell her it was up to her, and she could no more stop the explosion than she could reverse gravity.

"Good stuff?"

"The best, as always." Colleen nestled in, her head beneath Elizabeth's chin. She listened to the lub-dubs from Elizabeth's heart. With the passage of a little time and some quiet afterglow conversation, her own heart settled into a calmer cadence and her breathing returned to normal. They lay peacefully as twilight turned to darkness.

"How are things at the office?" Colleen asked. "I hardly ever get to talk to you, and your e-mails are always so short."

"About like usual. Work will take every single minute I'm willing to give it."

"I know. I called your office at least twenty times and never managed to find you. Toni told me you were in meetings off-site."

"I'm looking for a new distributor and a new warehouse. That takes a lot of time."

Colleen sensed a shift in Elizabeth's mood. "I know you're busy, and I wasn't accusing you of avoiding me. I was only calling to say hi."

"Since you're one of Triple S's authors, it might not be a good idea for you to call me at the office unless you've got a question about what's happening with your book or an issue with the contract—stuff like that. And some of those things, Toni can probably handle."

Colleen withdrew from Elizabeth's arms. "Sure. I understand. I guess I wasn't thinking about how it might look. Sometimes I just like to hear your voice."

Elizabeth eased into a sitting position. "Don't be upset. Let's not start the weekend with a fight."

"Who's fighting?" Colleen kicked the covers back and got out of bed. "We hadn't talked about whether or not I could call you at work. Now that I know you don't want me to, I won't do it any more."

"Collie—"

"No, really. It's okay." Colleen pulled her sweatshirt on and sat on the chair by the dresser to tug on her jeans and tie her sneakers. "I'll go let Buster and Muggins in." She took two steps toward the door. "If you're hungry, come on out to the kitchen. I made lasagna for us. I'll heat it up while I'm feeding the dogs."

ELIZABETH WISHED SHE hadn't said what she had to Colleen about calling the office. Well, almost wished. Over the past three months, Colleen had called almost every day. At first, she took her calls, but because of the paper-thin walls that separated her private space from the outer office, she told herself it wouldn't be wise to have intimate conversations with her new lover — conversations that could be easily overheard by Toni, Alex, and Joanie. No need to let things get out of hand with Colleen.

Out of hand? Good God, Elizabeth, you chase down here to LaGrange most weekends like a sailor on shore leave. It's already out of hand.

She saw little point in trying to fool herself. Pretending that Colleen calling her at work was the key issue was only a smokescreen. Once in a while, she'd even admit as much to herself. After all, Standing in Sappho's Shadow was her business (both as enterprise and as affair, so to speak.) If she wanted to strip to her undergarments, dip herself in semi-sweet chocolate, sit on top of her desk, and talk to the president, the pope, and the prime minister of Canada — let alone Colleen McCrady — no one on her payroll would dare to so much as say "boo."

Her discomfort ran a lot deeper than worrying what her staff might think if they learned about her and Colleen. One day soon she'd broach the real source of her unrest. Maybe even this weekend —

Her contemplations were interrupted by Colleen's voice calling from the kitchen. "What kind of salad dressing do you want?"

Okay, maybe not this weekend. Maybe next time we're together after this.

Chapter
Four

LaGrange, Georgia
December 2005

ELIZABETH AND COLLEEN were having coffee in Colleen's living room on Monday morning, December twenty-sixth.

"What's your favorite childhood Christmas memory?" Elizabeth asked between sips.

"I'd never thought about it." Colleen looked into her mug as though the answer might be spelled out in the swirls of the creamer still waiting to be stirred.

"Then what better time than today? Did you open presents Christmas Eve or Christmas morning?"

"It varied."

"Why was that?"

"You know, farm stuff. If my dad got hung up in the barn late on Christmas Eve, we'd wait 'til after morning milking Christmas Day."

Elizabeth drank more coffee waiting for Colleen to elaborate and to answer her original question. Instead, Colleen merely clinked her spoon in her mug. "What was the best present you ever got?" Elizabeth hoped a new prompt might get Colleen to open up a little.

"Every year was pretty much the same—socks and underwear. Pajamas. Some books. Maybe a game or a toy." Colleen shrugged indifferently. "Speaking of presents..." She reached behind the chair she was sitting in and pulled out a package. "I know this is kind of an unusual Christmas present, but I hope you like it." Colleen handed over a box wrapped in paper decorated with dogs wearing Santa Claus hats.

"I thought we agreed only one gift apiece. You already gave me this gorgeous brushed cotton running suit yesterday." Elizabeth fingered the collar of the jacket she was wearing.

"Yeah, but this is sort of a gift that keeps on giving. At least I hope it will. Open it."

Elizabeth made a face of mock disgust at Colleen, but undid the bow and pried the tape off the end of the package. Perhaps after this little diversion with the gift, she could steer the conversation back to Colleen's past.

She lifted the lid off the file-folder box. Inside, was most of a ream of paper. On top, was a cover page that said, "*Patchwork,* a novel by Colleen McCrady."

"Your next book." Elizabeth looked up and beamed at Colleen.

"Only if my publisher likes it. I know it's supposed to go through the submissions process, but I finished it right before you got here on Friday, and since Triple S's office is closed down until after New Year's, I thought maybe you'd let me bend the rules a little."

"I guess this is what's had you leaping out of bed in the wee hours of the morning every time I've come down to spend the weekend with you."

"I can't help it, LJ. When I get going on a story, I feel like I have to keep punching the keys until all the words are down on the page. I guess I neglected you a little over the past couple of months, huh?"

"I've spent enough time around writers to know that when the muses come, we lesser beings need to get out of the way and let the creative process happen."

Colleen slipped out of her chair and dropped to one knee beside Elizabeth. "I'll do better in the future. I promise. I'm still getting used to the idea that I might actually make a go of being a writer. I appreciate how patient you are with me." She laid her hand on Elizabeth's upper leg. "You're sure you weren't mad that I spent so much time writing instead of being with you?"

"I didn't have to come to LaGrange all those weekends. I could have stayed in Columbus if I'd thought it was a better way to spend my time." Elizabeth gave Colleen a quick kiss. "And it let me get better acquainted with Buster and Muggins. We had a lot of nice walks around the neighborhood." The dogs, lying in the sunshine streaming through the front window, stirred at the mention of their names and the word 'walk' in the same sentence.

"Not today, guys," Elizabeth said. "I've surrendered my dog W–A–L–K badge for the holidays.

"And I'll return the favor and not work on my B–O–O–K–S so that I can have the time with you."

"So, what's this one about?" Elizabeth asked as Colleen resumed her seat.

"It's a sequel to *Scrapbook.* It tells what Caitlin does to help her mother learn new ways of using motion to mimic dance and how Caitlin and LuAnn's daughter decides to follow in her grandmother's footsteps — well, I should say dance steps, to continue the metaphor."

"Sounds like a great story line."

"I guess you'll let me know. I mean, your reviewers will let me know." The Colleen McCrady blush showed itself in full force.

"What are your plans for the rest of the day?" Elizabeth put the manuscript box on the floor beside her.

"You mean other than taking you back to bed to pay you back for all the opportunities I've missed over the past few months?"

Elizabeth felt a tingle in her lower abdominal region. "Okay, yes, other than that."

"Nothing. What do you have in mind?"

"After catching up in the bedroom, how about we look through your book? I don't get many chances to edit anymore, and I kind of miss it."

"You mean like we did with *Scrapbook* that first day when I met with you at your office back in March?"

"Uh huh. Unless you'd rather not."

"No, I'd love it." Colleen perched on the edge of her chair. Her eagerness was overflowing. Then her face clouded. "But that's not very fair to your other authors. They don't get to have their books edited by Elizabeth Albright. It's not right for me to take advantage of our relationship that way."

"It's not like you asked; I offered."

"But still—"

"Come on." Elizabeth stood up and took Colleen by the hand. "First things first. First, let me have my way with you in the bedroom, and then we'll see how you feel about letting me have my way with your book."

THREE HOURS LATER, Colleen was in the kitchen making their lunch—sandwiches from the leftover Christmas ham. Elizabeth was in the bedroom, savoring the last lingering memories of their marathon on the mattress.

She caught the feeling—almost like a homesickness—creeping up on her, but no matter how severely she chastised herself, she couldn't stop it from washing over her like a tidal wave. All those Christmases with Alana Montaigne. All those dreams. All those hopes. All that anguish. All that heartache.

Seventeen years was a long time to spend with a first and only lover. And ten years was a long time to spend alone. Alana's departure from Elizabeth's life a decade ago did more than convince Elizabeth never to mingle her personal and professional realms. It convinced her that having feelings for someone was, at best, mostly a waste of time. At worst, it ruined both worlds—personal and professional.

Alana wanted to write books—or at least she *said* she wanted to write them. In their early years together, Alana had penned a number of manuscripts, but none of them had been accepted by any of the publishers to whom she submitted them. A couple of times, she had asked Elizabeth to critique chapters, but that never went very well. Elizabeth would point out parts of the plot that needed better development or revamping to fit what she knew were the existing standards for lesbian fiction. Elizabeth's comments would either anger or discourage Alana. Then Alana would toss the book in a box on the floor of the closet, and it would never see the light of day again.

After she came into her inheritance, when Alana encouraged her to launch Standing in Sappho's Shadow, Elizabeth knew part of Alana's motivation for being such an enthusiastic cheerleader was having a fast track to a publisher who simply couldn't tell her no. She always framed her comments in terms of Elizabeth no longer having to kowtow to the constraints of the industry, but it didn't take a translator to know what Alana meant at the essence.

The first couple of years that the company was in existence, simply getting it established took every ounce of energy either of them could generate. Alana was too busy helping Elizabeth at work and keeping the household running to spend much time writing, so Elizabeth was spared the difficult task of telling Alana she didn't think her conscience would let her publish her life partner's books. She had seen the harm the comparatively closed world of lesbian fiction would inflict on its members when it felt the "incest quotient" grew too high. Why tempt the fates?

Three-and-a-half years after Standing in Sappho's Shadow made its foray into the arena, Alana presented Elizabeth with a new manuscript titled *Call Me Tomorrow*, which read far better than anything Elizabeth had seen from Alana previously. The characters were multi-dimensional, believable, with flaws as well as talents. The protagonist was a lesbian, but the relationship between her and her lover was little more than a passing part of the action. The plot was intricate and detailed, overlaid with universal truths that would have made their English professors at Brown University (where Elizabeth and Alana had met) proud to the point of popping buttons. And her book was the sort of thing Elizabeth hoped to one day make a regular component of Triple S's offerings — literature — *literature* — by and about lesbians. She wanted to publish books that made the characters' sexual orientation merely another word of description, like "teacher" or "tall" or "afraid of snakes."

Yes, that had been her vision for Triple S. But she didn't feel she could have a book written by her lover as the house's first offering that ventured so far away from the norm in the genre. No. Too many risks, too much potential for the whole thing to blow up in her face.

She was finally doing what she felt was her life's work. She wasn't going to jeopardize it to appease Alana Montaigne's need to be a published author.

Alana was devastated when Elizabeth told her Standing in Sappho's Shadow wouldn't publish her book.

Devastated and, apparently, hell bent on revenge. A short time after multiple screaming matches over Elizabeth refusing to publish *Call Me Tomorrow,* Alana took up with the layout artist. Six months later, Elizabeth's home life and professional life were both in shambles.

And what was she doing now? Flirting with disaster all over again. She had already gone against her principles by publishing one book by her lover (even though she'd offered the contract before she'd offered open arms), and now Colleen had finished another book that she hoped Elizabeth would accept for publication. The manuscript was still lying on the floor in the living room, and unless she came up with a foolproof excuse, before the day was over, she'd be reviewing it with Colleen by her side. Elizabeth wasn't sure if she hoped she loved Colleen's new book or hated it. Either way, something was going to have to change.

How much longer could she keep her relationship with Colleen under wraps? Did it matter if it became common knowledge? Would any of her other authors care if Elizabeth and Colleen were a couple? Triple S Publishing was on solid footing now. She wasn't nearly as vulnerable to lunges and parries from her competitors.

Never mind all that. Was Elizabeth willing to put her heart above her head and acknowledge her love for Colleen — Colleen the person?

And then there was that other little problem that always cropped up when Elizabeth held this internal debate with herself: *Just who the hell is Colleen McCrady?*

"THIS IS ANOTHER very solid story, Collie," Elizabeth said as she scanned the final page in *Patchwork* later that evening. They sat side by side on the sofa. "I think you still need to work on your tendency to rush through some important parts of the plot by throwing information at your readers instead of letting it evolve as part of the development, but comparing this against your first draft of *Scrapbook,* you've substantially improved your skills as a writer." Elizabeth placed the manuscript on the end table and gave Colleen a peck on the cheek.

"I hope you're not saying that only because we're...uh...involved."

"I'm saying it because it's true."

"Do you think Triple S will publish this one, too?"

Elizabeth sensed the effort, but try as she might, Colleen couldn't stop the flush from whooshing up her neck and turning her face bright red. "For both our sakes, I think the right thing to do is for you to submit it to the submissions team and let them evaluate it as though it were another manuscript coming through the door. Then, when they forward it to me for my approval, I'll already be ahead of the game because I've had the privilege of a sneak preview." Elizabeth hoped the adoring look she bestowed on Colleen took the worst of the sting out of her message.

"Should I do the rewrites we talked about today before I send it in?" Colleen picked at the seam on the leg of her jeans.

"Your choice, but taking the time to fix the gaps I noted now will make that much less you have to do when it hits the editing cycle."

"How many books by each author do you put out each year?"

"Depends. Generally no more than two, especially if they're sequels. You want to give the buying public time to build up a hunger for the next installment. If they come out too close together, you run the risk of overwhelming their appetites."

"So even if *Patchwork* makes the cut, maybe it shouldn't be my next book anyway. I mean, *Scrapbook* is on the schedule for March, so you wouldn't want *Patchwork* to be slated until at least late next year, right?" Colleen was nigh unto squirming as she sat next to Elizabeth.

Elizabeth moved so that she was facing Colleen's profile. She wasn't much inclined toward intuition, but something about the look on Colleen's face and the hunch of her shoulders prompted her to ask a question that surprised them both. "Do you have another book you want me to look at?"

Colleen took a long time to answer. "Sort of, but probably not. It's not done yet. I don't know if I'll ever finish it." Colleen absent-mindedly traced the pattern in the fabric on the sofa.

"Why wouldn't you?"

"It's probably not something you would want to publish."

"Only one way to find that out—submit it and see what the reviewers think." Elizabeth intercepted Colleen's hand and stopped her from continuing her whirls and swirls on the brocade.

"I'm not sure I could ever be comfortable putting it out there."

"Because?"

Colleen pursed her lips before replying. "Because it's not like anything else I've written."

"A little too racy?" Elizabeth guessed.

Colleen laughed nervously. "No, not by a long shot."

"What then?"

Colleen got up from the sofa and flopped down on her stomach on the floor between Buster and Muggins. She stroked Buster's ear while she rubbed Muggin's belly. Elizabeth waited, but evidently, Colleen wasn't about to say anything more. She eased off the sofa and sat with her back against it. Elizabeth stretched her leg out to its fullest extension so that she could use her toes to gently kick the bottom of Colleen's foot. "Tell you what. How about you give me a few chapters of this mystery book of yours? I'll take a quick trip through it and we can talk about whether or not it would be worth your time to keep working on it."

Still nothing from Colleen.

"No extra charge, Colleen. It's part of the holiday package plan at Standing in Sappho's Shadow Publishing."

Colleen rolled over and lay on her back. She drew her knees up and put her feet flat on the floor. Muggins scooted over so that he could rest his head on her abdomen.

"I guess I could do that." Colleen patted the dog's head. "But if you hate it, don't tell me how to fix it. Tell me to throw it away and move on to something else, okay? I don't think I want to go through a line-by-line evaluation of it like we did with *Patchwork* and *Scrapbook*."

"Whatever you say, kid." Elizabeth edged closer to Colleen and laid her head on the other side of Colleen's midsection so that she and Muggins were lying crown to crown across Colleen. "Where is this masterpiece?"

"In the closet in my bedroom, but you don't want to read it tonight, do you?"

"I might. When I edited for Brazen Girls Press, I liked to read the opening pages of a book right before I went to sleep. When I woke up in the morning, if I was wondering what happened next, I knew it was likely to be a good book." Elizabeth gave a short laugh. "Of course, if I couldn't remember what I'd read the night before, I knew I'd have a long, hard slog through a ho-hum novel."

Colleen slid Muggins's head back onto the floor, then used both hands to comb through Elizabeth's hair. "I probably never should have mentioned this book. I can't imagine that you'll like it at all."

"Don't poison the well, sweetie. Let's go get it, and by this time tomorrow, we'll both know how I feel about it."

Colleen paused in her finger combing. "Promise me something."

"What?"

"No matter what you think about this book, promise me it won't change how you feel about me."

Elizabeth got to her knees and leaned over Colleen. She kissed her softly, then kissed her again.

"Deal." She got to her feet and offered both hands to Colleen. "Now, where is the McCrady secret library?"

Back in the bedroom, Colleen rummaged around in the walk-in

closet until she found the apple box she was looking for. As Elizabeth watched her pull the box out, dust off the lid, and haul the manuscript from the stacks inside, it evoked such strong reminiscences of Alana and her rejected manuscripts that Elizabeth thought she might be having a flashback.

As Colleen set a heap of binders on the corner of the bed, a small bundle of newspaper articles paper-clipped together slipped to the floor "What's this?" Elizabeth asked as she picked up the packet. She could only read half of the headline because of the way the page was folded. "Car bomb" and "local family" was all she could make out.

"That's some old research I was doing for a book once." Colleen grabbed the clippings from Elizabeth and jammed them back into the box.

"What about this?" Elizabeth held out a wedding photo that had slipped out of the stack. She looked at it more closely. "That's you!" she said as she pointed to a young girl standing in front of a bride who was stood between two smiling, middle-aged people. A solemn young man who looked to be in his mid-teens was beside the older woman. "Who are these people?"

"My mom and dad." Colleen's voice was totally devoid of emotion.

"But who's the bride and this boy beside your mom?"

Something flashed across Colleen's face, but she recovered quickly—too quickly for Elizabeth to decipher its meaning. "My cousins. Everybody always thought she and I looked a lot alike. My mom thought it would be fun to have a picture of me with her and her brother on her wedding day."

"You do look like her." Elizabeth stared at the photograph. "Have you got any other pictures of you when you were a kid? I'd love to see them." Elizabeth could see several photo albums that Colleen had taken out of the box. Colleen hastened to stow them away.

"Some. We can look at them another time." She took the wedding photo from Elizabeth and tossed it into the box. "Here's that manuscript." Colleen hefted the ragged-edged pages while she used her foot to slide the box back into the closet.

Elizabeth reached for the document, but Colleen pulled it back. "We said you'd only look at the first couple of chapters, right?"

"Okay, that works for me." Elizabeth opted not to press the matter.

"I think I want to look through this again before I decide for sure to have you read it." Colleen folded the manuscript against her chest. "While I flip through this, maybe you could put some food down for the dogs and turn the burner on under that pot of soup on the stove for dinner."

"Sure," Elizabeth said as she headed for the door. "If you decide you want me to take a peek, leave what you want me to see on the nightstand on my side of the bed." With that bit of encouragement, she left the room.

AFTER THE EVENING meal, the two women and two dogs wandered back into the living room.

"Did you pull an excerpt from that book for me, Collie?" Elizabeth asked as she sat in the recliner. "I might as well get started on it."

Colleen's already-pale complexion blanched even whiter. "I don't know if I can go through with it. It's not very good. I put the first few chapters by the bed, but I probably should just run the whole thing through the shredder."

Elizabeth got out of her chair and went to stand behind Colleen who was staring out into the darkness through the big, front window. "I've seen your stuff, remember? At its worst, it's not fodder for the shredder."

Colleen heaved a sigh. "All right. I asked for this." She turned to look Elizabeth in the eye. "I'll get it for you, but I can't sit in this house while you read it. I'm going to dump it in your lap, and then I'm taking the guys for a long walk." On cue, Buster and Muggins leapt up, agitating to get their leashes clipped on.

Colleen hurried back to the bedroom, grabbed a heavy sweatshirt from the dresser, and scooped up the stack of pages from the nightstand. "Here," she said to Elizabeth as she passed through the living room. "If you're gone when I get back, I'll know what you thought of these first four chapters."

She didn't wait for Elizabeth to comment, but rather hurried out the front door behind the dogs.

Elizabeth settled back in the chair. She undid the large rubber binder around the pages and removed the blank page atop the stack. *The Curse of Canaan*," said the title page. An epigraph followed: "Cursed be Canaan; a slave of slaves shall he be to his brothers." Beneath it, Colleen had noted, "Genesis Chapter 9, Verse 25, Revised Standard Version."

What in holy heaven is this about? With a shrug, Elizabeth turned the page and began to read.

Chapter
Five

The Curse of Canaan
Coon River Rapids, Minnesota
September 1956

"THERE'S COON WILLIE." Emil Schmidt canted his head in the direction of a man walking on the opposite side of the street. Ginny, Emil's five-year-old daughter, cast her gaze on the fellow in question.

What she saw was an odd-looking black man. He didn't walk in the same way everyone else did. His forward progress was more like miscellaneous movement resembling a double-jointed half-jig radiating from a ball joint located somewhere in his midsection. (Emil had been heard to compare Willie to Arthur Duncan, the black man who danced on the Lawrence Welk show. "Darkies don't have as many bones as white people," Emil said. "That's what lets them dance so good.")

No matter where or when they saw him, the people of Coon River Rapids, Minnesota, could count on Willie to be smiling, his gold capped front tooth gleaming like a jewel flanked by alabaster and surrounded by India ink. He was a tall, slight man, his arms and legs appearing almost too long and angular for his lean — bordering on gaunt — body.

Willie earned his keep by mopping floors and doing stock boy duties at the Woolworth's Dime Store in downtown Coon River Rapids — all six blocks of it. Sometimes, if the regular clerk was at lunch or out sick or on vacation, the store manager let Willie weigh out the candy purchases from the rows of glass bins that served as the main display in the center of the store. Every kid around knew that you had to be sure Willie was looking directly at you before you said, "I want a nickel's worth of malted milk balls," or "Give me ten cents' worth of gumdrops," because Willie was deaf and mute. He relied on reading lips and pointing to communicate, the whole time bobbing his head vigorously and grinning like a jackass eating briars.

How this lone Negro came to be living in Coon River Rapids in 1956 was anybody's guess. No one seemed to know. Or care. Willie ducked into the dime store; Emil and Ginny entered the establishment across the street.

Emil had made the six-mile drive from his quarter-section farm into town that Wednesday afternoon to pass a couple of hours at the snooker and billiards parlor. The name on the sign that hung outside the door said Bud's Lucky Spot, but everyone in Coon River Rapids called it The Spot. Emil and Danny, his fourteen-year-old son, had finished baling and stacking third crop hay last week – good thing, too, since Danny's school year had started two days earlier, right after Labor Day. In a few days, the corn and sorghum would be ready to chop for silage, so Emil was taking advantage of the lull in major farm chores to hang out with the other farmers who were, likewise, glad for the break, however brief, from the rigors of coaxing a living from the land.

Emil and Ginny entered the smaller of the two rooms at Bud's. "Hi, Schmitty." Marvin Booth, their neighbor, said to Emil. "Brought your good luck charm along, I see."

It wasn't unusual for one of the regulars at The Spot to bring a child along for the afternoon, so Ginny wasn't a stranger to the smoky, noisy pool hall. Ginny's brother and sister, Danny and Rose, had spent long hours priming Ginny on her colors and numbers and reading story books to her, so she was verbal and extremely mature for her age. If her birthday had been a month earlier, she'd be in school, putting her skills to good use. Instead, she was amusing herself (and her elders) in any way she could find.

"My daddy is such a good pool player that he doesn't need a good luck charm," she told Marvin. "But if you'll give me a nickel for an ice cream cone, I'll cheer for you."

Her father took Ginny by her arm and frowned. "Ssst. What have I told you about begging money from people?"

"Oh, let her be, Emil." Marvin boosted Ginny up onto the bench behind the pool table where her father and his friends would wile away the afternoon. Her blonde ponytail bounced and swayed; her hazel eyes twinkled with delight when Marvin tickled her ribs as he set her down. "We both know I'd have given her a nickel within the next ten minutes anyhow." He fished the coin from the pocket of his overalls and held it out to Ginny between his thumb and forefinger.

"Thank you. For sure I'll cheer for you now." Ginny shucked her jacket and wadded it up beside her on the bench, then slid off the edge and dropped to the floor. She swam through the swarm of men gathered around the five tables and emerged in the high-ceilinged front room of The Spot. One side was devoted to the jukebox and the coin-operated games – pinball, skittles, pachinko, and others. A long wooden bar lined with vinyl-topped stools ran the length of the other side.

Ginny walked halfway down the bar and stood in the opening that permitted access behind it. The top of her head was almost perfectly level with the top of the bar.

"Doris?" Ginny called.

"Hi, Hon. Did you come to town with your daddy today?" Doris was one of the regular waitresses who shuffled trays of beers and an occasional greasy hamburger to the pool-playing patrons. She and Ginny were the best of buddies.

"Uh huh. Mr. Booth gave me a nickel. Would you get me an ice cream cone?"

"What kind today? Strawberry?"

"Yes, please."

Doris pulled a cone from a box and lifted the freezer's lid near the far wall behind the bar. She scooped out a generous portion and tamped it into the cone and let the lid slam shut. "Here you go. Watch yourself on your way back to the bench. Don't let any of those guys hit you with their pool sticks."

"I won't. Thank you." She handed over Marvin Booth's nickel.

Ginny had lots of practice negotiating around pumping pool cues. She knew how to dodge and weave to avoid an errant rubber-heeled thump against the side of her head (or worse, to the top of her ice cream cone). Soon she was comfortably situated among the men's jackets and heavy outer shirts heaped on the bench behind the pool tables.

Ginny settled in for the afternoon's entertainment of laughter, curses, and conversation. She watched the men chalk the blue-tipped ends and then slide the sticks back and forth in the little loop they made with their fingers. The balls made loud snick-snick sounds as they caromed off one another and then dropped into the pockets and rolled along the tracks below. The men used their cues to slide little discs along a wire strung over the table to keep track of who was winning. She knew that when one of them took his cue stick and rapped the rubber end of it hard against the floor, that meant that the game was over, and someone from behind the bar would come in a minute to rack the balls and collect for the next game. That was also the best time to suggest to her father — or one of his friends — that another ice cream cone wouldn't be a bad idea. They already had their hands in their pockets, fumbling for the dime they'd lay on the edge of the table. Might as well make the fumbling worthwhile.

By the end of the afternoon, when the time came for Emil and Ginny to leave The Spot and go home to do evening chores, Ginny knew the Gages had a new boar pig, the Knutsons were digging a new well, the Trosvigs had traded tractors, and her daddy and four of the neighbors were going to pool their equipment, time, and labor to help one another get their silos filled. Though an annual occurrence, every fall the men went through the discussion process as if it were a brand new event, acting as though it were a barter when the deal was already done.

"Well, those cows won't milk themselves," Emil said. "Get your jacket on, Ginny."

She hopped off the bench, slipped into Danny's hand-me-down from several years earlier, and readjusted the rolled-up cuffs.

"Ready?" Emil asked, extending his hand. Ginny slipped her soft, tiny hand in his big, callused one, and they stepped out into the late afternoon light. Ginny had to blink hard several times to help her eyes accustom to the much brighter light of the outdoors.

"Look, Daddy. There's that man again."

Willie came out of the dime store at almost the same moment Emil and Ginny exited the pool hall. He was making his way across the street toward them.

"Yep. Coon Willie." Emil tightened his grip on his daughter's hand.

"Why do you call him Coon Willie?"

"Look at his eyes. See how the white parts of his eyes show up all bright and shiny? He looks like a raccoon. You know how raccoons always look like they're wearing a mask—like they're up to no good? Well, like raccoons, coloreds are shifty and cagey and up to no good. That's why they're called 'coons.'"

As always, the black man bobbed his head as though in perfect agreement with whatever was being said. He wore his trademark broad grin, his gold capped tooth his most memorable feature. He cut his eyes sharply at the little girl as they passed in the middle of the street. Ginny was hard-pressed to see any resemblance whatsoever to the raccoons she had seen at home on the farm or in her picture books.

"I don't think I'd like someone calling me 'coon,'" she said.

"He doesn't mind. He's used to it. For one thing, coloreds don't have the same feelings as white people. And in his case, he's deaf as a post to boot, so he doesn't even know that's what folks call him."

To prove his point, Emil Schmidt stopped on the far side of the street and turned back to face Coon Willie's retreating form.

"Coon Willie," he shouted. "Hey, Coon Willie! Hey, you dumb feller, come here and I'll give you a dollar." Ginny stood with her father, looking at the black man fading from their sight.

Of course, the deaf mute didn't so much as slow his pace let alone turn around or acknowledge Emil's offer.

"See?" Emil concluded. "It doesn't make any difference."

Little Ginny Schmidt was too young to argue, but had she been able to describe it, she would have sworn that she saw Willie tense his shoulders and ever so briefly clench his fists. Then he ambled on.

WILBUR ALPHONSE RICE, better known as Coon Willie, walked through town to the northern edge of Coon River Rapids. The owner of the Woolworth store, Kent Shelby, had arranged for Willie to rent a room at the Able Apartments situated on the fringe of the community. Olive Able was a widow woman, nearly seventy years old, nearly deaf, nearly blind, and — according to most residents of Coon River Rapids — nearly crazy.

The Able Apartments were a U-shape of three multi-unit buildings in varying stages of decay and disarray, prompting some people in Coon River Rapids to refer to them as the "Unable Apartments" or the "Able Stables." Two of the three buildings were completely given over to housing Olive's ever-growing collections of once-useful or previously-functional objects — now broken, obsolete, or downright dangerous. The one building which housed tenants was a duplex with only three occupants: Willie, in the smallest habitable unit, and in the other, two young men from the Mormon Church who were on a mission to convert the citizens of Coon River Rapids.

The Mormon missionaries were returning from their day of proselytizing as Willie approached the door to his unit. The three men waved and dipped their heads at one another as they went into their apartments.

"Poor ignorant heathen," Elder Benson said to Elder Kishel as they stepped inside.

"Unfortunate descendant of Canaan, the son of Ham and grandson of Noah," Elder Kishel added as he closed the door.

"Sanctimonious, self-righteous, blind devotees," observed Willie to the walls of his twenty-by-thirty cubbyhole.

Willie set about his evening routine. First, he went into the tiny bathroom and used the facilities, then set to work with a sponge to wipe off the pedestal sink, the top of the commode tank, and the cracked tiles lining his two-foot square shower stall. He took a straw broom from its place in the corner and swept out the bathroom.

Then, he went to the corner of his living space which Olive referred to as his "kitchenette." It contained a two-burner propane range, three feet of Formica-topped counter with a chipped enamel sink, and an eight-cubic foot refrigerator. He took a sponge from under the sink and wiped all of the surfaces, including the interior of the refrigerator. Next, he took an old sock and dusted the small wooden table that sat near the kitchenette, the wooden rocking chair that sat in his living room, the painted three-drawer dresser next to his mattress on the floor, and the tops of the orange crates that served as his bookcase. Lastly, he swept the rest of the faded linoleum floor and returned the broom to its corner.

Satisfied that his home was clean, he prepared his evening meal. Most days, the short-order cook at the Woolworth lunch counter made sure that Willie got breakfast and lunch. His breakfast usually was the order of fried eggs some customer said were supposed to have been scrambled, the burned toast, or the sweet roll with only a bite or two taken out of it. But Willie didn't care. The food was free and nutritious. Lunch might be the scrapings from the pan of chicken and gravy over the last of the hardened mashed potatoes or the sandwich that slipped off the plate. Sometimes, he got the piece of pie that should have been sold two days ago but hadn't been or the last piece of cake with the crystallized frosting. No matter. Willie smacked his lips, and rubbed his stomach to show his appreciation for the cook's generosity.

Willie took a pan of pork chops and lima beans from the refrigerator. Since only one burner on the stove worked, he often made up a week's worth of meals in a single session and then reheated portions each night. He warmed enough for a plateful and sat down at the table.

"Thank you, oh Lord, for this food. Thank you for this home, for my job, for my life. Please keep my mama safe until I can see her again. Amen."

As he ate, Willie reflected on his day. Things had been calm at the Woolworth's. No one had given him an order to do something, then changed their mind or criticized him for the sake of picking on him and laughing at him as he pretended not to comprehend their instructions. He had found twenty cents on the floor while he was mopping up—not much, but every little bit helped. With school back in session, the lunch counter didn't have much traffic, so he had fared better than usual there, too. Instead of rejects and left behinds, he was given small portions from the food the cook made up to sell to the paying customers.

Willie finished his supper and cleaned up his dishes. As was his habit, he stepped outside the door of his apartment and took a few steps up the walkway toward the unit where the Mormon boys were staying. He could hear their radio playing the evening broadcast of the "Back to the Bible Hour" from the all-religious programming station in Fargo, North Dakota.

Convinced that his only near neighbors were settled in for the evening, Willie went back inside and closed and locked the door. He went to his dresser and opened the bottom drawer. From its hiding place among the few warm clothes he owned, Willie extracted his battery-powered transistor radio. He slipped the ear plug jack into the radio and popped the earpiece into his right ear. With nightfall coming so early, the radio signals were carrying well even though the clock said only six o'clock. He tuned the dial to another of the Fargo stations, the one that employed a classical music format. He wasn't sure, but he thought the strains were from Dvorak's *Slavic Dances*. The tempo reminded him of the folk songs his mother had once sung to him.

Willie scanned his sparse library and selected Shakespeare's *Othello*. He eased into his rocking chair, and with quiet music as background, soon was immersed in the tale of the Moor's jealousy. He had hoped the drama would distract him from the lingering thoughts of the farmer's broad-brush bigotry on the street earlier that day, but he had been drawn to the work because he knew that he, like Othello, was black in a white man's world. That parallel alone would have been sufficient, but in the second scene of the first act, Willie faced another common theme.

Barbantio, father of the beautiful Desdemona, accosts Othello, saying, "O thou foul thief, where hast thou stow'd my daughter?" Barbantio calls Desdemona "a maid so tender, fair, and happy" and rudely states that she would never have run "to the sooty bosom" of someone like Othello. He accuses Othello of vile deeds: "Thou hast practiced on her with foul charms, abused her delicate youth."

For a man whom Emil Schmidt had characterized as stupid and devoid of feeling, Willie Rice certainly seemed possessed by something approximating thought and sentiment. He pulled the earpiece out and turned off the radio. He closed the book in his lap and lolled his head back against the highest part of the rocking chair. With a deep sigh, he let the memories overtake him.

Canaan, Mississippi
A fall Saturday morning, 1948

"WILBUR RICE! YOU get out of this house this instant or I'll take a switch to you. Put your book down and go finish your outdoor chores!"

At seventeen, Willie hadn't felt the business end of his mother's switch in a decade or more, but nonetheless, he heeded her dictates.

Willie was the youngest of Eunice and Edwin Rice's eight children. The four oldest—all boys—had all gone off to war, and praise God, all had come home alive. But now that they had seen something other than the workaday life of northern Mississippi, the young men had scattered to Detroit and Cleveland, Kansas City and St. Louis. The three girls had married and moved with their husbands, two to Tupelo and one to Memphis.

Willie had been something of a surprise to his parents, not only because his mother was already nearly forty-three when she discovered she was pregnant, but also because Willie wasn't much like his older siblings. He came out of the womb looking for information. His first word was "Wotdat?" followed soon by "Why" and "How does?"

Plessy v. Ferguson in 1896 used the words "separate but equal," but in Canaan, Mississippi in the thirties and forties, Willie and his colored friends attended school in a dilapidated, abandoned, bug-infested building while the white children went to class in a brick building erected specifically for that purpose. So long as someone was providing facts and data and urging Willie to think and reason, he didn't care what the surroundings were. Only one thing annoyed him: Canaan didn't have a library. When he wanted to know more than what his texts or his teachers could supply, he had to figure out ways to get to Ripley or Corinth or Holly Springs, all of which were at least twenty miles from Canaan.

Presenting himself at the library didn't assure him of service, either. While the "Coloreds Only" area remained constant, the days and times when the area was accessible were subject to on-the-spot revision if the librarian decided she wasn't in the mood to have "those people" in her haven of privileged information. Coloreds were never permitted to check out books, which meant Willie had to take quick notes for all he couldn't commit to memory.

"Mama," Willie asked, "do you think I can thumb a ride into Holly Springs today? We're studying world history, and the map in our book is old. It doesn't even show what happened with the boundary disputes between Poland and Lithuania and Yugoslavia and Bulgaria or what happened in Ethiopia and Albania or what's going on in the Middle East."

Eunice Rice had no more notion what her son was talking about than she did about how to conduct tests of nuclear fission. "Does the Holly Springs library have hours for coloreds on Saturdays?"

"It's supposed to, but even if it doesn't, sometimes I can get someone else to help find out what I need to know."

"You know that asking white folks to help you is the surest route to a head-banging."

"Oh, Mama, I don't come right out and ask. What kind of fool do you take me for? I never talk first. And I'm always real careful to let them do the offering as opposed to me doing the asking. Seems like some white folks feel real charitable and helpful if they're doing a small good deed for a poor little colored boy." Willie flashed his best "aw shucks" look at his mother.

"Hurry up and finish your chores, and I'll fix you a bite to eat. You know I hate to have you out on that road. I worry some whitey will come along and run you over like you're nothing but a raccoon."

"I know all the cars that run that road. I can tell which belong to white folks and which belong to coloreds. When white folk come by, I keep my head down and stay way off to the side. I've been thumbing rides out there for years. I know how to keep my skin on my bones."

"Why do you care about lines separating some countries I've never even heard about, son?"

"It's part of our world. I've been telling you about all the stuff going on in Israel and Palestine. It changes almost every day. I have to go to the library so I can keep up with it."

While Willie tore through his chores, Eunice warmed a plate of collards and fried chicken. When Willie came back inside, she was humming a tune.

"What's that song, Mama?"

"I don't suppose I know its name. The first time I remember hearing it, I was a little girl way down in Louisiana. I know both my mama and her mama used to sing it when they were working in the fields."

Willie looked at his mother and was struck as he always was by the remarkable mix of features on her face. No one had ever kept track of her exact heritage, but she was a blend of African, Native American, Roma (Gypsy), Cajun, Jamaican and/or Haitian, and at least a dash of Caucasian.

Eunice set the plate of food on the table in front of Willie. "Here. This should hold you 'til supper."

"Thanks." Willie dug in. "Talk to me while I eat."

"What should I talk about?"

"Tell me about when grandma was a little girl."

"Grandma Angelique was born in LaSalle Parish in Louisiana, we think around 1855, but we don't know for sure. We've always said it was before the war, because she was born a slave. The people who owned her mother lived on a huge plantation. They grew cotton and rice and sugar cane and soybeans. The main house was so big that they had four maids whose only job was to keep the furniture dusted."

"Tell the part about naming." Willie jabbed at the food on his plate.

"Whenever a new colored baby was born, the owners would let the baby's mother pick the child's first name, but whatever duties the baby's mama had on the plantation set what the baby's last name would be. They didn't pay any mind to the fact that slaves married each other exactly like white folks did. To them, naming a colored baby was about like naming an animal. So anyway, if the baby's mama worked in the cotton fields, his name might be Joe Cotton or Joe Ball—like the boll. If she worked in the kitchen, it might be Mary

Cook or Freddy Baker. If she was a house servant, they might call her Annie Easly, because working in the house was considered easy duty. Same for Sam Cane or Bessie Bean or Leroy Rice."

"So children who were no relation at all to one another might have the same last name."

"Right. And slaves got sold from one plantation to the next, so a boy your age might be known as Willie Rice on the plantation where your grandma was born, but then be known as Willie Ball if he was put to work in the cotton fields by the man who bought him."

"Which means for the most part we don't know who we are or where our birth families are?"

Eunice sighed. "Yes, son. Every time I tell you this story, you ask me that question, and every time, the answer is always 'Yes.' People my age almost always know at least one generation back, but that's about the best we can do. And for most of us, all we know is our mama's side. The plantation owners used colored folk like breeding stock. If they owned a man who was especially strong and easy to control, they'd want him to have lots of children, so they'd make him be with as many of the women slaves as they could. And you already know the owners and the owners' sons thought of the women slaves as their playground."

"Which meant that a woman who gave birth to five children might have had each one by a different man?"

"That hasn't changed since the last time we talked about it, either."

"But when you were born, things were different, right?"

"You know your history better than I do. Why do you keep asking me the same questions?"

"Because I can only change the future if I know the past. You could give me a bowl of that peach cobbler over there and tell me about how things were for you when you were little." Willie gave his mother another endearing look like the one he had used on her earlier.

"All right, but then you need to get on your way to Holly Springs, if you're still planning to go." Eunice heaped the cobbler in a chipped dish and handed it to him.

"Thanks, Mama." He ate eagerly.

"Your grandma was born a slave, but in 1863, the president —"

"Issued the Emancipation Proclamation," Willie finished for her.

"Are you telling this story, or am I?" Eunice chided gently. "And then two years later —" She paused.

"Slavery was abolished," she and Willie said together. Willie resumed his enjoyment of the cobbler.

"Angelique was ten years old when she and all of the coloreds on the plantation were set free. Lots of the slaveholders ignored the proclamation, but when the amendment to the Constitution was made, they knew the old days were gone and they'd have to turn their slaves free."

Willie spoke before Eunice could go on. "So Grandma's mama and her kids and a whole bunch of folks from the plantations in LaSalle parish took up farming as free men, and Grandma met Grandpa Easly and got married. Then they had you and Uncle Roman and Aunt Cherry and later moved to Memphis. And when you were sixteen you met Edwin Rice and got married and moved to Canaan. You and Daddy had seven kids, which you thought was enough, but finally you got it right and had a handsome, smart boy who you named Wilbur Alphonse."

"I take it you've had enough of the story for today." Eunice took the empty cobbler dish from him.

"If I'm going to get to the library, I need to go. I should be able to catch a ride out on Highway 72 with someone headed toward Memphis. Thanks for the good lunch." Willie kissed his mother's cheek, grabbed up some books and papers, and bolted out the door.

"Watch yourself, Willie," Eunice called after him.

She reached for the first of the dishes that needed to be washed. "Doggone it," Eunice said with a shake of her head. "I wish that boy could learn that just because things have changed a little, it doesn't mean people aren't still exactly like they used to be."

Chapter
Six

The Curse of Canaan
Holly Springs, Mississippi
September 1948

WILLIE DIDN'T FIND anything in the library's Coloreds Only reference area about the splitting of Palestine into Arab and Jewish states or the proclamation that established Israel as a sovereign nation. He went to stand near the demarcation line that separated the coloreds from the whites, hoping that one of the white patrons might be willing to acknowledge his presence and offer help.

After ten minutes, a white woman who had helped Willie twice before noticed him and spoke.

"Is there something that you needed, boy?"

"Thank you, ma'am. Yes, ma'am. I was hoping to find materials that would explain what's happening in the Middle East with the creation of the Jewish state of Israel."

As the woman was about to speak, the librarian—who had overheard Willie's question—broke her own rule about speaking loudly in her domain and shouted from behind her desk. "An ignorant colored boy doesn't need to know about the godless Jews. Get out of my library."

Willie knew better than to question or disobey. He hastened to gather his possessions and withdrew to the shade of the magnolia several hundred yards away. The library would still be open for another three hours, and he hated to hitch a ride back to Canaan so early. He lowered himself to the ground, leaning against the magnolia tree. Maybe there would still be some way he could get back in and find the information he wanted. Why did white people want to make everything so hard for him?

"I think the librarian was wrong to throw you out. In my opinion, your question was perfectly reasonable." A pretty, young girl with green eyes and curly light brown hair stood five feet away from Willie.

He raised his eyes enough to confirm that the voice addressing him was that of a white girl and quickly averted his gaze lest he be accused of molestation or harassment. "Yes, ma'am. I mean, no, ma'am. Thank you ma'am."

"You don't need to call me ma'am. We must be almost the same age. My name is Lila. Why don't you call me that?" She took half a step toward him.

"Thank you, ma'am, but I don't think I rightly could, ma'am. It wouldn't be respectful."

"Don't be silly. If I am asking you not to call me ma'am, how could it possibly be disrespectful for you to do so? In fact, doing so when I've asked you not to would seem to me to be even more disrespectful."

Willie had witnessed many instances where white people set up situations where they could bait and intimidate young black men and then entrap them on "assault" or some other trumped up charge. He felt like this was going that direction. But getting up and walking away was as likely to get him in trouble as staying and getting entangled. Inertia and confusion overtook him. He sat tongue-tied and unmoving.

"Will you do something for me?" Lila asked.

"Yes, ma'am. What would you like me to do?"

"I want you stay right there where you are until I get back. Will you?"

"Yes, ma'am."

Willie lifted his eyes enough to see the girl walk briskly back toward the library and disappear through the front entrance. He entertained the idea of leaping up and running for the highway, hoping for a ride back home, but he feared that if he weren't there when the girl returned, a potentially bad situation could become even worse. He sat and waited and worried, dreading she had gone inside to get her father who would give him a beating for treating his daughter improperly.

A quarter of an hour passed, and then she reappeared with a sheaf of documents in her hand, which she held out to Willie. "Here, this should tell you what you need to know about Israel. Everything is still very confusing. Resistance is evident, both in this country and around the world, to the idea of a Jewish homeland."

Willie sat mutely, not daring to look up to meet her eyes.

"These are periodicals. They're not even supposed to be taken out of the library. Do you want to see them or not?"

"Yes, ma'am, I do. Thank you, ma'am." Willie lifted his head, but avoided looking at Lila. He tentatively reached out to take the proffered documents. He was eager to read what Lila had brought him, but he still wasn't sure he could trust her. He didn't know if he should offer to take them somewhere else to read or if he should wait for instructions from her.

"I told the librarian I'd have these magazines and newspapers back inside within the hour, so you'd better get busy if you want to get them all read."

"Yes, ma'am. I will. And thank you, ma'am." Willie put his head down to scan the various articles Lila had given him.

"Now that I've done you a favor, you are obliged to do one for me."

"Yes, ma'am." Willie paused in his reading. "What's the favor?"

"You simply must stop calling me ma'am. It makes me feel like an old lady or a southern belle, and I most certainly am neither of those things. Wouldn't you agree?"

"Yes, ma'am."

"You're supposed to stop calling me that."

"I'm sorry. I don't know any other proper way to address a lady." Willie barely raised his head.

"I've told you. Call me Lila."

"Maybe I could call you Miss Lila?" Willie ventured.

"All right. That's at least an improvement. And I'd like it if you would look at me when you speak."

Willie drew his head back and tried not to stare at the young woman smiling down at him. She was unlike any white girl he'd ever seen, not that he was in the habit of studying the white girls in northwestern Mississippi. Yes, her eyes were green, but they were green with gold and darker shades of brown sparking around the edges. Yes, her hair was light brown, but it had strands of many different shades of blonde and soft browns running through it. A wild tangle of waves and curls and corkscrews framed her face and were gathered into a clasp at the nape of her neck. Her complexion had a luminance, almost like her skin was stretched over a low-watt light bulb and lit from within. She had a high forehead and prominent cheekbones; her eyes were close-set, her nose and chin crisp and chiseled.

As he took all this in, Willie felt an anvil on his lungs and a rope around his heart — the automatic reaction, he assured himself, of a poor colored boy looking directly into the face of a well-to-do white girl. "I appreciate you getting all this information for me, Miss Lila. That was very kind of you." Willie coaxed each word out, as he looked her straight in the eye.

"Not at all. I think anyone who wants to know about the movement to restore a rightful place for the Jews should be entitled to read what's in the news." Lila knelt nearby and rearranged her skirt around her. "By the way, what's your name?"

"Wilbur Rice, ma'am — I mean, Miss Lila. My family and friends call me Willie."

"May I call you Willie?"

"Oh, yes. That would be fine." Willie felt the anvil lift and the rope loosen.

"You'd best get on with your reading, Willie, so I can return the librarian's precious materials to her when I promised."

"How did you ever convince her to let her you bring these things outside?"

"I simply explained to her that my daddy, Jack Lowe, is the president of the new bank here in Holly Springs. You might be surprised at the number of impossible things that suddenly become doable once that fact is known."

"You're not from around here, are you, Miss Lila?"

Lila threw her head back and laughed with abandon. "No, I should say not. And I hope not to call Holly Springs home for long, either. Now, get busy on those articles. And when you finish with each one, give it to me so I can read it, too."

With as much effort as it had taken to will himself to look at Lila, Willie pried his eyes from her face and read the first article, handing it to Lila and moving on to the next one and taking notes when something struck him as significant. Occasionally, he looked up and caught a glimpse of the girl sitting near him, obviously as enthralled in the content of the articles as he was. Sometimes, she met his gaze, briefly, and a half-smile played across her face. Willie wondered at the tremor that raced through him.

Lila checked her watch. "Time's up. I may be the banker's daughter, but even that has its limits." She gathered up the magazines and papers and hastened back into the library. Willie stood and shook the cramps from his muscles. He stacked his books and notepapers together, regretting that he hadn't expressed his thanks to Lila before she left. He stole a last look toward the door through which Lila had vanished. With a sigh, he set off in the direction of Route 7, which would connect with Highway 72 and take him back to Canaan.

Willie was lost in his thoughts. And thoughts of the West Bank led to thoughts of the banker's daughter. One was as consuming as the other.

"You could at least have said good bye." From nowhere, Lila was beside him.

"I'm sorry, Miss Lila. Of course I should have said good bye, and thank you, too. I figured you'd be on your way home once you returned those things."

"As it turns out, this is the way home for me. Do you mind if I walk along with you?"

"No, of course not, but—"

"Please, I know what you're going to say. And in the immortal words written by Margaret Mitchell, frankly, I don't give a damn."

Willie angled his head so that he had a more direct view of Lila's face. Her translucent skin was flushed and dewy, her green eyes dark and intense.

"Do you know anything about Liberia, Miss Lila?"

THAT NIGHT, SEVERAL households in Holly Springs, Mississippi, buzzed with conversations about the new banker's daughter and the uppity colored boy who had been seen together on the streets that afternoon.

Eudora Willingham, active in the Women's Guild at the Marantha Baptist Church, leaned over the fence and said to her neighbor, Millie Butram, the butcher's wife, "Can you imagine? Talking to each other like they had things in common."

Mrs. Butram thought of her husband's antipathy for the Negroes and agreed that nothing good could come of that.

Chapter
Seven

The Curse of Canaan
Canaan, Mississippi
September 1948

FOR WILLIE, THE school week always felt as thought it were over in the blink of an eye, but this week, the days had dragged by, each one more interminable than the one before. At long last, Saturday rolled around. Willie was out of the bed and onto his chores before the sun had a chance to get a good grip on the day. "Mama, I need to spend the day at the library in Holly Springs. Would you pack a lunch for me so I can get an early start?"

"What is it today, son? More worries about world maps?"

"Something like that." Willie went to his room to change clothes and get his books. When he returned, his mother handed him a grocery bag containing two sandwiches, an apple and a pear, and four cookies.

"Thanks. That should hold me 'til I get home tonight."

"You look mighty sharp today. I don't remember you dressing up to hitchhike to the library before."

Willie wore his nicest pair of trousers and his newest shirt. He'd even polished his shoes. "I might want to see some materials that aren't in the Coloreds Only section. I figure the more respectable I look, the better my chances."

"Even though it's wrong to be prideful, I think you're a handsome young man."

"Oh, Mama." He accepted his mother's kiss.

"Promise me you'll be careful."

"You know I will." Her kissed her cheek and let his gaze linger on her face. Until last Saturday, Willie would have argued with anyone who didn't agree that his mother was the prettiest woman in the county. Now, she was tied for first place.

Willie lucked up and caught a ride all the way into Holly Springs with a family from Corinth on its way to see their son at Rust College. He even got to ride in the backseat of the car instead of in the back of a pick-up truck, as was his usual means of transportation.

Willie was at the library when it opened. He knew to hang back from the entrance to ensure that the whites had ample opportunity to get through the door first. He scanned up and down the street while he waited, then went inside and hurried to his section, positioning himself to view the entryway and keep tabs on everyone who came in.

He saw her.

Miss Lila Lowe.

His mouth went dry. He wanted to wave and call her name, but he knew better.

Then she caught sight of him, too, and walked briskly through the library foyer and strode up to the rickety table where Willie sat. The dropping of jaws by the white patrons was practically audible.

"Hi. I was hoping you'd be here today. How are you?"

"I'm fine, Miss Lila, thank you." Willie dropped his already low voice. "I'm not sure it's such a good idea for you to be on this side, though."

Before Lila could reply, the ubiquitous librarian interceded. "You, boy!" She pointed at Willie. "Remove yourself from this building at once, and stay out for the rest of the day."

Willie pulled his few books and papers together and walked silently out the door, head down. He knew Lila was only a few paces behind him, but he didn't look back, nor did he slow down.

"That worked out perfectly." Lila caught up with him at the base of the exterior steps. "If I'd sat down with you in there, everyone would have watched us like hawks, and we would have had to whisper. This way, we have the whole day to ourselves. Isn't that wonderful?"

Willie didn't look at Lila until they were well away from the entrance. "Miss Lila—"

Lila cut him off. "No, Willie. I hate having you call me Miss like you're some kind of servant or something. It's 1949. The Civil War has been over for more than eighty years. That's enough."

"But it's not only what you want that matters. White people around here treat coloreds in certain ways and expect us to act in certain ways. I'm afraid of what they'll do to you if they see me treating you in ways they don't like."

"Then you're going to have to make a choice. You can worry about what other people want, or you can pay attention to what I want. Either you call me Lila, or you'll call me nothing at all— because I won't be within earshot to hear you."

For Willie, that wasn't much of a contest.

"All right, Lila," Willie said with effort. "We've been thrown out. Now what?"

"Let's go someplace where we can sit and talk. On Tuesday, I checked out two books about Liberia. I brought them with me, and I thought we could each read one and then tell one another what they said."

"I don't know of anyplace in Holly Springs where we could sit together."

"I do. Come with me."

Lila walked purposefully through town and marched onto the grounds of Rust College as though she had personally established the university for Negroes in 1866. The school year had been underway for a few weeks. Students were gathered in groups all around the campus grounds, studying, laughing, flirting, talking. Lila led them to a bench set back from the edge of a walkway away from the main part of the campus and sat down.

"This should do nicely," she said as she extracted books and a pad of paper from her oversized bag.

"Aren't you uncomfortable?" Willie asked as he sat a respectable distance apart from her.

"Why?"

"Look around. Do you see anyone who looks like you?"

"So? I'm used to feeling like I don't belong. But I'll bet we can sit here all day and not have even one person tell me that I have to leave. That alone makes it a better option than the public library." He could feel Lila's eyes fixed on his profile.

Willie faced Lila directly. Her eyes riveted him to his seat.

"You're more than the banker's daughter, aren't you?"

"What do you mean?"

"I mean you know how it feels to be hated because of who you are. Who are you, Lila?"

Lila looked to the far edge of the horizon. "My real name is Lilith. According to Hebrew folklore, the original Lilith was the first wife of Adam, in existence before the creation of Eve. In some versions of the Semitic legends, Lilith haunted deserted places and attacked children." Lila paused and let Willie digest this preface to her story.

"You're a Jew." Willie mouth hung agape.

Lila gave him a disarming look. "Once we've gotten to know each other better, you can decide which of those representations of Lilith is the better description of me."

Chapter
Eight

The Curse of Canaan
Holly Springs, Mississippi
May, 1949

"I MISSED SEEING you last Saturday," Lila said as she and Willie sat on "their" bench at Rust College.

"I missed you, too. My mama counts on me to help out at home with the garden and with our field of beans and with the chickens and our three cows. And it's my job to keep the roof patched and the yard picked up. I've always got so much to do to around home. I tried to get away, but by the time I had all of Mama's projects done, it was too late to catch a ride over here. I'm sorry."

"You've never mentioned your father."

"My daddy died when I was fifteen. I'm the only one left on our farm. After he passed, my brothers and sisters wanted Mama and me to come live with them, but I drive the tractor and keep up with our garden and do the rest of the outdoor chores. I've got family in Cleveland and Detroit, Kansas City, St. Louis, Memphis and Tupelo." Willie ticked each city off on his fingers to make sure he hadn't left out any of his siblings.

"I understand, but I've gotten used to seeing you every week."

The early May air was warm and inviting. They had been meeting weekly (and more frequently when they could) for nearly eight months. Willie had become accustomed to watching the light play off the brown and gold highlights in her hazel eyes. He only wished he knew what Lila thought when she looked at him.

"I brought this newspaper article," Lila offered. "The Arab unrest in the Middle East seems to be increasing." Their hands accidentally brushed against one another as they traced the lines of the latest boundary skirmishes on the map accompanying the article. For a moment, neither dared speak nor move nor breathe, lest the earth pitch off its axis and hurl out of control forever.

"Would you like to take a walk, Lila?" Willie asked, his pulse climbing ever higher.

"Yes, I think that would be nice. Where should we go?"

"I've noticed an old, abandoned barn outside of town. I pass it on my way from Route 7. It sits way back off the road—"

"I know the one you mean. I see it when we drive to Memphis."

"Maybe it would be better if we went there separately."

"I think you're right. I'll go first. Give me a fifteen minute head start."

"Okay."

Lila scooped up her belongings and virtually ran to the meeting place. Willie waited fifteen minutes, watching the clock in the tower in the center of campus. At last, the sluggard minutes ticked off. He did his best to act like an insignificant colored boy as he hastened through town and made his way to the barn.

Willie was careful in his approach. He circled to the far side of the building, all the while checking to be sure no one was observing him, even briefly, from a passing car or a neighboring farm yard. Satisfied no one had seen him, he went into the weathered, rotting building. Early afternoon sunlight filtered through several holes in the roof.

"Lila?" he called softly.

"Over here." Standing near several bales of gray-green hay, she beckoned. "Did anyone see you?"

"No, I don't think so," he answered as he walked toward her. "I looked all around the building before I came in. What about you? Do you think anyone saw you?"

"No, but remember, nobody will challenge me—I'm the banker's daughter."

"So what are you doing in this old barn with a Negro boy from Canaan, Mississippi, little miss banker's daughter?" Willie's stab at lightness was more for his benefit than for hers.

"I'm hoping to find out if your arms will feel as good around me as I've imagined." Lila took a step toward Willie.

"Lila," Willie's voice wavered, "do you know what a terrible risk we're taking?"

"If your arms don't feel good around me, then I'll ask you to let me go." Her beauty turned his knees to rubber.

"People will flog every inch of skin off both of us if they find out we're together." Willie wasn't sure which he was more afraid of— actually touching the stunning young woman or being found out and lynched if he did.

"Then the least we can do is make it worth their while." Lila lifted her arms and laid them on Willie's shoulders, edging in nearer still to him. Willie looped his hands around her so they rested in the small of Lila's back. He flexed his fingertips into the hollow on either side of her spine. It felt like a summons to destiny. With a sigh, Lila fell against him and was lost in the muscular embrace of his lithe, lean body.

He drew his face away from its resting place atop her head and ran his lips down her cheek. She met his kiss.

They pulled away from one another and searched each other's eyes. Ever so softly, almost inaudibly, Lila whispered, "Yes."

Willie took two of the bales, broke them down and scattered the hay to make a bed. Wordlessly, they helped one another undress and used their clothing to cushion the sharp edges of the alfalfa.

The earth paused in its rotation and the moon froze in its orbit. Every other human ceased to exist. They had gone into the barn a Jewish girl and a Negro boy, but by afternoon's end, no black or white, no Jew or Gentile remained — only two people in love, bound to one another with the firm belief that they were meant to be together forever.

Chapter
Nine

LaGrange, Georgia
December 26, 2005

ELIZABETH HAD HEARD Colleen come in through the back door with the dogs at least twenty minutes earlier. As far as she knew, Colleen was still in the kitchen.

She set the manuscript aside and stretched her arms over her head. Colleen appeared in the doorway.

"How was your walk?"

"Good. The boys always like to ramble for a while after dinner." Colleen called back into the kitchen, "Release." Buster and Muggins thundered into the living room, jubilant at having been freed from their long "down-and-stay" that Colleen had imposed so that Elizabeth could read uninterrupted.

"How was your read?"

"Where in the world did you come up with that story?"

Colleen leaned against the doorjamb between the living room and kitchen. "Nice try, but that doesn't answer my question."

Elizabeth narrowed her eyes and squinted hard at Colleen while she considered her answer. "Okay, let me put it this way. If this book came through the door at Triple S, the first member of the review team to see it would write on the evaluation sheet, LWL."

"LWL?" Colleen echoed without shifting her posture.

"Yes. In-house short-hand for 'Lesbians? What lesbians?'"

"I told you this book wasn't like any of my other stuff."

"You could get an award for understatement of the year."

"Did you hate it, LJ?" Before Elizabeth could speak, Colleen held her palm up to stop her. "Never mind. I don't want to hear those words come out of your lips." She looked past Elizabeth so that she wouldn't have to meet her eyes.

Elizabeth rose and joined Colleen in the doorway. "Come sit beside me and tell me about the book."

Colleen shook her head hard. "No, I thought I was ready to bring this out of the shadows, but I was wrong. Let's drop it, okay?"

Elizabeth put her hand on Colleen's forearm and felt the shudder pass through Colleen's body.

"It's your book. Nobody—not even your publisher—can force you to put it in front of the reading public's eyes until you're ready to." Elizabeth pulled Colleen into a half-hug. "Did you get cold when you were out with the dogs?"

"No." Colleen tried to laugh, but it wouldn't materialize. "Cold feet, maybe."

Elizabeth waited a few seconds. "Let's go warm them up. Race you to the bedroom."

"I'll give the dogs one more chance to make sure their bladders are empty and lock up the house. I'll meet you there in a minute." Colleen gave Elizabeth a brief kiss and summoned the dogs to accompany her to the back door.

That's a welcome reprieve, Elizabeth thought as she made her way down the hallway. *I was afraid I was going to have another Alana Montaigne episode to deal with. I don't see a chance in a million that* The Curse of Canaan *is going to turn out to be a lesbian love story.* Elizabeth stepped into the bathroom. *Still, I can't help but wonder what happened to Willie Rice and Lila Lowe.* She squeezed toothpaste on the brush. *And if Colleen ever gives me the rest of the manuscript, maybe I can find out.*

Chapter
Ten

Columbus, Georgia
May 1, 2006

"I WOULD HAVE brought your royalty check along when I come to LaGrange next weekend." Elizabeth pushed some papers around on the top of her desk. "Or we could have dropped it in the mail to you. You didn't have to come all the way up here to pick it up."

"To tell you the truth, I had forgotten that royalty checks are issued on May first." Colleen perched on the edge of the guest chair in Elizabeth's office as though she thought the back of it might be wired to give her a jolt of electricity if she leaned back. "I missed having you at the house with me this past weekend. That's why I made the drive to Columbus. Even if it's not for more than a minute or two, I wanted to see you."

"Huh," Elizabeth said with a snort. "Does that mean you've finished the manuscript you were working on? When I was down there weekend before last, you didn't spend more than fifteen minutes at a stretch with me. I figured I might as well stay here and try to get caught up on some of my paperwork instead of wasting my time listening to you swear at your computer."

The bitterness in Elizabeth's voice cut Colleen to the quick. "I was rude. I'm sorry. I can't seem to make any of my story lines work out right now, and it's driving me crazy."

"It's not doing much for my state of mind, either." Elizabeth closed her center desk drawer forcefully.

Colleen shifted uncomfortably in her chair. "Do you think maybe I could take you out for an early lunch or that we could go for a walk or something?"

"I can't up and drop everything because you decided to invite yourself to my office, Colleen." Elizabeth looked up and saw Colleen's lower lip start to tremble. She softened her tone. "But since you're here, why not?" She pushed back from her desk. "Do you want to wander in the great outdoors or eat?"

"Let's walk. I don't feel much like eating."

"Okay. Where?"

"We could go to that big park over on the Chattahoochee."

"Good idea." Elizabeth gave a couple of quick instructions to Toni, then escorted Colleen out of the office. Each took her own car, and ten minutes later, they claimed two parking spots farthest away from the water access.

Colleen looked around to be sure no one was close enough to have their "Honk if you Love Jesus" bumper sticker curl in spontaneous combustion and gave Elizabeth a lingering kiss. "I don't blame you for being mad at me. I've been a total shit the past few times you've come down to LaGrange."

Elizabeth let her hand tarry on Colleen's shoulder as they stepped back from one another. "I'll tell you the truth, Collie. On my drive back from your place ten days ago, I was about ready to call the whole thing off. I know you get wrapped up in your work. I get wrapped up in mine, too, but when we finally have a chance to spend some time together, I don't think it counts if the two of us sit in the same room while I look at invoices on my laptop and you sweat out a dialogue scene in your next book."

"You're right. No less than thirty times that weekend, I told myself I'd hit the save key and rip off my clothes and pounce on you, but I couldn't seem to do it."

Elizabeth slipped her hand down Colleen's arm and clasped her fingers momentarily. "Wanna walk down the footpath a ways?"

"Sure. It's a pretty day."

They walked a while in silence. Too many others were on the path enjoying the pretty spring weather for them to hold hands or make much physical contact, but Colleen savored the nearness of Elizabeth. They made small talk about Colleen's dogs and the rowboats on the river.

Colleen stopped and studied a trillium blooming beside the path. "If I tell you what the problem is, do you think it might help us sort this all out?"

"Couldn't hurt. Might help." Until Colleen spoke again, Elizabeth watched dragonflies diving and hovering over the water.

"Remember that book I had you take a look at when you stayed with me at Christmas time?" Colleen looked briefly into Elizabeth's eyes, but then stared off across the river.

"Uh huh. Canaan something or other, wasn't it?"

"The Curse of Canaan."

"Willie and the Jewish girl."

"Right."

"What about it?"

"It's like I literally opened Pandora's Box when I took that manuscript out of the closet that night. Every time I try to write something else, it crowds into my mind, and *The Curse of Canaan is* all I can think about."

Elizabeth rubbed her hand on the bark of a nearby dogwood tree. "So finish it."

"I'm trying, but I keep hitting dead ends. And I know no one — not even you — is ever going to publish it, so I'm throwing good time after bad. Nothing will ever come of it."

"Lots of authors write books that don't get published. I remember one of the very first conversations I ever had with you. You told me that writing was cheaper than therapy. Write it for the sake of writing it. Think of it as putting a new cartridge in your printer or paying your bills — a housekeeping chore you need to get out of the way so you can move on to the important tasks."

Colleen contemplated Elizabeth's observation. "But isn't that like a musician playing music when nobody's listening?"

"What if it is? Even a pianist likes to hear the sounds of the notes she hits." Elizabeth glanced at her watch. "I wish I could spend the afternoon with you, but I need to get back to the office and swing a machete over that jungle on my desk."

"I understand."

"I can see this is bothering you a lot. I wish I had a magic pill that would cure writers' block. I could make a fortune from it." Elizabeth patted Colleen's back reassuringly. "Let me give you a suggestion, okay?"

"What?"

"Put *The Curse of Canaan* aside for the rest of the week. When I come down this weekend, I'll take a fresh look at it and see if I can't help you break the logjam that's keeping you from making any progress. Can you do that?"

"Maybe."

They retraced their steps up the path toward the parking area.

"Thanks for coming to the park with me," Colleen said. "I wish we could spend the day together." She lowered her voice in deference to the others on the path within earshot. "And the night, too."

"That would be delicious." Elizabeth enjoyed the buzz that unexpectedly sprang in her gut. "I don't suppose you can stay?"

"No, I didn't arrange for anyone to take care of Buster and Muggins, and besides, you've got a boatload of work to do."

They covered the last distance to their cars.

"It's only four nights 'til I'll be in LaGrange." Elizabeth reached for her door handle. "We'll have to hope we can make it until Friday night."

"I'll be counting the minutes."

"Me, too."

Elizabeth was about to slide behind the wheel, but Colleen used her arm to bar Elizabeth's access. "I...I want to ask you something."

"Ask me."

"Um." Colleen gulped a deep breath, then tried again. "Um, do you think you'd be willing to read another part of that book—*The Curse of Canaan?* I brought four more chapters along today."

"That's what prompted you to come up today, isn't it? You wanted to give me the next part of the book."

"I've wanted to talk to you about it for months, but I can't seem to make my brain form the words and push them off my tongue."

"Of course I'll read it. If it's only another four chapters, I'm sure I can have them read by the time I come down on Friday."

"You're the best, the absolute best. I wish I could lay you down in the backseat and—"

"Easy, there, buckaroo. Don't go getting a sex-starved woman all worked up when we know we can't get our tickets punched."

"Then count on two round trips when you get to LaGrange on Friday." Colleen blushed until Elizabeth feared her hair would ignite. "I'll get the manuscript." She walked around the back of both cars and lifted a grocery bag from the floor of the front seat of her car. Elizabeth met her at the rear fender. "Note the exquisite carrying case," Colleen said with a laugh as she slipped the handles of the Ingles Store bag from her fingertips to Elizabeth's.

"We'll talk about what's going on with this book while I'm at your house this weekend, okay?" Elizabeth asked as she placed the bag in the car.

"Right. For sure we'll talk about it then." Colleen's face belied her words.

Elizabeth backed out and drove away, wondering why her lover was so nervous about the manuscript.

Colleen waited until Elizabeth's car was out of sight. She went back to the path and walked until she thought she couldn't walk any farther. And then she walked some more.

IT WAS NEARLY eleven o'clock Thursday night before Elizabeth remembered her promise to Colleen. She trudged out to the garage and claimed the manuscript from the front seat. She sat down in the living room to skim the first four chapters to remind herself of what she'd read more than nineteen weeks earlier, and then she picked up where she had left off.

Chapter
Eleven

The Curse of Canaan
Holly Springs, Mississippi
Spring, 1948

JACK LOWE HAD made a rare midday trip from the bank to his residence. He strode through the living room of their home, one of the largest, plushest houses in Holly Springs, and summoned his daughter and wife from their lunch at the mahogany dining table.

"Lila Lowe, I will not have you keeping company with some colored boy. After all we went through to get here, I would hope you'd have the good sense not to jeopardize our standing in this community. Have you forgotten what happened in Atlanta?"

"First of all, I am not 'keeping company' with Willie Rice. He's a nice person I meet at the library sometimes. You know that awful librarian, Mrs. Carruth, won't allow the Negroes to use any of the new reference books or periodicals. He's deeply interested in the Zionist movement. So what if I help him with his research?" Lila sat on the edge of the divan and cautiously watched her father. Her mother stood near her.

"I'll tell you so what. The people of this community don't like to see white girls socializing with the coloreds, especially colored boys. They think if I allow you to associate with him, that means I approve of it—and in short order, they'll take their banking business elsewhere."

"Yours is the only bank in town. Where else would they take their business?"

"To another town, until they can drive me out and replace me with someone more to their liking, like they did with the last banker. I've heard talk, Lila. If I don't put a stop to this, the men of this town will. I'm ordering you to have nothing more to do with that Willie Rice."

"But Daddy—"

"No buts. You are never to see him again. That's my final word on the subject." Jack Lowe marched out the front door and slammed it behind him.

Stella, Lila's mother, sat down on the divan and cupped her daughter's face in her hands. "He's more than a nice boy you help do research at the library, isn't he?"

"Of course not. What else could he be?"

"I see your face when you come back from an afternoon with him. I know the feelings that cause a girl to look like that."

Lila pleaded silently with her mother.

"Oh, child. Maybe if we were still in New York, there might be a chance for a romance between the two of you, but here—" Stella shook her head forlornly. "Your father is right. It will never be tolerated. If you care for the boy, you should end it. Yes, your father's bank might suffer, but that's only money. What could happen to Willie is far worse than losing a few dollars."

"I can't believe you and Daddy, of all people, are being so narrow-minded about this."

"It's not us. It's the world around us. We know firsthand what's done to people for the sake of hatred. I can't fault your father for wanting you to get out of a situation that can only end in tragedy. Better that you should choose to end it before someone ends it for you."

Lila drew away from her mother. "I respect you and Daddy— you know I do. But it's precisely because of what happened to us in Atlanta and to millions of us in Europe that I won't be scared away from Willie by other people's prejudices." She squared her shoulders and faced her mother directly. "First, we left New York because Daddy felt that the influx of Jews after the war was raising too much negative attention. Then, we moved to Atlanta and were confronted by such strong anti-Semitism that we fled the city, changed our names, and drifted from town to town until we wound up here in Holly Springs. You have forbidden me to go to Israel to join a kibbutz because you feel it's too dangerous. Now you're telling me that having feelings for a Negro is likewise too dangerous. How much more of my identity will I have to surrender before I'm acceptable?" Stella opened her mouth to speak, but Lila held the palms of her hands out to stop her.

Lila took a deep breath and continued. "And how much more of your identity are you willing to deny? You used to be Esther Rachel Lebowitz Levy. You used to sit Shiva and bake challah and keep a mezuzah on the door." Stella looked away, tears in her eyes. "Now you're Stella Lowe. I actually overheard you say to someone that you think that you might have some distant Jewish relatives. Distant? Do parents qualify as 'distant?' Daddy was Jacob, now he's known as Jack. I was born Lilith; now I'm Lila. Shall I cut off all my hair and have my nose bobbed? Should I forget that I know about places like

Auschwitz and Dachau? Should I disregard what Ben-Gurion and Ralph Bunche are doing in Palestine?"

Lila ignored the tears pouring down her mother's face. "Pretending we're not who and what we are doesn't make us what we pretend to be, Mother. All it makes us is liars." Lila fled from the room and dashed out the door.

Lila stomped along the sidewalk, then detoured around the back of their palatial home onto the well-manicured grass. Fists clenched, she dodged around the hammock under the burr oak and headed for the woods. She often walked this way where no one could interrupt her thoughts. She wished she could bring Willie sometime, but even though they were regularly sighted at the Holly Springs library and on the Rust College campus, being seen alone — just the two of them without other people around — was too dangerous. Whenever they were in public, she hated how they had to be so careful about not sitting too close or laughing too much. Certainly, they never touched. She thought of all the times they'd been so formal in parting — and then they'd run to the old barn where they could satisfy their need to belong completely to one another. Their entire relationship existed in lies and shadows, hidden from truth and light.

She lifted her fist to her mouth and bit down on her knuckle. She wanted a physical pain — one that would interrupt the fear of thinking she might never be with Willie again if her father's order were carried out. She had thought she and Willie had been so cautious, mindful to let no one see or suspect, but if her father knew about them, Holly Springs must be agitated to the point of frenzy.

They had been lovers for slightly over two months, but their time together wasn't mere physical passion. Much more than sex connected them. She knew they were both fascinated by the parallels between the history of the Jews (driven from their homeland, persecuted and reviled, longing for a place to call their own) and the history of the Negroes (stolen from their homeland, persecuted and reviled, longing for a place to call their own.) She loved that Willie shared her affinity for literature, music, and history. They talked of shedding Holly Springs and making their way north where they could be open about their feelings for one another. Some day, she hoped they would get the chance to go to Liberia and Israel and work for the betterment of their homelands.

She reached a dense part of the woods where the path forked, one way leading to the creek and the other back out to the gravel road. She stopped, tears in her eyes, and put out of mind the distant future and all the countries far away. She had more immediate concerns now. When they had parted company last Saturday, she and Willie had made plans to meet today in the barn as soon as

Willie could catch a ride from Canaan to Holly Springs. After the scene with her parents, Lila was convinced that the only hope for her and Willie was for them to run away.

She knew the time had come to get out of Mississippi — or die trying.

"WILLIE, I THINK we need to make plans to get away from Holly Springs." Lila was wrapped in Willie's arms, lying in their makeshift bed in the barn.

"That's what we've said all along. I thought we'd decided on Chicago," he said thoughtfully, "but I need to find a way to earn some money for us to live on while we're traveling and to hold us over until we get set up."

"I don't think we can wait. My father is upset by what people at the bank have said to him about not banking there any more, and my mother is worried there are men in town who want to teach you a lesson about staying away from white girls. I'm afraid for you."

"White men around here make a big show of saying they're going to hunt a man down, but that's all big talk to scare him into doing what they want him to do."

"All the same, maybe we shouldn't see each other for a while to give the town time to cool down some."

"Is that what you want? Not to see me?" He burrowed in at the base of her neck.

"You know that's not what I want. I'd see you every day if I could. I hate that you have to ride in the back of trucks to get here." She locked her fingers in his thick, textured hair. "I don't want you to get hurt. You're the very heart of my life."

"I'll find a job somewhere this summer. I'll save every dime. Whatever money we have when summer's over, that's what we'll use to strike out with. We might have to stop along the way and take odd jobs to earn enough to get to Chicago, but by New Year's Day, 1949, we'll be married and calling Illinois home." He propped himself up on his elbow. "You do still want to marry me, don't you?"

"Yes, Mr. Rice. From the day I heard you ask that woman at the library for information about Israel, I knew you were special. I fell in love with you that very afternoon under the magnolia tree. You're so smart and so handsome. I can't wait to see what our children will look like." She kissed him soundly. "But now I need to excuse myself to the woods, and then I'll have get ready and get back to the house. My father is already on the warpath. No sense in making him angrier still." She pulled on her skirt and blouse, then slipped out of the barn to relieve herself in a nearby grove of trees.

Willie lay on his back for a few moments contemplating his

future life in Chicago with his beloved Lila. He rolled to his side and reached for his pants. He heard a noise from the direction Lila had gone. "Lila? Are you back already?"

Silence. The hairs on the back of his neck prickled. He looked around for a pitchfork or a shovel—something he could use as a weapon—but saw nothing. He jumped to his feet to put his pants on, when suddenly, two men sprang through the narrow doorway of the barn. Each carried a single-shot shotgun. Willie stood aghast, his pants clutched in one hand.

"Well, looky here, Nate. Seems we got us a fresh, naked, young buck. Too bad the poor stupid thing is color blind, though." The man leered at Willie and waved his shotgun angrily as he approached. "I hear they're fun to watch if you shoot 'em in the nuts. Some say they dance like a monkey on a string."

As they drew nearer, Willie realized he'd seen them working on cars in the bays at the gas station on Main Street in Holly Springs. They came to a stop a dozen feet away. Willie seized the opportunity to hastily draw his trousers on.

"As I see it, Jimpsey, now we gotta make a choice. I'm thinking that since the fool is already color blind and don't have the sense to stay with his own kind, we ought to finish the job and make him blind once and for all. Seems a shame to waste two shells, though. Should we watch him dance, or should we help him go blind?" They laughed menacingly.

Willie looked from one man to the other. The stench of cheap liquor and human perspiration filled the air. Their clothes were dirty from the oil and grime of the garage.

He quickly buckled his pants and prayed silently that Lila had heard or seen the men and either hidden in the woods or raced for home.

His prayers went unanswered.

"Willie, I—" Lila came through the door and froze in her tracks.

"Willie, is it?" Jimpsey sneered. "I see you've been making deposits to the banker's daughter, Willie. I think we'll have to close your account for good." He raised his shotgun to his shoulder, pointed it at Willie's head, and held it there with one hand.

"What's wrong with you people?" Lila screamed. "We're not hurting anybody. If I want to be with this man, what business is it of yours?"

Jimpsey kept his eyes on Willie as he spoke. "If one gets away with it, they'll all think they can. We ain't gonna have our race contaminated with blood from the likes of him."

"Your race," Lila shouted. "What race is that? The Jews? The twelve tribes of Israel? Are you Jewish like me? Would you be so concerned if you knew that Jack Lowe's real name is Jacob Levy? My given name is Lilith, and my mother's name is Esther Lebowitz. We're Jews from New York who came here by way of Atlanta. You don't know anything about what you think you're defending."

Nate swung toward Lila as he spoke. "Don't you lie to us to try to protect this nigger's hide. We should've known he'd poison your mind and tell you to make up some wild story to throw us off." He hacked up a wad of sputum and spat it out the corner of his mouth, barely missing his cracked work boots as it landed at his feet. The gaps in his brown teeth gave him the appearance of an evil jack-o-lantern.

"If you want to hurt or kill Willie, then you'll have to kill me first." Lila took several quick steps across the barn and positioned herself between Willie and the men.

Jimpsey glowered. His rheumy blue eyes watered and he swiped at his runny nose with the back of his hairy hand. "Now why would a pretty white girl like you ever want to defend something so useless as a no-account nigger boy? What kind of demon spell has he put on you?"

Lila's tone was scathing. "Something that louts like you wouldn't know anything about, obviously. He loves me and respects me. And I love him. If that offends you, then kill us both, because you won't harm him so long as I draw breath." Lila moved back until she bumped into Willie, then took his arms and drew them around her. She lifted her hand behind her head to Willie's face and caressed his cheek.

"Don't that make you want to puke, Nate?"

At that instant, a rat knocked against an old tin pail along the far wall behind the men. They turned in the direction of the noise. Willie gave Lila a strong push toward the door. "Run!" he commanded. At Willie's shout and Lila's movement, Jimpsey and Nate swiveled back and fired. One moment Willie saw Lila's beautiful head of brown and blonde curls; the next moment, her head was nearly blown right off her neck. She crumpled to the ground. In horror, Willie looked toward the men and saw that Jimpsey's shot had torn through Nate's middle immediately above his hips.

"Stupid son of a bitch." Nate groaned as he fell to the floor atop his gun.

Jimpsey dropped his weapon. He lunged for his fallen comrade. Willie took one look at the two men on the floor, then dove for Jimpsey's shotgun. He used it to take a roundhouse swing at Jimpsey's kneeling form. The stock landed with a crack against the side of Jimpsey's skull, and he slumped on top of Nate's bleeding body.

Willie dropped the shotgun, leapt over the two men, fell to his knees, and gathered Lila to him.

"Oh, my darling. My brilliant, priceless Lila." She hung like a rag doll in his trembling arms. He wanted desperately to kiss her, but nothing remained of her dazzling, captivating face. He laid his head against her bosom one last time. The smell that assailed him was a mix of blood and urine, and he thought he was going to be sick. He wasn't sure how long he knelt, holding Lila, rocking and whimpering.

He heard the wail of a police siren in the distance. "Oh, God."

He could barely breathe. On shaky legs, he carried Lila over to the place where only a little while before she had lain warm and promising in his arms. He laid her gently on the hay and lovingly draped his shirt over her ravaged form.

"I will always love you." He looked down at her one last time. "Lila."

Despite the warmth of the day, Willie shook with a chill that intensified as he struggled into his shoes. He tore into the woods as the police car skidded to a halt on the other side of the barn. He ran until he feared his lungs would burst, and then he ran some more. Near nightfall, he hazarded out of the woods on Route 306 and thumbed a ride west, away from Holly Springs, away from Canaan, away from hell.

An old black man in a barely-running Chevrolet pick-up took him as far as Route 51 and gave him a shabby shirt that had been under a tire in the load bed. Willie spent the night in a drainage culvert beneath a gravel road. At first light, he caught a ride with a farmer hauling melons into Memphis. By nine a.m., he made his way to his sister Pearl's house.

"Lord, you've gone and done it this time, child." Pearl pulled him inside and closed the door.

"They killed her," Willie sobbed.

"Hell, 'they' didn't do nothing. It's all over the news. The way it's told, two Holly Springs businessmen were out doing some practice shooting when they came upon a colored boy raping a white girl in an abandoned barn. When they tried to pull him off her, he grabbed their shotguns, killed the girl and shot one of the men, and then clubbed the other one in the head. The police from Holly Springs knocked on Mama's door last night and said she'd better turn you over to them if she knew what was good for her. They carried on all through the night and finally gave up about five o'clock this morning. She called here right after that crying her eyes out."

"Mama knows I'd never kill anyone, especially not Lila. I loved her."

Pearl's eyes flew open wide. "Willie, you're crazy, boy. Folks like us don't fall in love with rich, white bankers' daughters. Mama said she'd never heard of Lila Lowe."

"It doesn't matter now. She's dead." Willie cried harder than ever.

"Stop it, Willie. You look like an old man."

"Pearl, Pearl," he said, trying to make her understand, "she was the best thing that ever happened to me. We were going to go away up north and get married."

"We ain't got time to talk. God's truth is you have to get out of here. Mama thinks once the police find out you've got people here in Memphis and in Tupelo, they'll come looking for you. If I could, I'd feed you a good meal and put you to bed, but I don't dare. Where do you want to go? Detroit with Rudy maybe? Or Kansas City with Eddy? Mama hasn't called any of the boys yet. She figures it'll take the police a while to find out where all your kin lives. The less everybody knows, the less they can tell the police."

Willie looked at her, confused and heart-broken, and couldn't bring himself to speak.

"Where do you want to go, Willie? Pick a place so that we can make some plans."

Willie searched his mind and uttered a familiar-sounding city's name. "Chicago," he said. "I want to go to Chicago."

Chapter
Twelve

The Curse of Canaan

WILLIE'S MOTHER'S PREDICTION was right. By noon that Friday, the Memphis police were standing at Pearl's door asking questions about when she had last seen her brother Wilbur and what she knew about his involvement with a white girl named Lila Lowe. The Tupelo police were asking the same questions of his other sisters, Lacey and DeeDee.

By the time the police got to Pearl's house, Willie was long gone. Pearl took him to the Hopewell Baptist Church on Kimball Road and, with a kiss and a hug and a promise that somehow everything would turn out all right, left him in the capable care of Reverend Wright.

Willie sat in a windowless room with the minister. "What am I supposed to do, Reverend?'

"You stay right here in this church. Don't so much as look out a window to check the weather. On Sunday, after services, I'm leaving Memphis to drive to Little Rock for our church's annual meeting. When I go, you're going with me. Between now and then, though, you stay out of sight. Do you understand?"

"Yes, sir. But I didn't kill Lila. Those men shot her by accident. They were drunk, and I know they hate me, but shouldn't I go back to Holly Springs and tell the truth?"

Reverend Wright clamped his hand on Willie's shoulder. "Son, there's truth, and then there's truth. From what I've seen on the news and heard from Pearl, the citizens of Holly Springs have already held your trial, found you guilty, and set your sentence. The sooner you get gone, the greater your chance of seeing your next birthday."

Willie wanted to cry. He bit his lip to help fight the tears.

"I'm sorry, Willie."

"But what about my mama? When will I see her again?"

"I don't know. I do know that if you try to see her now, it'll put both you and her in danger. The police will be watching for you to show up at a relative's house. My advice is that you stay clear of your family for at least the next year — maybe longer. Maybe forever.

Hate has a long memory."

Willie hid all weekend while Reverend Wright quietly gathered clothes and personal care items for him. Other than Pearl and Reverend Wright's wife, no one at the Hopewell Baptist Church knew that the fugitive was being harbored there. By Sunday night, Willie and the Reverend had traveled to Little Rock where he was handed off to a friend of one of Reverend Wright's fellow ministers.

Without a penny or a plan, Wilbur Alphonse Rice set off on his own and learned to live by his wits. He picked up day labor jobs and took to sleeping under railroad trestles and highway overpasses. He worked for meals, for repair to his shoes, and for the right to rinse out his few clothes in someone's wash tub. He labored for the privilege of riding a few more miles down the road to the next town where he'd trade his time and his muscles for what he needed to hold body and soul together for another day.

From Little Rock he went to Shreveport, from Shreveport to Jackson. Then to Montgomery and Atlanta, Chattanooga, Nashville, Louisville, Indianapolis—and all of the little towns in between. Sometimes he stayed a day or two. Sometimes, he stayed a week or more. Atlanta was nearly two months, but as soon as he had the money for a bus ticket or got wind of the possibility of shagging a ride for free, he was gone from where he'd been and on his way to who-knew-where.

Mid-December 1949, was a cold and frigid time, and Willie had been on the run since May. He had read about snow and seen pictures of it in his school books, but experiencing it first hand without a warm coat was another matter altogether. He stood in a rail yard in Indianapolis with other men who had no coats, no homes, and no prospects.

"I hear Chicago is the place to be," one of them, a man called Max, said. "Tonight's the night I hop a freighter and give the Windy City a try." Max rubbed his hands together over a fire, which was struggling against the spitting snow.

"Would you mind some company?" Willie asked.

"Nope. It's a free country." All of the men—black and white—laughed ruefully at his statement.

Sometime in the early hours of the morning, a long, lumbering Chicago, Rock Island, and Pacific Railway train rumbled through the yard. Several of the boxcar doors were standing ajar.

"Come on, boy." Max shook Willie to rouse him from his fitful sleep. "If you're going to Chicago, your ride's here."

Max and Willie ran alongside the train as it swayed through the rail yard. With deadeye aim, Max tossed his bundle through the cracked door into the boxcar and then took Willie's satchel from him and did the same. With a perfectly timed leap, Max landed on the lip of the boxcar and wedged himself into the door's opening.

"Don't think about it or you'll lose your nerve," Max called. "Get a good running start and push off hard. I'll catch you."

Only the dim light from a few distant security lamps illuminated the track, and Willie could picture himself slipping in the slushy snow and falling under the wheels of the train. He didn't feel he had a clear view of the doorway for which he was aiming. He pumped his arms and legs harder as he ran, trying to likewise pump up his courage to make the jump onto the moving train.

"Hurry up, boy. Train'll be out of the yard soon and pickin' up speed. You can do it," Max said. "I'll count three and you jump, okay?"

"Okay." Willie gulped.

Max counted and Willie leapt. Both of his feet slipped out from under him the instant his hands made contact with the ledge of the boxcar. He flung his hand out and grasped the metal ladder that hung beside the open door. His forward momentum carried him into the cold steel, and he smacked his face against the hard edge of one of the rungs. It stunned him so badly that he nearly lost his grip. He was grateful that Max was there to grab his arm.

"Thanks." Willie rolled up on his knees. "I guess I should have practiced that in the daylight a time or two before trying it at night in the snow." Willie let Max help him to his feet.

"Looks like you hurt yourself," Max observed as they flashed past a bright light on a lamppost near the edge of the rail yard.

Willie wiped the back of his hand across his lips. He could taste the blood. He ran his tongue around the inside of his mouth and located a gap where a front tooth used to be. "Must have knocked a tooth out."

"That'll hurt like the devil once the shock wears off. Here." Max pulled a dented flask from inside his shirt. "Not exactly smooth sippin' whiskey, but it'll numb the ache a little."

"I don't drink liquor."

"Oh hell, boy. Under the best of circumstances, this ain't liquor, and tonight, it's medicine. An hour from now, you'll be begging me to do something for you to kill the pain. Save us both the bother and have a little nip now."

Willie did as the older man directed and gagged at the taste.

"The next one will go down a little better," Max assured him as he reclaimed the flask from Willie and took a long pull from it himself. "Might as well try and get some sleep. It'll be four hours or more 'til we get to Chicago."

Max went to the far corner of the boxcar and poked around in the darkness. "Hey, we're in luck. I found a whole bunch of old empty feed sacks over here. Come on. I'll share 'em with you."

Willie crept into the pile of sacks near Max, grateful for the warmth they provided. Max passed his flask to Willie several more times. As the throbbing in his face intensified, Willie was ever more grateful for Dr. Max's pain tonic. They dozed and talked as the train rocked on through the night.

The cold steel wheels of the freight car squealed to a stop in Chicago's teeming rail yard. Willie groaned to his feet, feeling all of the knocks and knots from his awkward attempt at boarding the train. He moved to the doorway and looked out the slit at the door's edge. A dismal day had dawned an hour or two earlier. Morning light, the color of dirty dishwater, greeted him.

"Good luck to you, boy," Max said as he offered Willie his hand. "I hope Chicago is your dream come true." Max jumped from the car and looked back at Willie in the doorway. "And by the way, Happy New Year, a week or two early." Max walked away and was swallowed up in the throng of men in the yard.

Chicago. Dreams. A new year. Without Lila, what was the point?

Willie wandered out of the rail yard and watched the crowds of people on the streets. He discerned that, for the most part, Negroes were coming from one direction, but whites were coming from everywhere. He walked in the direction from which the Negroes came. The more he walked, the more evident it was that he was headed in the right direction. Soon, everyone he met was dark skinned. The business establishments were operated and patronized by Negroes. The children playing along the curbs were nappy-headed. In some ways, it reminded him of being on the colored side of town in Canaan, Mississippi, only the beat-up houses were crammed much closer together, and the noise and the smells weren't what he was accustomed to.

Willie wished he could take another swig from Max's flask. What little numbing effect the alcohol had provided for the raw edge of Willie's broken tooth had completely dissipated. Since he knew no one in Chicago, even if he'd had the first clue about how to get around in the city, he had no idea where he might find a Negro dentist. And if he could find one, he had no way to pay for the care he needed. Still, the screaming pain in his tooth demanded something be done.

He roamed up one avenue and down the next until finally, on 110th Street, he saw a sign for James J. Rice, DDS. He climbed the stairs to the second floor, pushed open the wooden door, and stepped into the waiting area. A stooped man with a tufted row of white hair above his ears on either side of his head came out from an interior office.

"Can I help you, young man?"

"Are you Dr. Rice?"

"What's left of him, yep, that's me."

"Sir, my name is Wilbur Rice. It's not at all likely that we're related in any way. I got to Chicago this morning," Willie hefted his small satchel to emphasize his point, "and I don't know a soul here. I had an accident earlier today and broke off one of my front teeth." Willie pinched his top lip with his thumb and forefinger and raised it for the dentist's benefit. "I need to find someone who can do something about this tooth. The pain is making me crazy."

"Put your bag in the corner and come on back here with me."

"I need to tell you, sir, I don't have any money to pay you, so maybe you don't want to bother with me."

The dentist faced Willie. "I'll be the one who decides if you're worth bothering with or not. I don't expect any patients for another hour, so I might as well take a look at that mess in your mouth."

Willie followed him into the cramped examination room and sat in the high-backed mechanical chair.

"Broke it off clean as a whistle," Dr. Rice noted. "It needs a cap, the sooner the better. You've got bruised nerves exposed to the air. You must be one tough fellow not to be crying like a baby." He washed his hands in a small sink in the corner of the room and returned to his patient's side. "Okay, let's get to work."

"How much is this going to cost?" Willie made a move to get out of the chair.

Dr. Rice laid a hand on his shoulder and held him in place. "We'll work out my fee after we see how this goes. Now, try to relax. I'm going to give you an injection that will make your face go dead. It'll be easier for both of us that way."

An hour later, Dr. Rice finished the procedure.

"Take a look." He held a handled mirror out in front Willie.

Willie strained to part his lips. He was surprised to see a bright, gold false tooth shining back at him.

"I appreciate what you've done for me, sir," Willie slurred, "but I'll never be able to pay for it."

"Don't worry about it. A patient of mine ordered that gold cap six months ago, but durned if he didn't up and get himself killed in an accident in the freight tunnels before we could get the tooth put in. It's been sitting here in my drawer waiting for someone like you to come along. It's almost a perfect fit—I only had to make a couple of little adjustments to make it do. Consider it a gift from old man Wilcox."

"But I still owe you for your time and supplies."

"Indeed, that you do. Maybe you could work it off."

"Yes, sir. I'd be glad to do that. Tell me what you want done."

"The first thing I want you to do is take your bag and go to my house where my wife will see to it that you get a bath, a decent meal, and some rest. That injection I gave you will wear off soon, and a few hours sleep would be the best thing in the world for you."

"I couldn't impose on you that way."

"Don't argue with me, young man. Remember, I have all these implements of pain right here at my disposal." His tone was light and teasing as he gestured at the drill and tray of scalers, probes, and clamps. "If you're going to work for me, it's to my advantage to have you in good condition. I'll write a note for you to give to my wife and tell you how to get to my home. Follow me."

Willie felt shaky, as if he'd been hit in the head with a hammer. He followed the old dentist to a cluttered desk in the reception area and waited for him to scribble out directions and a note for Mrs. Rice.

The dentist handed the two pieces of paper to Willie. "Now, go." Dr. Rice retrieved Willie's bag from the corner.

He lifted a garment from the back of the chair at the desk. "Here, you better take this coat, too. It's too cold out there for you to be roaming around with nothing more than that light jacket. I've got another one in the closet." He helped Willie slip into it and pointed him toward the door. "I'll see you at home later."

Willie opened his mouth to thank the doctor, but his words were dismissed with a wave of James Rice's hand. Willie descended the stairs and emerged in the city's infamous swirling winds. Using the doctor's directions, he made his way through the neighborhood to the Rice residence. Ordinarily, his pride would have kept him from accepting such outright charity, but he was tired and cold, hungry and in pain.

The dentist and his wife lived on the bottom floor of a five-story walk-up. The building was old and run down, but looked to be in better repair than many of the others around it. Willie knocked, and a female version of the man he had left at the dentist's office — but with more hair — answered.

"Mrs. Rice? Your husband sent me. Here's a note from him." Willie's mouth hurt too much for him to offer a more comprehensive explanation.

She scanned the page that Willie handed her. "Come in, child. You look like you've been in a war."

"Thank you, ma'am. I feel like it, too."

"Call me Neecy, son. That's how everybody knows me."

In short order, Neecy directed Willie to the bathroom where he had his first real bath in longer than he cared to remember. She outfitted him in some of James's clean clothes. The next order of business was a bowl of hot soup that didn't require much chewing. Willie could barely hold his head up to finish the last spoonful. Neecy gave him two aspirin and led him to a tiny second bedroom that obviously doubled as Dr. Rice's library of reference materials. She got him settled in a cot. Willie's thanks to Neecy were lost in the pillow. He was asleep as soon as he got his feet off the floor.

Willie woke to the sound of muffled voices. Dazed and disoriented, his new tooth twanged, jarring his memory, and reminding him where he was. Because he was shrouded in darkness, he assumed it must be nighttime and that Dr. Rice had recently come home from his office. He made his way down the short hallway toward the voices he heard. The dentist and his wife were sitting in the living room. A horsehair sofa with sagging springs sat along the wall under the narrow, oblong window. Two mismatched armchairs were opposite it. A lamp without a shade sat on a small, square table between the chairs. The long wall that backed to the hallway was lined with book cases stuffed to overflowing. A record player was on one of the shelves.

"Ah, there's our sleeping prince. Good morning. How's that tooth?" Dr. Rice inquired.

"Morning?"

"Yes, indeed. It's about six a.m. You fell asleep after Mother gave you lunch yesterday and slept clean through the night. We were discussing whether or not we should wake you, but you've saved us the trouble."

"I'm sorry, sir. I thought I'd nap a couple of hours and then get on those chores you wanted me to do to pay you back. Give me a minute to get my shoes and things, and I'll be ready to go."

"No hurry. We're going to have breakfast in a little while. Would you like some?"

"Thank you. It's kind of you to offer, but I've already taken too much from you."

"Oh, nonsense," Neecy said. "We're glad to help out. That little bit of soup you had yesterday won't begin to hold you over. Let me fix us all some eggs and toast and sausage. How about a cup of coffee?"

"Oh yes, that would be nice, Mrs. Rice."

"I told you yesterday, call me Neecy. Father told me your name is Wilbur."

"Yes, but most folks call me Willie."

"All right, then, Willie. I'll be back in a minute with coffee for three." Neecy withdrew to the kitchen tucked in the far corner of the apartment.

"I don't know how to thank you and your wife for all that you've done for me. I promise you, I'll work off every penny."

"I'm sure you will." Dr. Rice looked Willie in the eye as he stood in front of him. "I pride myself on being able to judge a man's character. Helping some folks is only throwing your time away, but others are good people who've fallen on bad times and who need a chance to get themselves set right. I've seen plenty of times where the kindness of strangers has made the difference in a person's life."

Neecy came back and served three steaming cups of strong coffee. "Sit down, Willie." She gestured to the chair near him. "Now, tell us about yourself." She sat next to her husband on the sofa.

Willie hesitated as he lowered himself to perch on a chair's edge. "I don't mean to be rude, but it probably would be better if I didn't go into details."

"Trouble down South, son?" Dr. Rice asked kindly.

Willie recoiled as though he'd been slapped. "How did you know that?"

"It's an educated guess. You're a well-spoken young man with a strong Southern accent. You show up in Chicago in the dead of winter without any decent clothing or a cent to your name. When you came to my office yesterday, you told me that you don't know a single person here.

"Generally, there's three reasons folks like you come to Chicago. One is that you've got kin here and are looking to tie up with them. The second is that you got fed up with the treatment of the Negro in the South and decided it's time to be part of the northward movement to improve your lot in life. When that's the reason, it's usually done with at least some planning and preparation, and usually with other family. The third reason is that something has gone wrong, and you run out in a hurry and run on 'til you run out of road or run out of reason to run. It seems to me that you fit into that last category."

Neecy added, "And even if my husband is right, Willie, you're under no obligation to tell us anything. We decided a long time ago that the only real reason to offer help is because someone needs it."

Since the day he'd fled through the woods outside Holly Springs, Willie hadn't spoken of Lila Lowe to anyone other than his sister, Pearl. Every time he fell asleep, he had dreams of her—and nightmares of her death—but until now, he had remembered Reverend Wright's admonitions and kept his own counsel.

He meant to continue that practice, but while sitting and drinking coffee with these gentle people, for the first time in more than six months he didn't have to look over his shoulder every second. He dropped his guard.

"They say I killed a white girl down in Mississippi."

"Did you?" Dr. Rice set his coffee cup down on the end table.

"No, sir, I did not. I loved her. We were planning to find a way to move to Chicago so that we could get married and—" The crush of the memories was too much. He had tried so hard to wipe from his mind the last moments he had spent with Lila, but the anguish of acknowledging her death—her gruesome, needless death—took the blood from his brain and the air from his lungs. He stared at his hands in his lap, hoping to regain his composure.

Dr. Rice waited a moment before speaking. "I'm afraid you've got some misguided notions about what life in Chicago would have been like for you. The expectation is that we know our place and stay there. The outright discrimination might not be as bad up here as in the South, but don't be fooled into thinking that Negroes can do as they please because they're above the Mason-Dixon Line."

"James is right, but all the same," Neecy said softly, "I'm sorry for your sadness."

Neecy Rice was the first and only person to acknowledge that Willie had suffered a heart-wrenching loss. Even if she had never done anything else for him, he would have cherished her forever for that kindness.

"Well, Mother," James said abruptly, "we'd better have our breakfast if I'm going to get to the office in time to show Willie what I want him to do."

Whatever other questions or concerns James and Neecy Rice might have had over Willie's past, they kept them to themselves. And that two-sentence conversation in the aging dentist's apartment was the next to last time Willie ever mentioned Lila Lowe.

Chapter
Thirteen

The Curse of Canaan

FOR THE NEXT four months, Willie worked for Dr. Rice. He
sorted through the backlog of papers in the office. He made order out
of the chaos in the second bedroom at the apartment. He brought
ledger books up to date, inventoried every item in the doctor's
practice, and threw out years' worth of outdated supply catalogs. He
organized reference materials, sent out billing notices, and updated
patient files. He scrubbed floors and washed windows, and when
Neecy would let him, he cooked meals and did their laundry.

In late April, on a mild Tuesday night after dinner, Willie,
James, and Neecy were sitting on the stoop in front of the apartment
building. "Willie, you have long since paid off your debt to me for
fixing your tooth. I wish I had enough work for you to do to hire you
as an employee, but I'm afraid you've about gotten everything
caught up."

"You have been kinder to me than I ever dreamed anyone could
be. I wanted to show you my appreciation."

"You've done that and more, but I can't let you keep doing the
work of three people—and I can't afford to pay you what you're
worth."

"I was talking to one of your patients the other day who was
telling me that the Chicago Tunnel Company is hiring. I was thinking
I might try to get a job there—if you're sure I don't still owe you."

"No, you don't owe me anything. I hear the work in the freight
tunnels will break your back. Are you sure you want to get into
something like that?"

"Yeah, the fellow said it's hard work, but the pay is real good. I
need to save some money so I can send for my mama. I don't guess I
can ever go back to Mississippi, so I'll need to bring her up North to
live with me."

"James and I have talked about the fact that you'd probably be
striking out to find work soon." Neecy cleared her throat. "We'd be
real glad to have you stay with us for as long as you want to."

"That's nice of you to offer, but I feel I've already overstayed my welcome."

Neecy held Willie in her gaze. "It doesn't make sense for you to go out and find a place to rent when you could live here. If you're wanting to save money, you'd get that done lots faster not throwing away fists full of money every month on some dirty, little room. But we won't press you, son. We want you to know it's an option for you."

"Would you let me pay you room and board?"

Neecy patted Willie's forearm. "I'd tell you no, but I know you'd do it anyway."

"I suppose I could stay longer—maybe for a month or two until I can get set up—but only if you're sure you wouldn't mind."

By nightfall, they had come to terms for the particulars of Willie's continued lodging at James and Neecy's apartment.

The next day, Willie went to the management office of the Chicago Tunnel Company and was hired as a freight handler. The following Monday he began his job loading and unloading shipments of business supplies, mail, coal, and cinders on the three thousand freight cars that negotiated the sixty-mile maze of tracks that ran forty feet underground beneath nearly every street in downtown Chicago.

It didn't take Willie very long to figure out that he could have stopped any number of people on the street and nine out of ten of them wouldn't have believed Chicago had such a subterranean freight system. He learned it had been a long time in the making. Excavation of the tunnels began in 1899, supposedly for the purpose of housing telephone cables, but the construction company also installed two-foot gauge railroad tracks. In 1906, the tracks opened for business, serving warehouses, office buildings, and stores. He was surprised when one of the senior freight handlers told him that at the peak of operations, every day, about three hundred trains comprised of ten to fifteen cars each cruised unheard and unseen in tunnels six feet wide by seven-and-a half feet high beneath the busiest part of Chicago's loop.

Nowhere in the system did the locomotives or freight cars appear above ground. Willie was fascinated by the fact that specially constructed cable-driven elevators were used to raise and lower the train cars to and from the surface. Ironically, this ingenious way to transport goods in what was rapidly becoming one of the nation's most congested metropolitan areas had the same characteristic as both its greatest virtue and its greatest detractor: it was unseen. Many businesses were completely unaware of the underground freight system's existence, and consequently, it had a difficult time drumming up customers. But Willie didn't care much about that. He had employment, and the Chicago Tunnel Company became his subterranean home.

The unspoken caste system that operated above ground was, likewise, in place in the tunnels. White men had the managerial jobs, served as foremen, and got the prime shifts. Negroes did the heavy lifting and took whatever shifts they were told to take.

In a few weeks' time, Willie had adapted to the routine of his job. He was an able, eager worker liked by his co-workers and generally not hassled by his supervisors. Any number of his co-workers offered to exchange small talk with him, but other than answering direct questions related to the task at hand, Willie kept a closed mouth.

One day, after several months on the job, Willie lifted his self-imposed restriction on conversation. "Hey, Franklin, let me ask you something."

"Look at this, brothers, the silent one is asking a question." Franklin reeled in mock disbelief. "What can I do for you?"

"Are any of you guys going to put in for the management job that opened up? I hear the pay is lots better. I was wondering why none of us—" Willie gestured to the gaggle of black men around him—"has been picked as a supervisor. I know some of these men have been here way longer than the white men who got the last two promotions."

Franklin rolled his eyes. "I'd have thought a bright boy like you would have figured that out by now. Whitey gets real nervous if he thinks we're acting too big for how he thinks we ought to be. If we stand too tall or use words that sound too smart, he wants to knock us down and help us remember where we belong. If we act like poor, dumb slaves, he lets us be. It's an easier way to get along. We're all doing what we have to do to survive and get by. Probably the worst thing in the world a Negro can do is get noticed by a white man."

"Franklin is right," a man named Henry said. "You could ask any one of the foremen down here which of us is Willie or which is Joe, and he wouldn't be able to tell you. Bet you a dollar if you asked him to describe one of us from the other, he couldn't do it. 'They all look the same' is what he'd say. But one time, get in trouble for something or do something that makes you stand out, and then they'll remember you."

"Yeah, Henry's speaking truth," Franklin said. "The more you blend in and the less you say when whitey's around, the better your chances of staying on the job and never getting knocked upside the head. As best I can tell, the guys in charge think you're basically deaf and dumb because you never say nothing to nobody. I've even heard a couple of them call you 'The Dummy' behind your back."

"The man who hired me knows I can talk," Willie said.

"Sure," Franklin said, "but that man stays in his warm, dry office above ground. Once you come down here, you're nothing but a faceless, nameless colored who pulls and pushes things on and off these rail cars. You could walk back into that same office tomorrow and give him a new name, and he'd look at you like he'd never laid eyes on you before in his life."

"Doesn't it make you mad, though," Willie asked, "to have to act like something less than you are?"

"Where'd you come from, Willie?" Henry asked.

"Why?"

"You talk like you're from down South someplace is all. I wonder if you didn't have to do the same thing down there. Did you ever have to step and fetch and dance to the man's tune?"

"Sure, but I heard things were different up here. What's the point of moving North if we can't claim a place?"

All of the men listening to the conversation laughed.

"What's supposed to be and what happens in reality don't always match," Henry said with a shake of his head. "If I was you, I'd keep those crazy ideas to myself."

"Yep," Franklin agreed. "Be one of the bunch. Don't say anything that could ever be used against you. Hang with the brothers, and let whitey think you're too dumb to ever have a thought of your own. Lord knows he don't think you're smart enough for something as special as being a supervisor."

Henry gestured to indicate that a foreman was making his way toward the group. Willie watched the men shift their demeanor to fit what they'd talked about.

The foreman had spoken to Willie on many occasions, so Willie was sure the man would remember him. Willie decided to try a little experiment to see if Franklin, Henry, and the others were right.

"How long 'til you'll have this car unloaded, boy?" the foreman said to Willie.

In the past, Willie would have faced the man squarely, looked him in the eye and answered, "Ten minutes or so, sir."

This time though, he flashed his capped-tooth grin and held up both hands and waved his fingers in front of the foreman's face, then pointed to the man's watch.

"Ten minutes, boy?" the foreman asked.

Willie grinned again and inclined his head sideways like an idiot might.

"Okay. Fine. Keep up the good work." The foreman walked off down the line without another word.

"Yassuh, boss," Franklin said under his breath.

"Don' hit me no mo-ah, Massah," Henry added.

If that was the way it worked, Willie decided he would use it to his advantage. If saying as little as possible and acting like a simple-minded dolt meant he might better escape difficulties — and increase his odds of never being found and dragged back to Mississippi to be hanged — then so be it.

Willie walked over to Franklin and leaned close to his ear. "From now on, I'm Willie, the deaf mute. Will you make sure the others know?"

"You got it, brother." Franklin corrected himself. "Oh, I mean—" and energetically waggled his head up and down, grinning like a fool.

WILLIE'S CHARADE WAS easier than he expected and surprisingly satisfying. With a little practice, he mastered the ruse so effectively that people immediately concluded he was profoundly deaf and incapable of speech. He quickly learned he should only react to people if they were standing directly in front of him. He made a study of pretending to read lips and amused himself pretending to misunderstand words that "looked" like other words when they were spoken.

Even though many of the men with whom he worked in the tunnels knew he wasn't deaf and mute, he acted the part so well that, within a few months, they, too, only spoke to him if he was facing them and never called after him if they thought of something more to say when he walked away. Although he shopped in the same stores he'd frequented all along and passed the same people on the streets, in time, everyone came to regard him as the deaf man with the gold tooth.

Willie was both entertained and appalled by what people would say in his presence now that they regarded him as incapable of hearing. The presumption always seemed to be that, if he couldn't hear or speak, it would reasonably follow that he was slow-witted, as well.

He took perverse comfort in the knowledge that if through some outrageous confluence of circumstance the police from Holly Springs, Mississippi, should get wind of his working in the freight tunnels in Chicago and come hunting him, he was now a deaf and dumb ignoramus with a gold front tooth — hardly the well-spoken, presumptuous young Negro the locals of Holly Springs would have described. And his deception would provide a better cover for when he could pull together enough money to send for his mother.

The only time Willie dropped his façade was when he was with James and Neecy Rice inside their home. The three of them so rarely went out in public together that he didn't feel it necessary to tell them about his artifice out in the world. Most evenings, the three of them stayed in and listened to music. They used James's small record player with his collection of LPs, or they tuned the radio to the various Chicago stations and heard everything from the music of Dizzy Gillespie to Vladimir Horowitz, Eubie Blake to Leonard Bernstein, Gershwin to Mozart, Copeland to Ellington.

Willie was learning to put his life in little cubbyholes: his boyhood in Canaan, his love for and tragic loss of Lila, his time on the run, his safe haven with James and Neecy, his fraud as a speechless, deaf man. Soon, he hoped, he would build a new compartment—one where he could resume a more common life, reunited with his mother. But he still remembered Reverend Wright's caution about hate having a long memory. He didn't dare take the chance of trying to communicate with anyone in his family, as much out of fear of harm for them as for being found and extradited to Mississippi.

One year passed, and then another. Willie continued to work in the freight tunnels. He stayed on with James and Neecy. At first, he felt it wiser than finding a place of his own and laying out the money, but in the fall of 1952, James took ill and couldn't keep up with his practice. Willie was the family's support while James lay in his bed and wasted away.

When James died in February, 1953, Willie felt like he had lost his father all over again. After the funeral, Neecy and Willie were sitting in the living room of the apartment. Neecy was inconsolable. She and James had been married for nearly sixty years.

"I don't know where I'm going to go or what I'm going to do, Willie."

"Why would you go anywhere?"

"I can't pay the rent on this apartment. We sold off all James's office equipment and used up all our savings for James's doctor bills. I've got no family, nowhere to turn."

"You're staying right here, Neecy. I make enough to pay the rent and take care of the bills."

"No, you're supposed to be saving your money so you can bring your mama up here. You can't go throwing it away on an old lady like me."

"You've been my mama for the last four years. My mama in Mississippi wouldn't want anything to do with me if I up and left you now, not after all you and James have done for me."

Willie, the deaf mute, continued to labor in the freight tunnels. Two years later, Neecy passed over to join James. Willie wept for weeks. He kept a few things he could use, cleaned out what was left of their belongings, and returned the keys to the landlord.

By 1955, residents and businesses in Chicago were gradually switching from coal to natural gas to heat their buildings, and since coal had been one of the major commodities hauled in the tunnels, the company's business slumped drastically. A lot of men were laid off in the freight tunnels. Improvements in the motor truck industry cut into the remainder of the Chicago Tunnel Company's revenues, and Willie knew the company would soon fold completely. With James and Neecy gone, nothing held him in Chicago.

In the six years since Lila's death, Willie had, in effect, lost the ability to summon her face to his mind's eye. He knew he'd recognize her voice if he ever heard it again, but that was never going to happen. Lila had contracted down from her human form into an essence—a spirit—a force that Willie felt but couldn't describe, a tool he needed but couldn't employ.

In some ways, he was grateful that Lila hadn't lived to see what a disappointment life there would have been for them. As an interracial couple, they'd have met with no more acceptance in the Windy City than they did in Holly Springs.

Willie went down to the Chicago train yard on the first of December, 1955, and hopped a westbound train. All the years of hard labor in the tunnels had strengthened his muscles and given him grace and coordination. Unlike his first experience boarding a passing train, he didn't have any trouble at all hopping into the car. In addition to the little satchel of personal possessions he had brought with him six years earlier, he had a small suitcase of books he'd kept from James's library.

In Minneapolis, he clambered on a Burlington Northern freighter headed for Canada. He might have made it to Manitoba, but the stationmaster in a little whistle-stop along the way caught sight of him climbing back into the boxcar after he'd gotten off to relieve himself in the woods.

"Hey there! You! We don't allow coons to hitch rides in our boxcars. Get outta there!"

Willie grabbed his satchel and suitcase and fled the train. He planned to lie low and catch the next train in either direction. Meanwhile, he was hungry. Maybe he could find a place that would fix him a sandwich for a quarter.

Welcome to Coon River Rapids proclaimed an arch over the town's main street. *Friendliest town in Minnesota.*

"Why not?" Willie asked himself. "The stationmaster has already declared me an honorary citizen of this snow-capped hamlet. I may as well be Coon Willie of Coon River Rapids."

He walked under the arch and headed up Main Street, past the hardware store, the J.C. Penney, the bakery, the bank, the movie theatre, the furniture store, the barber shop, the pool hall, the grocery. The citizens of Coon River Rapids forgot that they were supposed to be friendly; they were too busy being stunned at the sight of a real, live Negro.

Willie saw the neon sign flashing in the Woolworth's window. *Good Food.* He went to the lunch counter at the rear of the store, sat down on the last of the dozen ladder-backed swivel chairs, and lifted the menu from the rack behind the napkin holder.

The waitress had been standing with her back to the counter, talking to the cook through the pass-through window. When she turned around, she was so flustered by Willie's presence that she dropped the three plates of customer's food she was balancing. The commotion brought the cook out from the kitchen.

Willie saw the mop and bucket tucked in the far corner behind the lunch counter. He got up from his seat, stepped behind the counter, and grabbed the mop to clean up the jumble of broken plates and spilled food. A man strode over from the notions department. He hadn't witnessed the waitress's clumsiness. Willie could see him off to the side, watching while he mopped.

"At least he knows his place," one of the customers remarked as she watched Willie tend to the mess that wasn't of his making.

The woman's comment sparked his ire. Willie was about to respond, but then thought better of it. On the way from Chicago, he had decided he would discontinue his game of playing deaf and dumb, but Henry and Franklin's advice about never doing anything that would get him noticed or saying anything that could be used against him rang in his ears. As far as he knew, Mississippi still regarded him as a man wanted for murder. He didn't so much as look up from the floor as the women continued their observations.

The man who had been watching walked over as Willie returned the mop and bucket to their place. "Thank you for taking care of that. My name's Kent Shelby. I'm the manager here." He offered his hand for Willie to shake.

Willie grasped Mr. Shelby's hand, tipping his head in Mr. Shelby's direction as he did so.

"I take it you're only passing through Coon River Rapids."

Willie made a motion like moving a pencil across the palm of his other hand. Mr. Shelby pulled a pen from his pocket, picked up an order pad from the counter, and handed them to Willie.

Willie wrote, "My name is Willie Rice. I can't hear or speak, but I can read and write and I read lips. Yes, I was passing through, but if there's work here, I would be glad to work off what I owe you."

"I'll be damned." Mr. Shelby took two steps away from Willie. "Come with me." Willie stood stock-still as Mr. Shelby moved away. When the manager realized Willie wasn't dogging his heels, he wheeled around and repeated "Come with me," enunciating as he did so. Willie picked up his two bags from under the lunch counter and followed.

They walked up a flight of cement steps to the small, second floor office. Mr. Shelby conducted a few more tests of Willie's ability to comprehend and carry out instructions. Willie played the part perfectly.

Mr. Shelby sat back in his chair, a pencil in his hand. "I've been toying with the idea of hiring someone to help sort and move inventory and take care of miscellaneous chores around the store."

Willie waited, a hopeful look on his face.

"I've been the Woolworth's manager for nearly twenty years, doing many of the odd jobs. I could use someone to spare my aching back and do the more demanding physical tasks." He let out a sigh. "I hate to pay a salary to someone to do what I could do myself. Hmm..."

Willie watched the calculating look that came over the man's face, and as expected, he offered Willie about half of what he'd pay a white local boy. Willie indicated his acceptance of the offer.

"I'll have to pay you in cash," Mr. Shelby explained. "Saves a lot of government paperwork that way."

Willie didn't much care. He didn't expect to draw Social Security, and if he didn't file a tax return, that was one less means for anyone to find out where he was. Besides, he wasn't likely to live out the rest of his life in Coon River Rapids. He knew he had no hope of blending in here, but surely it wasn't the sort of place the Holly Springs police would ever think of looking for him, either.

As long as he had enough money to get by on—and maybe tuck a few dollars aside to one day bring his mama up North with him—that would do. What little he had saved while he was working in the freight tunnels had all been used to help with James and Neecy's illnesses and funerals, but he didn't regret that.

"Do you know of someplace I could get a room cheap?" Willie wrote on a piece of paper.

"Sure. I guess that means you want the job. I'll take you over there myself."

Within the hour, Willie was a paying tenant at Olive Able's past-its-prime apartment house. The few dollars a month it would cost him for rent didn't seem a bad bargain, especially since he knew he'd never survive the sub-zero weather of northern Minnesota hiding under railroad bridges.

He could see Olive was torn, and because she thought he was deaf, she wasted no time telling Mr. Shelby that she wasn't sure she was comfortable having a colored man in her establishment, but then, she also admitted that his rent money would be a welcome addition to her scant resources.

"Don't worry about it. I'll vouch for him," Mr. Shelby assured her. "I don't think you'll have any trouble from that coon, Willie."

No one was ever clear if Olive thought that his name was "Coonwillie," or if she thought that "Coon" was a title or form of address, but she told neighbors and people she met on the street about her new renter. Inside of a week, all of Coon River Rapids claimed to have seen and exchanged greetings with the deaf darkie in the Able Apartments.

Chapter
Fourteen

The Curse of Canaan
Coon River Rapids, Minnesota
September 1956

WILLIE'S HEAD FELL forward. He awoke with a start with Shakespeare's *Othello* still in his lap. He rubbed the back of his neck and rolled his head from side to side to stretch out the kinks and saw it was nearly midnight. Time to wash up and go to bed.

Willie had been in Coon River Rapids for nine months. He hadn't expected to stay nearly that long, but ironically, despite the fact that he was the only Negro in the community, he felt completely anonymous and unthreatened. To his surprise, the people *were* friendly — in a look-at-the-oddball sort of way — and the pace of life was far more to his liking than Chicago had been. He was in no hurry to move on.

In the seven years since he'd left Mississippi, Willie had never dared write to his mother for fear that someone at the Canaan post office might intercept his letter and harm her or track him. But now, Eunice was sixty-eight. He was worried that if he didn't send for her soon, she'd be too old to make the trip.

Shortly after arriving in Coon River Rapids, Willie had taken a chance and written to his brother Rudy at his last address in Detroit. The letter came back undeliverable. He'd never had addresses for Eddy, Lowell, or Reggie. As for his sisters, as far as he knew, Lacey and DeeDee were still in Tupelo, and Pearl was still in Memphis. On foot in Tupelo or Memphis, he could find their houses with no problem, but he didn't know what streets they lived on or their house numbers. He didn't have phone numbers for any of them, and even if he could get them, how would he explain a deaf man standing at a pay phone making a long distance phone call?

He lived as frugally as he could, but his salary didn't provide much excess to devote to savings. And without money to buy a bus ticket, he was beginning to despair of ever seeing anyone in his family again. His dreams were often a jumble of images of his mother as he had last seen her, of their little farm in Canaan, and of all his big brothers and sisters fussing over him like they had done when he was a child. And every memory was overlaid with visions of Lila, one minute vital and radiant, the next, disfigured and inert. Willie was glad everyone thought he was mute—that way he never had to speak of his impossible longings.

Early the next morning, Willie walked through town to the Woolworth's. Early autumn in northern Minnesota was a gorgeous time. The multicolored leaves reflected off the sky blue lakes, doubling the effect of the panoply. That day, Mr. Shelby put Willie to work behind the candy counter. He had often heard Mr. Shelby mention to other clerks how candy sales were always highest on the days that Willie weighed out the sweets. In part, it happened because customers seemed to think it their civic duty to patronize the colored man. Willie did his share to boost the till by intentionally "misreading" the item or quantity that the customers spoke, thus prompting them to buy more of the item they wanted or to buy two things instead of one.

He was surprised to see the little blonde girl and her father come into the store. They had been in the day before, and it was usually a week or more between their visits. He overheard Emil Schmidt speak to his daughter.

"Here's a dime, Ginny. You go pick out your candy while I get that notebook Danny said he needs for his Future Farmers of America projects. When you're done, go stand by the door and wait for me, and don't go wandering off. I need to get out to Edgetown Equipment and pick up the part I need to fix my corn picker. I don't have time to be searching all over the store for you. Do you understand?"

"Yes, Daddy."

Willie watched as the girl carefully inspected the glass-fronted bins.

Regulars at the Woolworth candy counter knew that, when the female clerk was on duty, you tapped your coin against the glass to get her attention and signify that you'd made your selection. Ginny was too short to see over the counter to know Willie was behind the counter, not the lady. She used her dime to rap on the cinnamon-flavored jelly dollars bin.

Willie was having a hard time shaking the vestiges of his ruminations from the night before. Without thinking, he walked over to the place in the circular counter where the little girl was clinking her coin. He peered over the edge and opened his mouth to speak. In the nick of time, he caught himself and looked inquisitively at Ginny.

"What are you doing here? I thought the lady with the long face would give me my candy."

Willie used his index finger to point to his chest, then waved his hands in widening circles to indicate he was in charge of the candy sales today.

Ginny was a frequent buyer at the counter and knew how to strike the deal no matter who was doling out the treats. She held up her dime in one hand and her nickel in the other. With the dime, she gestured to the cinnamon dollars, and with the nickel, she pointed to the red licorice bites. Willie went to the scales in the center of the candy display to dip and weigh the appropriate portions.

As was often the case, Ginny changed her mind. "Hey mister, I don't want the licorice bites. I want these caramel drops instead."

Willie rarely slipped up, but that morning, he forgot he was supposed to be deaf. Without ever looking at the little girl, he left the scoop in the licorice bin and moved over to the caramel drops instead. His hand froze in midair when he realized what he had done. He looked quickly around. To his relief, no one other than Ginny was anywhere in sight. Thank goodness. He chastised himself silently for his lapse in attentiveness, then folded the tops of the white bags and handed them to Ginny. She surrendered her coins to him and went to wait by the front door as she'd been told to.

"What kind did you get today, babes?" her father asked.

"Chewy hot dollars and caramel drops."

Emil held out his hand for a sample. Ginny carefully unfolded the bag tops and extracted one piece of each candy for her father.

"Come on. We need to go out to the John Deere place." Emil and Ginny stepped out into the bright, autumn light.

"Daddy, doesn't 'deaf' mean that people can't hear you?"

"Yep. And since you have to hear things to learn to talk, most people who are deaf can't talk either."

"I thought you told me that the dark man who works here is deaf."

"He is."

"I don't think so. He heard something I said to him when he was putting my candy in the bag."

"You're all the time making up stories about things. Why can't you take what people tell you and let it be? Why do you always have to pretend about everything?"

"I'm not pretending about this. Really."

"I'm not going to argue with you. But I'm telling you, stop making things up, okay? Pretty soon, people are going to start calling you a liar. You don't want that to happen do you?"

"I guess not. But I didn't make it up. He did what I asked him to do, but he wasn't looking at me when I told him."

"Ginny," Emil said trying to control his exasperation, "that's enough. Everybody in Coon River Rapids knows that he's deaf.

Nobody's going to believe you if you try to tell them different. Now, drop it." He opened the passenger door to the pick-up truck and offered to boost Ginny up.

"I can do it myself," she assured him, struggling to hoist herself in.

"You are an independent little cuss, I'll say that for you. Now if only you could learn the difference between what's real and what you make up in your head."

Chapter
Fifteen

Columbus, Georgia
May 4, 2006

DAMN. DAMN. DAMN. Elizabeth clomped around her house cursing everyone from Guttenberg to the Babylonian who invented cuneiform. She was mad at the Chinese for discovering how to make paper and ink. She hated Smith and Corona and whoever else was responsible for typewriters that evolved into word processors that morphed into computers. If those things didn't exist, no one could be writing books and making her life a contorted mess. *Damn.*

She ran a lesbian publishing company, dammit.

Lesbian.

She was eight chapters into Colleen's novel, and no character on any of the pages or waiting in the wings of the plot could even spell "lesbian," let alone be one.

What was most upsetting was the fact that she liked the book. If she didn't know better, she'd have thought Alana Montaigne had set up this whole situation just to fuck with her head.

"Now I won't have to listen to you carp about the lackluster options coming out of lesbian fiction houses," Alana had said. Elizabeth could almost hear a sinister snigger reverberating off the walls.

I never should have agreed to read this book. I never should have gotten involved with Colleen—at least not both as a lover and as an author. Shit. I'm screwed no matter what I do with this book.

Elizabeth tromped up and down the stairs a few times to try to calm herself.

If I tell Colleen it's a good book, she'll want me to publish it. I could lie to her and tell her it needs work, but I can't point to anything seriously wrong in her story, so she'll know I'm lying. If I tell her I won't put it under contract, then what? Will she continue her Alana impersonation and leave me—leave Triple S?

Elizabeth flung herself on her bed and went through the motions of trying to sleep. What few moments she did doze off were plagued with convoluted dreams involving Colleen McCrady and Willie Rice. She'd awaken and try to sort fact from fiction, only to find herself more confused than when she started.

By Friday morning, she was more tired than she'd been when she climbed the stairs for the last time Thursday night. She was worse than worthless at the office on Friday, and by the time she stopped the car in Colleen's LaGrange driveway Friday evening, she had worked herself into a state where she could barely put together a three-word statement.

"HOW ARE YOU?" Colleen had heard the car pull up and met Elizabeth at the front door.

"Too tired to breathe."

"It shows," Colleen said sympathetically. "Did you eat?"

"I had a couple of pieces of fruit and some cheese on the drive down."

"Go draw a hot bath, and I'll make you something," Colleen offered.

"I'd rather go to bed. Would you mind?"

"No, not at all. Would you like me to rub your feet or back — or maybe your front?"

"Inviting as that sounds, more than anything on this planet, I need a solid night's sleep."

Colleen kissed the back of Elizabeth's neck. "Climb into bed. I'll keep the dogs out here with me 'til I'm sure you're asleep and try to slide in beside you without waking you up."

"Unless you clang a gong next to my ear, I doubt I'll hear a thing."

Elizabeth padded through the house to the bedroom. When Colleen peeked in on her fifteen minutes later, she was deep in slumber, so she blew a kiss from the doorway and pulled the door nearly shut.

A melancholy settled over Colleen as she tipped back in the recliner in the living room. This would be the first time she and Elizabeth hadn't made love within the first few hours of a reunion. She wondered what it portended for their relationship.

Then again, if she convinced Elizabeth to read the rest of what she'd written in *The Curse of Canaan*, would they still have any relationship at all by the end of the weekend?

THE RING TONE of Elizabeth's cell phone shortly after six a.m. startled them both out of their dreams. In her sleepy stupor the night before, Elizabeth had forgotten to set it to go to voice mail when she crashed into bed.

Elizabeth finally managed to pull the phone from the belt of her slacks lying on the floor beside the bed.

"Hello? Elizabeth Albright."

Colleen shushed the dogs. They weren't any happier about Elizabeth's noisy, ringing pants than the women were.

"Toni? Slow down. I can't understand what you're saying."

Colleen watched horror spread over Elizabeth's face.

"I'm out of town, but I can be back in Columbus by eight. Meet me at the office." Elizabeth used her free hand to sweep her hair back from her temples. "No. Don't call anyone else. Don't answer the office phone. Let everything go to voice mail. I'll see you as fast as I can get there."

Elizabeth flipped the phone closed and jumped out of bed. She grabbed her clothes and began fumbling into them.

"What's wrong? What happened?"

"I'm sorry, but I can't tell you anything. I've got to get back to Columbus."

"I picked that up from what you said to Toni. Is someone hurt?"

"Colleen, I can't discuss this with you. Help me get my stuff pulled together. I'll call you once I know more of the details, okay?"

"Whatever you say." Colleen got out of bed and reached for her robe. "What do you need me to do?"

"Where's my laptop? My briefcase?"

"They must be in the car. You didn't bring anything in last night."

"What about my keys? My glasses?"

"Your glasses are right there on the nightstand. You're keys are on the table by the front door."

"Okay, that should be all I need for now."

"Don't you want something to eat?"

"I don't have time."

"I've got some bagels and bananas in the kitchen. You could eat that on the way." Colleen took two steps toward the door. "I'll start the coffee."

"Can't wait for that. I've got to roll." Elizabeth bolted out of the bedroom, nearly tripping over the dogs on her way. "Get these damn yapping fools out of the way, Colleen!"

The sharp tone in Elizabeth's voice sent Buster and Muggins slinking back to the bedroom.

Elizabeth retrieved her keys and was out the front door before Colleen could catch her to tell her good-bye. She heard Elizabeth's Lexus laying rubber as she peeled around the first corner.

Muggins and Buster tentatively crept into the living room. "It's safe, guys. She's gone." Colleen gave them pats of reassurance. "She was kind of over the top, wasn't she? I don't think she meant it, though. Something must be terribly wrong at work." She gave Buster a final scratch on his belly, then yawned. "C'mon, guys, let's go see if there are any squirrels in the yard." She led the way to the back door and let them out.

As she punched the button on the coffee maker and sat at the kitchen table to wait for it to brew, she noticed the manuscript she had hoped to have Elizabeth finish reading over the weekend. She thumped it lightly with her fist. Oh, well, whatever the crisis was at Triple S Publishing that had called Elizabeth back to Columbus, it would probably be resolved by noon. Maybe she'd be back to spend the night with Colleen, or Colleen could drive up to Columbus in the morning.

The contents of *The Curse of Canaan* had already waited nearly a half century. Tomorrow would certainly be soon enough to see if they drew a reaction from Elizabeth Albright.

Chapter
Sixteen

COLLEEN DIDN'T GET to see Elizabeth again the next day or even the next week. She had to wait until Memorial Day weekend before things settled down enough for Elizabeth to spend more than six hours at a whack away from her office. She drove to LaGrange for the day on Sunday, the twenty-eighth of May.

"It's good to see you, sweetheart. It's been a long, lonely month without you."

Elizabeth accepted Colleen embrace as she got out of the car. "I agree. I'm glad to see you, too."

Colleen thought Elizabeth looked like someone had sucked all the color out of her skin, but she was wise enough not to say so.

"You know I'd have gladly come down to Columbus so that you didn't have to waste the time on the road. You could have used the extra hour to sleep."

"I only wish. Sleep and I haven't exactly been on good terms lately. I don't think I've slept four hours end-to-end since the last time I was here."

"I'm sorry, LJ." They started toward the front door. "You should have let me help out with what you've been going through."

Elizabeth's shoulders slumped. "Don't start, okay? I've told you a hundred times that I couldn't bring you into this mess."

Colleen had called Elizabeth at least daily since that early morning call, and Elizabeth had reluctantly shared more of the full story with Colleen than was generally known around the lesbian fiction circle.

The mess that Elizabeth was referring to was a lawsuit brought against Standing in Sappho's Shadow Publishing by the parents of one of Elizabeth's authors, Wendy Westmuller. Wendy and her lover had gone through a nasty break-up the preceding fall. In her subsequent depression and accompanying delusion, Wendy got it in her head that if Triple S had published more of her books, her lover wouldn't have left her. When she downed a half a bottle of sleeping pills on the first Friday in May, she left a suicide note that blamed Triple S in general and Elizabeth Albright in particular for destroying her "promising career as one of lesbian fiction's brightest young authors." Wendy's parents filed the suit, claiming Triple S had acted capriciously in its treatment of Wendy and had caused extreme emotional distress which led to her suicide attempt. Though Wendy's stomach had been pumped soon enough that she suffered no long-term physical effects, the fallout from the attack on her publisher made the odds of her resurrecting her reputation as a writer pretty slim.

Elizabeth's legal beagles had quickly defused the law suit as baseless, but word of the situation had leaked out, and the shock waves rocked not only Elizabeth's company, but all of her competitors, as well. The mainstream right-wing fundamentalists and their media minions were having a field day flinging mud on Elizabeth, her company, lesbian writers, the lesbian publishing industry, and the entire lesbian community. Damage control had been going on 24/7, and Colleen hated how badly Elizabeth was showing the strain of it.

"You know I'm here for you if you need to discuss anything at all."

"I mean it, Colleen," Elizabeth continued as they neared the stoop. "Now that the furor is finally dying down, I'd rather cram bamboo shoots under my fingernails than talk about it, okay?"

Neither spoke again until they were inside the house. Muggins took one look at Elizabeth and bolted behind the sofa.

"He'll get over himself in a minute," Colleen said. "I don't think he's seen anyone come through the front door since you were here the last time." She crouched down on the floor near the end of the sofa. "Muggsy, you remember LJ, don't you, buddy? Come say hello."

"Pretty sad commentary that my looks are enough to scare a dog into hiding." Elizabeth's fatigue was evident in her voice.

"You've been dragged backwards through a barbed-wire fence. You're entitled to be at less than your best."

Elizabeth cocked her head, almost as if she'd been backhanded across the face. "Thanks. That's *precisely* what I needed to hear." Sarcasm dripped from every word.

"You may not recall it, but last time you left here, you yelled at the dogs and almost kicked them on your way down the hall. They may not be human, but they remember stuff like that." Colleen rose. "All I'm saying is that you've had a hell of a month." She advanced toward Elizabeth. "You're still beautiful to me."

Elizabeth stepped away before Colleen could reach her.

"Are you mad at me?" Colleen asked tentatively.

"Mad at the world, I think." Elizabeth dropped heavily onto the sofa. "Maybe I don't have what it takes to run a publishing house after all."

"You said the lawsuit has been dropped. No real harm was done." Colleen crossed the room and sat on the recliner.

Elizabeth stared at Colleen. "You're joking, right?"

"I didn't think I was."

"What about my reputation? The legal expenses? The crap that's been all over the newspapers from Columbus to Atlanta? One of the wire services did a story that ran in a dozen major cities."

"No such thing as bad publicity," Colleen said, hoping to inject a lighter note.

Elizabeth leapt to her feet. "You simply don't understand how much of my life I've poured into this company." She balled her hands into fists. "You don't know how close I came to losing everything."

Colleen lifted her hands, palms up. "How can I understand? I've tried for the past three weeks to find out what's happening — how you're feeling — offering to do something, anything — to take some of the pressure off you. I don't think we've had a phone conversation lasting more than four minutes since you blew out of here that morning Toni called about Wendy's suicide attempt. For that matter, Toni has been a better source of information for me than you have."

Elizabeth glowered. "You just don't get it, do you? You're one of my company's *authors*. How would it look if I were to cozy up to you and tell you every detail of this wretched pandemonium that has eaten me alive every minute of every day for what feels like a hundred years?"

Colleen weighed her response carefully. "Like we're a couple. Like I'm someone who means something to you."

"When we're here in LaGrange, we're a couple. At my office in Columbus, I'm the publisher of Standing in Sappho's Shadow, and you're an author under contract with my company." Elizabeth got to her feet and stood without moving, her hands clamped on her hips.

Each of Elizabeth's words hit Colleen like a dart striking a tightly-filled balloon. Deflated, she sank deep into the recliner.

Tension hung in the air for several minutes. Colleen spoke first. "I thought I could help. I only wanted to make things easier for you." A tear spilled down her cheek.

"But you couldn't." Elizabeth's tone still held a harsh edge. She resumed her seat and looked at Colleen. "I guess I'm rubbed a little raw right now." She laughed flatly. "It's trite, I know, but I need some space."

"What do you mean by that?"

"I don't think I've got the strength to face another firestorm at Triple S right now."

"Why would you have to?" Colleen asked.

"If it came to light that you and I are involved —"

The hopes that Colleen had harbored for joyfully reuniting with Elizabeth died like a moth against a flame. "I see." She hated that she sounded like a little girl who had just been told her parents never loved her at all. She fought the wave of nausea that threatened. "Do you even want to spend the day here with me today?"

Elizabeth was silent for a long minute. She opened her mouth to speak, but instead of words, a sob escaped her. She tried to stifle it, but failed. "Oh, Collie. Yes. Yes, I want this day with you. I need this day with you."

Colleen rushed across the room and flung her arms around her. Elizabeth leaned her head on Colleen's shoulder and cried until the well was empty.

"Could we lie down? I feel lousy all over." Elizabeth swallowed hard and mopped the last of her tears.

They went to the bedroom and stretched out side by side on the bed. Colleen placed her hand on Elizabeth's chest, and Elizabeth covered it with her own.

The raspy rise and fall of Elizabeth's breathing was the only sound Colleen heard. When Elizabeth's breaths came more evenly, Colleen said, "Can I get you something? Maybe a Coke to settle your stomach or some toast?"

"I think noon yesterday was the last time I ate."

"No wonder you don't feel good. Tell me what you'd like, and I'll go fix it." Colleen tried to extract her hand from beneath Elizabeth's.

"Don't go yet. I think we should talk about some things first."

"Okay."

Buster and Muggins eased into the room, but lay down right inside the doorway instead of coming to the bed. Colleen cast them a glance that said, "Don't you dare do anything that upsets this woman."

Elizabeth rolled from her side onto her back. "I'm thinking about making some changes."

"What kind of changes?"

"I've entertained everything from simply tightening up the language in my contracts to selling out altogether."

"Sell Standing in Sappho's Shadow? Oh, LJ, I know you've had a horrible month, but you can't be serious about selling out. Triple S is doing so well."

"Depends on what measuring stick you're using. Sure, we're turning a decent profit, and I've got plenty of books under contract to easily keep me in business for the next two years."

"But that's not enough for you, is it?" Colleen propped up on her elbow so that she could rest her head on her palm and see

Elizabeth's face.

"No. Sappho's Shadow Publishing has become a junior league Brazen Girls Press. Everything I publish is exactly like everything I've already published. This whole nasty muddle over Wendy's lawsuit has forced me to take a hard, honest look at what's going on in my company. I've lost sight of my vision. I was going to be a pioneer and break new ground in the wonderful world of lesbian fiction. Instead, I'm cranking out pabulum."

"Your publishing house has a great reputation. Why are you so down on it?"

"The books I publish are cookie cutter copies of each other — worn out and trite. Sappho's Shadow isn't going anywhere."

"You're too tired to think clearly, LJ. In a few weeks after things have gotten back into a routine, you'll feel differently."

Elizabeth tipped her head from side to side in the indentation between the pillows. "I don't think so. On the drive up here today, I got to thinking that if I ever get run through a wringer again like with Wendy's situation, I want it to be for something that matters, not for some dime-store novel that gets read at the beach and then forgotten."

Colleen wanted to evaporate. Even though she knew Elizabeth wasn't intentionally castigating her work with her broad vilifications, the words sliced through her like a fillet knife. She lay lightly by Elizabeth's side, almost as if she hoped Elizabeth might forget she were there if she didn't move so much as a fraction of an inch.

"Sure, some of my authors — like you, for instance — write books that step away from the usual prescription for lesbian romance, but for the most part, it's all interchangeable plots and characters." Elizabeth's exhale was nearly a lament. "I don't think I can do it anymore."

Colleen took heart from Elizabeth's indirect compliment in reference to her writing. She kissed Elizabeth's forehead. "If you don't run your publishing company, what will you do?"

"Damned if I know. Move back to Atlanta and sell kosher hotdogs in the Toco Hills neighborhood, maybe. At least I'd have Saturdays off."

"I still think all you need is a break. Take a vacation. Go away for a week or two, and when you come back, Triple S will seem like the place it's always been."

"I can't possibly take time off now. The production schedule was blown to hell and gone by all this legal bickering. Besides, you're missing the real point. Even if I did go away — two weeks, two months, two years from now — it will be exactly what it's always been, and I'm not sure how much longer I can live with that."

"Have you definitely decided to give up publishing?"

"I don't know that I'm capable of definitely deciding if I'll floss my teeth before I go to bed tonight. I don't trust my brain for much of anything these days."

Colleen let a thought rumble in her mind before saying it aloud. "Why don't I come up to Columbus and help you in the office for a while? That way, I'd have a better idea of what you deal with every day, and I'd be a whole lot more help to you in figuring out what to do with it, long term."

Elizabeth noticeably tensed. Colleen would have given a king's fortune to grab the words from the air and stuff them back into her mouth.

"Bad idea. I never should have mentioned it. Sorry." Colleen reached to bring Elizabeth nearer to her, but Elizabeth resisted.

"That would only complicate my life. The shellshock from this past month's ordeal has me questioning a lot of things."

Once again, Colleen wished she could slip off to a parallel universe and not hear what she dreaded Elizabeth was about to say.

"Like your feelings for me," Colleen said. What difference from whose lips the words came?

"No, that's one thing I'm not questioning." Elizabeth patted Colleen's hip distractedly. "But I'm not sure I didn't make a mistake thinking we could be both lovers and business associates."

"Are you saying I need to pick which one I want to be?" Colleen willed herself not to cry, wondering if Elizabeth would force her to choose.

"I honestly don't know. Either way, something changes between us, and I don't want to think about what that might mean."

"So let's not think about it right now." Colleen could only hope she didn't sound as devastated and desperate as she felt. She dropped her elbow prop and lay down on her back.

"We have to."

"No, we don't. You're exhausted. You're up to your neck in worries over what to do with your company. A little while ago you said you weren't sure you could trust yourself to make a decision about little things, never mind something that will affect the rest of your life. Why borrow trouble?"

"But I feel like I'll be a candidate for the psych ward if I don't get some of these issues resolved." Elizabeth made a motion with her index fingers like screwing pegs into the sides of her head.

"We could go on auto-pilot for the summer." Colleen felt around on the covers until she touched Elizabeth's hand.

"What?"

"We could agree to be together like we've been for the past year—you coming down here for weekends if you wanted—"

"You know I care about you, Collie."

Colleen felt like she might cry again, but this time for happier reasons. "You haven't said anything like that to me in almost a month."

"I should have. I do, you know—care about you, I mean." Elizabeth gripped Colleen's hand more tightly. "But I'm not in a very good place mentally or emotionally right now."

Colleen didn't want to risk hearing Elizabeth tell her again that she needed time and space away from her. "That's okay. I can wait for you to sort through things." She raised her leg from the bed and draped it lightly over Elizabeth's thighs. "We're good together, LJ. Please don't throw us away."

Colleen inched in closer to Elizabeth to wait for Elizabeth's reply. A minute later, a soft snore was the only answer she received.

Chapter
Seventeen

Columbus, Georgia
September 2006

"I'M SURE I know what you'll tell me about this book, but I decided it's better to hear it from you so I can stop second-guessing myself. It's not at all like anything else I've given you. You'll probably hate it." Colleen stood in the outer office at Standing in Sappho's Shadow's headquarters. She clutched a manuscript in the crook of her elbow.

"Maybe we should we go into my office and talk about it." Elizabeth struggled to keep her voice level and professional.

"No, I can see you're busy, but I knew if I didn't get it off of my desk and onto yours, I'd never be able to move on to a new project." Colleen shifted from foot to foot and moved the manuscript to her other arm.

"It's a little early, but let's get some lunch and we can turn a couple of pages while we eat. Let me get my jacket and keys." Elizabeth walked briskly into her office and reemerged shortly. "You guys can keep a lid on things here for a couple of hours, can't you?" She directed the question at Toni.

"We always do, boss," Toni answered. "Take your time. We can lock up if you don't make it back by quitting time."

Elizabeth chose to ignore the unspoken suggestion in Toni's remark. If Toni or any of the other staff members had anything further to say, they had the good sense to keep it to themselves until Elizabeth and Colleen were safely on the other side of the door.

They stopped at Elizabeth's car, and Colleen dropped the manuscript on the passenger seat. "I'll meet you at the Cork and Cleaver," Colleen said as she hurried to her car.

At the restaurant, Elizabeth didn't bother with niceties. Instead, she jumped right in with a strident tone. "I thought we'd settled this. You know my office staff suspects there's more than firm handshakes between us, Colleen. Why do you insist on pouring fuel on the flames?" Elizabeth slapped the tabletop of the booth they were sharing at Cork and Cleaver.

"We do a hell of a lot more than shake hands, or have you forgotten where you face and fingers were most of last weekend?"

"As I remember it, once again *your* face was plastered to your computer screen and your fingers to the keyboard for all but an occasional recess, while I was left reprising my role as Auntie Elizabeth to Buster and Muggins."

"At least the dogs don't think of you as some evil step-mother." Colleen changed her tone. "I was working on the book I brought you."

"Yes, I know. I've played second fiddle to your books on many occasions." Elizabeth pounded on the seat as she spoke. "I thought I was supposed to be an important part of the plot of your life."

"Pot calls kettle black. Film at eleven. Why am I such an embarrassment to you? We've been a couple for almost a year-and-a-half now, but the only time you'll have anything to do with me is when it's pitch black outside, and we're miles away from Triple S's offices."

"We've had this discussion. I'm not ashamed of our relationship." Elizabeth looked around to be sure they weren't being overheard. "I thought we agreed we'd take things slow and easy for a while. You're the one who suggested it. What was the phrase you used? 'Go on auto-pilot,' I think it was." Elizabeth studied her cuticles rather than look at Colleen.

"It's been more than four months since you told me you wanted some space between your professional connection to me and our personal relationship. You wanted some time to decide where things were going between us and what you were going to do about Sappho's Shadow. I've tried to be patient, but you still won't admit to Toni and the others — or to anyone else, for that matter — that you and I are anything more than casual business acquaintances — even though you just said you're sure people know what's going on."

"I told you when we talked about this on Memorial Day weekend that, after trying to sweep up the pieces of my business because of that lawsuit, I don't want to do anything that's going to pitch my business into the path of an on-rushing train. It hasn't been easy getting back on track. I know a lot of my authors contemplated leaving Triple S in case I couldn't keep it rolling. Telling everyone we're lovers might alienate the very women who've stuck with me through thick and thin."

"And it's better to dismiss me — no, make that better to break my heart — by treating me like I'm little more than another filly in your stable so that your precious business doesn't lose a dollar or two. You sure know how to make a girl feel special, Elizabeth."

"You should talk." Elizabeth fought to keep the rancor out of her voice. "You're perfectly content to have me sit like an indoor yard ornament while you hammer out some glitch in a story line." She kneaded her fingers in her palm. "And as long as we're pointing out one another's shortcomings, you still don't trust me enough to tell me anything more than the barest details about your life. I have to beg for every tiny scrap of information about what you did for the past fifty years. For all I know, you're an escaped mental patient or an ax murderer."

Colleen's face burned flame red, but not from a blush. "That's it. I've had enough. I don't care if you read the damn book I brought you or not." Colleen grabbed her keys from the tabletop. "Thank God I was smart enough to drive my own car over. Have a hell of a nice life. Thanks for nothing." Colleen fled the restaurant in tears.

Elizabeth stared out the window as Colleen leapt into her car and left the parking lot. *My own stupid fault. I couldn't decide if I wanted her in my bed or in my business. Looks like I won't have her either place.*

Elizabeth was too upset to go back to the office. She made the twelve mile drive to her two-story brick house on Livingston Drive. Colleen's manuscript lay in the passenger seat. Elizabeth carried it into the house with her and dropped it on the table beside her favorite wing chair.

"Maybe some music will help." She scanned her collection of CD's and selected a compilation of old show tunes. She slipped it in the player and stretched out on the sofa in hopes of soothing her troubled mind. The second song hit her like a ton of bricks. The touching lyrics from "We Kiss in the Shadow" brought Colleen's livid remarks to mind: *The only time you'll have anything to do with me is when it's pitch black outside.*

What stung the most was that Colleen had illuminated the very issue that Elizabeth had struggled with for a year and a half — did she have the courage to admit to others what she almost dared not admit to herself? She was in love with Colleen McCrady. But she hid it from everyone — kept it in the darkest shadows. Should she — could she — put her feelings for Colleen out in the open and let them have life in the light of day?

Elizabeth leapt up and punched the stop button. "Damn you, Oscar Hammerstein."

She went upstairs and changed into the running suit Colleen had given her for Christmas, then went to the main floor and looked in the fridge for something to eat since they'd left the Cork and Cleaver without ordering. Thinking about the anguish on Colleen's face as she stormed from the restaurant made her stomach churn, and she closed the refrigerator door. She wandered into the living room and saw the book.

This might be the last thing I ever get from Colleen McCrady. She eased into the chair, lifted the manuscript to her nose, and caught the barest fragrance of the Chanel Number Five Colleen always wore. The poignancy of the scent brought her to the edge of tears.

She untied the yarn that held the protective cover in place and removed it. "Oh, good God. This is the book I started reading last Christmas — Willie's story." She let the irony of the outfit she was wearing bring a sardonic smile to her lips.

Elizabeth skimmed through the first chapters of the book to refresh herself on the details. She flipped forward to where she had left off the last time she had read *The Curse of Canaan,* more than five months earlier.

For the good times.

And then she began to read.

Chapter
Eighteen

The Curse of Canaan
Coon River Rapids, Minnesota
September 1956

"IF YOU'RE GOING to be out here watching us," Emil said, "you've got to stay way back from the machinery. Do you understand?"

Ginny displayed her most solemn expression. Right after morning chores, the four neighbors who, with Emil, were working together to get their silos filled, had arrived at the Schmidt farm with their tractors, silage wagons, auger blower, and corn chopper. Ginny had gulped the last of her bowl of Rice Krispies and dashed out the door to greet the men and be part of the day's activities.

The first task was getting the auger blower positioned so that the chopped corn and sorghum could be fed up a nine-inch diameter chute and forced through an opening in the silo roof. The blower didn't have a motor of its own, but relied instead on a belt/pulley arrangement run by the power take-off from a tractor. Once the blower and tractor were in place, Gordon Gage hooked up the chopper to his Massey-Ferguson and drove it out to the first cornfield. As he drove up and down the rows, Marvin Booth drove along side pulling a V-shaped silage wagon that held about two-and-a-half tons of chopped corn. When his wagon was full, he drove back to the silo in the farmyard where he and Emil and Howard Trosvig unloaded at the auger blower while Elmer Knutson drove the second wagon alongside the chopper.

The auger blower deposited all of the silage in the center of the structure. Between loads, to better distribute the silage as the level of chopped corn in the silo rose, Emil climbed through a narrow, steel enclosure on the silo using metal rungs that scaled the side of the storage cylinder. Inside the structure was a series of vertical trap doors. When he reached the door above the last layer, he used a wide, flat pitchfork to move the silage toward the edges. In the winter, as the animals fed on the silage, Emil or Danny unloaded from the top of the silo down, using the trap doors to toss silage to the floor of the lean-to that connected the silo to the main barn.

The curved half-circle enclosure hung on the outside of the silo itself, covering the rungs toward the top half of the silo. One of Ginny's favorite pastimes was to stand at the bottom of the rungs and yell up to her father as he climbed up and down. She liked the echo of her words in the metal tube.

In the early part of the day when the silage was low, he had only a short climb, but by mid-afternoon, Emil was climbing twenty feet up to get access through the trap doors. As he finished working after distributing each load, he made sure the trap door was properly double-latched so the outward pressure of the chopped fodder couldn't dislodge it.

She watched until she saw her father's feet emerge from inside the tube and land on the rung. "Daddy!" she hollered. "Mommy said to tell you that afternoon lunch is ready."

"Okay." Her father's voice boomed down the side of the concrete silo and bounced off the metal enclosure. "Tell her to bring it down as soon as the next wagon comes into the yard."

"Can I ride in the wagon to take Gordon's lunch out to him?"

"You'll have to ask Elmer. He might not want to have you in the way out there."

Emil slapped at the second clasp on the trap door and descended the rungs. He jumped backwards off the third rung from the bottom.

"What did your mother make for lunch?" He grabbed the top of his daughter's head and twisted it playfully from side to side.

"Sandwiches and potato salad and cake with frosting." Ginny went back to the base of the rungs and looked up the side of the silo to the very top of the enclosure.

"Little Sir Echo, how do you do? Hello? Hello?" she sang at the top of her lungs.

Suddenly, a terrific pop and crack sounded from high up.

"Ginny! Look out! Get out of the way!" Emil lunged toward the child and pushed her aside as a two-foot-square trap door came rocketing down. Emil propelled Ginny out of the door's path, but he slipped and fell face down on the lean-to floor. The edge of the thirty pound trap door slammed squarely across the back of his legs, snapping both femurs like matchsticks. The pain was so intense that he passed out immediately.

Howard Trosvig heard the door clattering down the side of the silo and raced inside the lean-to. He arrived in time to see Emil lying on the floor unconscious. Ginny was frozen to the spot where she'd landed after her father's push.

"Did you see the door hit your daddy?"

"Uh huh."

"Where did it hit him?"

"Right here." She drew a line across the backs of her own legs to demonstrate.

"Oh, only his legs. Thank God." He'd feared the door had hit Emil in the head and killed him. "Ginny, you run up to the house and tell your mommy to get the car out. Can you do that? Tell her to drive it right down here by the barn. Run quick."

By the time Emma got the car down by the silo, Elmer was back in from the field. Howard met them at the doorway to the lean-to and explained what happened. "We've got to get him into town right away."

They didn't have time for shock or tears. Emma, Howard, and Elmer dragged Emil by the collar of his jacket over near the car. Ever so carefully they hoisted him onto the back seat, doing their best not to lift him by his legs or to put any pressure on them. Elmer slid behind the wheel and Emma got into the passenger's seat. Spewing gravel, they raced down the lane and headed for Coon River Rapids.

Howard unhooked the wagon from his tractor and set off for the field to tell Gordon and Marvin what had happened.

Ginny stood off to the side and watched, unblinking, as the adults tended to her father and raced out of the yard. Danny was still in school, Rose was at her teacher training institute, and all the neighbor men were out in the field. She was left alone.

Boots and Pepper, the dogs, came out of the main part of the barn and trotted over to the little girl.

"Come on, guys," Ginny said as she started back toward the house. "I know where there are some sandwiches we can have. I'll tell you a story about a man at the store in town. He has a big gold tooth right here."

FLASHING THE HEADLIGHTS and honking the horn the whole way, Elmer Knutson covered the six-and-a-half miles to the canopy over the hospital's emergency entrance in less than ten minutes. Emil moaned pitifully in the back seat.

Emma rushed inside the hospital and hurried two orderlies and a nurse back out to the car, explaining, "A heavy silo door fell across the back of his legs. He's been mostly unconscious since we got to him, so I can't tell you for sure, but we think his legs are broken."

"We'll take it from here," the nurse said. The orderlies got Emil out and on a gurney. "You go to the admitting desk and take care of paperwork," the nurse directed Emma. To the orderlies she said, "Take him to the ER to be checked. Probably have to take him to X-ray next and get shots of both legs, but we better find out what the doctor has to say. You'll need to move this car," she added over her shoulder as they hastened away with Emil.

A few minutes later, Elmer joined Emma as she paced in the enclosed waiting room next to the emergency desk. "Do you want me to sit and wait with you, Emma?"

"No, I'll be fine. I know you need to get home and get your milking done."

"I'll have to take your car."

"That's okay. I'll probably be here most of the night with Emil anyhow."

"I don't mean to add to your worries, but it occurs to me, we drove off and left Ginny standing by the barn."

"Oh my goodness. I was so worried about Emil that I didn't give her a thought. You're right. Well, maybe Howard or Gordon or Marvin kept an eye on her. She's real grown up for her age. It's easy to forget that she's not even six yet." She checked the clock on the wall; a few minutes past four o'clock. "The bus drops Danny around four-thirty and Rose gets home by five fifteen or so. Ginny's probably sitting someplace with a pile of storybooks. I'll use the pay phone to call home in a little while. Danny will have to do the chores by himself tonight."

Another two hours passed before a doctor came out to the waiting room to speak to Emma.

"Mrs. Schmidt?"

"Right here." Emma stood up, clutching her purse with both hands. "How is he?"

"He's not good, but it could have been a lot worse." Dr. Ross took Emma by the elbow. "Let's go over here and sit down." He steered her to the far side of the waiting room, away from the reception desk and the noise.

"Is he conscious?"

"Yes, but groggy. We've got him on strong painkillers."

"What did you find?"

"The X-rays show that both of his legs are broken right above the knee. That's where he got by lucky. The emergency room nurse said a falling silo door hit him. Six inches lower, and it would have shattered his knees. Instead, these are clean breaks, but the femur is a big bone. It will take months for the breaks to heal. The muscles in the thigh are so strong that, with breaks like he's sustained, the muscles pull the two parts together like this." The doctor laid his index fingers together so that the tips overlapped. "We've had your husband in surgery for the past hour and a half so we could put pins in his legs above and below the fractures. We'll use traction to pull the legs so that the bones can be realigned.

"In about a week, we'll have to do surgery again to install pins and plates to actually hold them together. Once we're sure that they're knitting together as they should, we'll put him in casts that run from here—" the doctor swiped the edge of his palm across his upper leg below the groin "—to here." He drew another line across his mid-calf. "We'll need to be sure that his legs are completely immobilized to give the fractures the best shot at healing."

"Will he be able to walk?"

"After the legs heal, you mean?"

"Yes, after he's healed."

"We think so, but because it's both legs and because the fractures are so severe, he'll be bedridden for his entire convalescence. That means he'll need rehabilitation after the casts come off to build up his leg muscles. We can't tell yet if there's any nerve damage. If so, he might even have to be taught how to walk again once the casts are off and he's had some time to rebuild his legs. It's too early to say for sure. We'll know more in a few weeks."

"How long does he have to stay in the hospital? He hates to sleep away from home."

"Until he's out of traction and has the second surgery. Then probably we should hold him another couple of days to make sure there are no complications. Remember, he won't be able to get around at all while those casts are on. Taking care of him at home will be a tall order—bed pans, turning him over to prevent bedsores, making sure he's getting enough fiber and liquid to prevent constipation, rubbing his feet to prevent pooling of blood and the danger of clots. He'll need a lot of care and attention." Dr. Ross saw the look on Emma's face. "We'll have our home care office meet with you to discuss everything when the time comes."

"Can I see him now?"

"I suppose so, but don't expect him to carry on a conversation with you. He's heavily sedated."

Dr. Ross took Emma to the room where her husband lay. His usual ruddy complexion was ashen. Emma had always regarded her rugged, six-foot-tall husband as indestructible. Lying in the hospital bed, he looked like a poor imitation of himself. His short-cropped brown hair was plastered tight against his head. His eyelids fluttered open, but his eyes, usually so bright and animated, were dull, and his pupils so large they almost covered the blue of his irises. Despite the drugs, he was still moaning in pain.

"Emil. It's me. The doctor says you're going to be okay, but you won't be able to walk until the bones in your legs heal. I called home a little while ago. Danny knows he has to do the milking and other chores by himself tonight, so don't worry about that. He knows how to take care of everything outside. Rose will fix supper and look after Ginny. You try to get some rest, okay?"

Emil struggled to speak. "Ginny? Okay?"

"Yes, Daddy. Ginny is fine. Probably ordering Danny and Rose around and running the show like she always does."

That seemed to give Emil some peace of mind. He closed his eyes and mumbled, "Sir Echo, how do you do?"

Emma set her purse on the floor and pulled the molded plastic chair close to the side of his bed. She took one of Emil's hands in both of hers. "Hello? Hello?"

With snippets of one of their younger daughter's favorite songs playing in their heads, the farmer and his wife made their first steps on the long road before them.

"KEEP YOUR SHIRT on, Emil. I'll be there in a minute," Emma called from the kitchen.

The only thing worse than Emil in the hospital was Emil home from the hospital. Emma had run herself ragged for the twelve days he had spent at Coon River Regional. She had to locate a medical equipment supplier and make arrangements to lease an adjustable bed with an overhead lift trapeze and have it delivered to the house. That necessitated moving the living room furniture into the dining room and cramming everything together so all the furnishings would fit. Then there were the twice-daily trips to see Emil at the hospital and all of the sessions with the home care office to make sure that she'd be ready when he was discharged. Betwixt and between she canned tomatoes, dug potatoes, pickled cucumbers, and harvested the squash and pumpkins.

In the midst of all that, she and Danny had to keep up with everything that needed doing day by day on the farm. Most mornings, Danny wasn't getting to school until at least third period. Feeding, milking, and mucking out for thirty milk cows was a daunting task for a fourteen-year-old boy. If that had been all that needed doing, he might have been able to manage, but many of the cows were delivering calves, so that required hand-feeding the newborns with nipple buckets and making sure the new mothers were producing properly. Sixty feeder pigs needed tending, as did a hundred or so laying hens, and twenty steers required feed, water, and clean stalls daily. And that didn't even address getting the corn picked or the fall plowing done. Thank goodness the neighbors had gone ahead and finished filling the silo.

Several of the neighbors came by while Emil was in the hospital to pitch in with one session of milking or to provide some other service, but everyone knew that couldn't go on indefinitely. They were glad to help out for the short term, but they had full-time duties on their own farms and lots to do to get ready for winter. Short-changing themselves in deference to Emil's needs ultimately only robbed Peter to pay Paul.

Now that Emil was home from the hospital, Emma never got a minute's peace. When he was awake, he couldn't go ten minutes without needing her to bring him something or to help him do what he couldn't accomplish by himself. When he was napping, Emma shifted into high gear to tackle the dozens of chores stacking up while she was doing her Florence Nightingale impersonation.

"What is it this time?" Emma tried to keep the edge out of her voice.

"It's almost noon. I want to watch the market reports on channel six."

"For heaven's sake. I've got three bushels of tomatoes blanching in the kitchen. What difference is it if winter wheat is up two cents or market hogs are down a penny? Why don't you call for Ginny when it's something as simple as changing the television channel?"

"She won't stick around for more than a couple of minutes. She hasn't said more than five words a day to me since I got home. I don't think she's even in the house."

"Who can blame her? You bark out orders like some kind of drill sergeant. She's scared to death of you." Emma rearranged the pillows under Emil's head. "She's not used to seeing you all laid up like this. She thinks it's her fault you got hurt in the first place. Try to remember she's a little girl. Stop yelling and try talking."

"You don't know what it's like to be trapped in these damn leg casts. I can't even stand up to pee. I can't run my farm, can't move my bowels, can't even sit in a damn chair. I can't sleep. Nothing tastes good. My back aches day and night. If I want something, I have to wait until you've got time to come and get it for me. I don't know how long I can put up with this."

Emma cranked the dial on the black and white TV and fled the room. She hurried back to the kitchen and resumed her assault on the tomatoes before Emil could say anything more. Wiping the tears from her eyes, she searched for a tissue in her apron pocket and then blew her nose. She hated being so short tempered, but four hours of sleep in sporadic doses for the past two-and-a-half weeks simply wasn't cutting it.

Ginny wandered in from outdoors where she had been throwing sticks into the cattle pond for the dogs to fetch. She hung her jacket on a nail behind the kitchen door. "Are we going to sit at the table and eat today, Mom?"

"Probably not. I'll have to fix something for your daddy in a little while. I'll find something for you then, too, okay?"

"Okay." Ginny inched herself onto the stool near the counter where her mother was peeling tomatoes. "Why is Daddy mad at me?"

"Daddy's mad at the whole world right now."

"He's mad because I made the door fall out of the silo, isn't he?"

"You didn't make that happen. It fell out by itself."

"Huh uh. I was singing up that metal chute to little Sir Echo, and then all of a sudden the door came down."

"That's what's called a coincidence. Do you know that word?"

"Not really."

"A coincidence is when two things happen right about the same time, but don't have anything to do with each other. Like, if you slammed the door, and I sneezed right when you did, that's a coincidence. I didn't sneeze because you slammed the door. I'd have sneezed anyway. See?"

"I guess." Ginny squirmed on the stool.

"So tell me another thing that would be a coincidence."

"I jump off this stool and you put a tomato in the jar."

"Right. I was going to put a tomato in the jar no matter what you did. You jumping off the stool didn't make me put it in there."

"I sang to Sir Echo, and the door fell out of the silo. It was going to fall out anyway."

"That's right. Daddy getting hit in the legs was a sad thing and a bad thing, but you didn't make the door hit him."

"I still don't know why he's so mad at me."

"Daddy's not used to having to stay in bed all day everyday. He's bored and lonely. And he's scared."

"Daddies don't get scared," Ginny said, more hoping she was right than having reason to believe she was.

Emma wished she hadn't planted that seed in her daughter's active mind. "I've got an idea. Why don't you go tell Daddy I'm going to fix his lunch soon? Then you can sit and eat with him, okay?"

"Okay. And I'll tell him not to be scared anymore, too." Ginny padded off through the dining room to Emil's makeshift infirmary in the living room. She approached the bed, but kept her distance.

"Why are you scared, Daddy?"

"Who said I was scared?"

"Mom did. She said you were bored and lonely, too."

"Your mom doesn't always know what she's talking about."

"So you're not bored and lonely?"

Emil chuckled in spite of himself. "Maybe a little."

"And scared?"

"Maybe for a minute, sometimes."

"Do you know what helps me when I get scared?"

"What, babes?"

"For someone to tell me a story. Pretty soon, I'm trying to think of how the story will end, and then I forget to be scared."

"Then maybe you should tell me a story."

"Okay." Ginny gingerly climbed onto the foot of her father's bed. "Should I tell you a story from a book or one I made up myself?"

"How about one you made up yourself?"

"Once upon a time, there was girl named — umm — Daisy and her brother named — uh — Dickey. They lived on a farm with their mom and dad and two dogs."

"Did the dogs have names?"

"Uh huh. Peppy and Socks."

"I see. So what happened to Daisy and Dickey?"

"They had a little sister named — umm — Janie. They used to say to Janie 'Let's play a game' or 'Do you want to read a book?' They would tease her and make her laugh, but then one day, they stopped doing that."

"Why would they stop playing with Janie?"

"Because everyone only had time to work all day. Daisy said, 'I guess I don't need to be a teacher after all,' and Dickey said 'I don't need to go to school anymore.' And sometimes they said mean things to each other and to Janie, and sometimes Daisy cried at night when she thought no one was listening. And the mom all the time was saying, 'Not now, Janie, I'm busy.'"

"What about the dad?"

"He had to go away for a while."

"So what happened to Janie?"

"She played with the dogs and stayed out of the way."

"Oh." Emil searched the little girl's face. "Is there any more to your story?"

"Janie growed up real fast and helped everybody do all their work so they could read stories and play again." She let herself slide off the side of the bed. "The end." She skipped out of the room, and Emil could hear her thumping up the stairs to her bedroom.

Emma came into the room carrying a tray. "Here's a hot roast beef sandwich and some fresh, stewed tomatoes. Are you up to eating?"

"Yes, thanks." He asked Emma to use the crank to elevate the head of the bed and then hooked his arms on the overhead trapeze to pull himself into a more upright position. He took a bite of the sandwich. "This is good. I'll probably want another one of these." He paused before taking another bite. "Aren't you having some lunch?"

She couldn't read the tone in his voice. "Well, I want to get this canning done — "

"I thought maybe you'd bring your sandwich in here and eat with me." He wiped his mouth.

"I guess I could take a few minutes to sit with you when I bring you your second sandwich."

"Good. I want to tell you the tale our little storyteller made up. Sometimes I'd swear that Ginny is an adult in disguise."

"I know what you mean. I never know quite how to take it when she starts her yarns with, 'When I used to be big.'"

"Almost like this is her second time around or something. Good sandwich, by the way." He took another bite. "I definitely want another one."

Emma was back in a few minutes with a sandwich for herself as well. She sat down on the straight-backed chair near the bed.

Emil didn't pick up his sandwich right away. "You haven't exactly told me the truth about what's going on around here, have you?"

Emma rearranged the contents of her sandwich, stalling for time. "What do you mean?"

"For starters, Rose is making noises about dropping out of her teachers' training program, and Danny is threatening to quit school. You're growling like a bear in a beehive, and, apparently, I don't live here anymore."

"Have you been taking too many pain pills?"

"No, I've been having story time with Ginny."

"Oh."

"You'd better fill me in, and this time, don't sugarcoat it."

"Yes, Rose has offered to drop out of her teachers' training program to help out. Danny is about to fall over from exhaustion. He's doing his best, but it's too much. Most days, he misses almost half of his morning classes. By the time he's done with evening chores, he's so tired he falls asleep over his homework. I've even caught him reading standing up, trying to stay awake. He's missed all of his 4-H and Future Farmers activities. As for Ginny, she's used to having the big kids read to her and spend time with her, but they're both too busy."

"And what about you?"

"I'm fine."

"Sure you are, if you don't count the fact you're drop-dead tired and overworked to the point of being ready to kill."

"These are tough times. What choice do I have? I guess I thought your broken legs were only your pain and your problem, but the truth is, this whole family is about to break in half."

"Then it's time we did something about putting a cast on it, isn't it?"

Chapter
Nineteen

The Curse of Canaan
Coon River Rapids, Minnesota
September 1956

EMMA SAT AT the kitchen table with her three children. She'd been thinking a lot about the long chat with Emil that afternoon. Up until her outburst that morning, she knew Emil had assumed everything was moving along all right in his absence — because no one had wanted to tell him anything to the contrary. Now that he knew better — and now that Emma had more fully explained how long his recovery was likely to take — he'd told her that finding someone to work on the farm was the only reasonable course of action.

She said, "Danny, you talk to all the boys in Future Farmers and to everyone in the 4-H club. Tell them to let us know about anybody who might be available to hire out for the next six months to a year." Emma shifted her gaze to her older daughter. "Rose, there are lots of girls in your teacher training class who aren't from right around Coon River Rapids. Maybe one of them has a brother or a cousin or an uncle or a boyfriend who'd be willing to hire on here. I spent all afternoon on the phone calling all the neighbors and both sides of the family. So far, we haven't come up with anybody, but we have to find somebody to help us out."

Rose looked concerned. "So Daddy honestly wants to do this?"

"Yes," Emma said.

"The doctor still thinks Dad is going to be in bed for six months?" Danny asked.

"Maybe not quite that long, but the doctor told me to figure on it being next fall before he's back to his old self. If it's sooner than that, then good for us. I guess our motto should be 'Pray for wind, but row toward shore.'"

Rose patted Emma's shoulder. "You know I'll drop out of my training program if that's what you and Dad want."

"As a farm hand, you'd make a good waitress, Rose," Emma

said. "You're too much like me to be any good in the barn or out in the fields. Neither one of us knows the first thing about tending the animals or running the machinery. I suppose we could learn, but by the time we did, Daddy would be back on his feet, and who knows what a mess we'd have made of things by then." Emma had a hard time picturing her tall, pretty daughter in overalls and work boots. Though Rose had inherited her father's genes for height and build, she not only bore a strong facial resemblance to her mother, but she shared her complete lack of interest in the outdoor labor of the farm. A willowy young woman, nearly five-ten, her face was full, framed by soft blonde/brown curls that went well with her hazel eyes. She'd be a wonderful teacher, but not a good farmhand.

Danny squared his jaw. "I can run this farm, Ma."

"I believe you could, but you've got your school work to keep up with, too. With all you're doing now, you're dead on your feet, and there's no time left for studying. Your father doesn't want you to miss out on everything because he's laid up. Even when we find someone to work for us, you'll still have all your chores like always."

"I could drop out of school for the next couple of months and pick back up when Dad's better."

"Let's save that as a last resort, Danny." Emma had contemplated that very move. If they couldn't find a hired hand, it might still come to that, but she hoped not. Danny was an excellent student, but an extremely shy adolescent. If he fell back a year, it might be enough to paralyze him socially for life. Like his big sister, Danny resembled both of his parents, but he had inherited Emma's smaller stature and Emil's looks. Stretched to his tallest, he barely made five-nine. If he didn't work so hard on the farm, he'd easily be pudgy, maybe even fat, but all of the physical labor kept his squat, roundish body toned and firm. His hair was the same deep brown that Emil's was, and his eyes the same engaging blue. When Emil and Danny sat side by side, no one could mistake he was his father's son.

"What about me, Mom?" Ginny piped up. "Isn't there something I'm supposed to do?"

"Your job is to keep Daddy entertained."

"You mean by dancing and stuff?" Ginny leapt from her chair to show her version of the gyrations she had seen Barbara Boylen and Bobby Burgess perform on Lawrence Welk. Her recent growth spurt had added almost two inches to her height. A yard stick was already half a foot too short to measure her. If she continued as she was going, she'd likely end up at least as tall as Rose, but with more blonde in her hair and more blue in her eyes.

"Not exactly," her mother replied. "I meant you should sit in the room and change the television channels or watch for the mailman and bring the newspaper. If he wants a drink, you can bring a glass of water. You can rub his feet and take him his lunch—things like that. That way, I can get a few things done and not have to run in there ten times an hour. Can you do that?"

"Sure. You should have told me before that's what you wanted."

Rose grabbed the first of the dirty plates to stack. "Are we about done discussing this, Mother? You know I have a date with Milton tonight. I need to hurry and get these dishes done so I've got time to get ready."

"Oooh, Milton," Ginny teased. She wrapped her arms around herself and made kissing noises.

"Why do you let her carry on like that, Mother?" Rose grabbed a handful of silverware and put it on top of the plates.

Emma sighed. "Because, heaven help me, I've never found a way to stop her. You go on and get ready for your date. I'll clean up these dishes. Ginny will help me. Won't you, Ginny?"

"I'll get Pepper and Boots to lick 'em clean."

Half an hour later, Milton Shelby pulled into the yard to collect Rose for their date. As always, Ginny was the first one to greet him at the door.

"Where are you taking my sister tonight, Milton? Someplace dark?"

"Oh, Ginny," Rose said as she and Milton walked out the door, "you're such a pest. Bye, Mother. I won't be late."

"I guess I should have spoken to your father," Milton said as they slid into the front seat of his Ford Victoria. "I haven't seen him since his accident."

"Probably better that you didn't go see him. He's been impossible to get along with since he got home from the hospital. I don't think he likes people to see him in his undershirt lying in bed."

Once they were out of the yard and safe from Ginny's ever-prying eyes, Rose moved from the passenger side to the center of the seat. "Where *are* we going tonight?"

"To Don Ahrens's house to play board games with Patsy and him. Does that sound all right?"

"Sure. The way things have been going at home, I wasn't even sure I'd get be able to get out for our date. Lately, it's looked like I might have to leave my training program to learn to milk cows and feed pigs."

"Oh?"

"Yeah, but now my mother and father have decided we need to hire somebody to help out on the farm until Dad is well enough to work again. It's too much for Danny to do by himself. You don't know anybody who's fond of the smell of manure and likes to work twelve hour days, do you?"

"Not off hand, but I'll ask my dad. He might know somebody. He's president of the Chamber of Commerce again this year."

"Some scrawny boy from town won't do, Milton. It's got to be someone strong who knows at least a little bit about farming."

"I'll talk to him tomorrow. If he's got any ideas, I can call you or tell you about it at church on Sunday."

"I'll keep my fingers crossed."

KENT SHELBY SAT in the Schmidt's living room/infirmary on Sunday afternoon, the last day of September. "I was real sorry to hear about your misfortune, Emil. I've been keeping up on how you're doing through Milton, and I've talked to several of your neighbors when they've come into the store, too. As steady company as Milton and Rose are keeping, I guess you and I are the next best thing to family." Kent waited for Emil to reply; he didn't.

"Anyway," Kent continued, "Milton tells me that you need someone to help out 'til your legs heal. I think I might have a solution for you. I know you've seen the colored man who works for me at the Woolworth's. His name is Willie Rice. He's a reliable worker, easy to give instructions to, never causes any problems."

"What good to me is a deaf colored man who doesn't know anything about farming?" Emil's face was serious, and though he seemed to be trying to mask the discomfort of being held prisoner in his own living room, Kent couldn't help but see his misery. Everyone he knew around Coon River Rapids prided themselves on being self-sufficient, and clearly, asking for help was killing Emil Schmidt.

"Turns out he does know something about farming. When Milton talked to me yesterday about your situation, I sat down with Willie and asked him some questions. Of course, he had to write out his answers, but he told me he grew up on a farm down south someplace. He's milked cows and tended chickens and raised crops. He hasn't had any experience with hogs, but that would probably be pretty easy to teach him. The only problem in dealing with Willie is remembering to stay right in front of him when you talk to him so he can read your lips. He almost always catches things on the first try. He's strong as an ox. I think he'd do fine for you."

"I don't know anything about giving orders to a colored fellow."

"It's no different than giving orders to anybody else. Tell him what to do, and he does it. He might need to come to you or Danny with questions, but he writes them out in a little notebook he carries. In some ways, he's the easiest man I've ever managed. You never get any back talk from him, and you don't have to worry about him standing around wasting time jawing with other folks. With Willie, it's all work." Kent paused. "And he works cheap, too." He laughed knowingly. "Problem is, though, he doesn't have a car. But chances are you'd want him to board on the farm to be here bright and early for chores every morning."

"I'm not sure how comfortable we'd be having a colored man on our farm all day every day. I'd worry about him being around Emma and Ginny. I couldn't get to them if he got out of line."

"I honestly don't think that would be a problem. He's been working for me ten months now. I've never had a minute's difficulty from him. He's real respectful. Keeps to himself, does what he's told."

"I appreciate your driving out here to make the offer, but I still think it would be borrowing trouble. Emma and the kids are asking around. We'll find somebody who'd be better than Coon Willie."

"Suit yourself, but I don't think you'll find anybody else who's willing to work for room and board and two dollars a day. You'd be lucky to get anyone else for room and board and six dollars a day." Kent stood and offered his hand to Emil. "Think about it. Let me know if you change your mind."

Over the next two weeks, three potential hired hands gave it a whirl at the Schmidt farm. The first one, a relative of one of Rose's fellow teacher trainees, lasted two days and quit. "I'll never drink another glass of milk," he swore after his first experience with a cow's mastitis.

The second one was a man from Ashby, a little town about forty miles down the road. One of Emma's sisters had suggested he make the trip to Coon River Rapids and look up Emil and Emma. He sometimes had a problem with a little too much to drink, so he had a long history of short-lived jobs. On his fourth day on the farm, he drove Emil's Allis-Chalmers tractor through the fence around the feeder cattle. When told, Emil left no question that, regardless of the condition of his legs, his lungs were still perfectly fine.

The third fellow was a man who worked in the Grant County Agricultural Extension Office. He fancied himself a person who could take what he knew in farming theory and readily apply it to the real world. For the better part of a week, he did fairly well. Then Emil explained to him that he and Danny would be castrating the young male pigs to make them into market barrows for fattening and selling to the slaughterhouse. At first, he thought Emil was making a crude joke when he described how Danny would hold the pig by its hind legs while he, Mr. Theory-into-Practice, excised the pig's gonads with a sharp knife. When he understood that Emil was stone cold serious, he barely made it out of the house before he threw up and passed out.

On a Saturday afternoon, Emil called for Rose. She came down from her bedroom and stood by her father's bed. He said, "I suppose you're going out with the wimpy town boy again tonight."

"Why are you so hard on Milton? We've been going out for four years now, and I don't think I've ever heard you say anything nice about him."

"He's so darned soft, that's all. When he shakes your hand, it's like shaking hands with a woman."

"You know that's because he's a musician. He has to keep his hands soft to play the violin."

"He couldn't even pick an instrument fit for a man — drums or the accordion or a brass horn." Emil's face was lined and leathery from all his time in the summer sun and the winter wind. His hands were usually cracked, stained, and callused from handling the animals and machinery. He hated that lying in bed had made his hands into what he thought of as women's hands — pale and smooth. It reminded him of what was happening to every muscle in his body, too, and Milton Shelby's somewhat effeminate demeanor only underscored Emil's unhappiness with his own state of being.

Rose's voice was firm. "Let's not do this again. Milton is Milton. And I happen to like him that way. Do you need me to break my date with him and stay home with you tonight?"

"No, I need you to go on your date with Milton Milquetoast, and tell him to talk to his dad again about that colored guy coming to work here."

"He's not 'colored.' What color is he? The right term is 'Negro.'"

"I don't much care what the right word is. I need somebody who can milk a cow and drive a tractor and get this place ready for winter. We've still got three fields of corn to pick and more than sixty acres that need plowing. Have Milton tell his dad to bring that colored man out here tomorrow so we can talk."

"All right, I will." Rose went in search of Emma. She found her mending Danny's coveralls in the utility room off the kitchen.

"Mother, do you know Dad is planning to have that Negro from the Woolworth's work on the farm?"

"He's talked about it. After what's gone on with those first three, I'm surprised he hasn't asked his seventy-year-old mother to come milk for him."

"You're all right with it, then?"

"It'll seem strange at first, I guess, but if he can do the work, what's the difference?"

"Are you going to have him eat at the table with us every night?"

"That's what we did with the others. Why wouldn't we with him?"

"No reason. But I've never eaten a meal with a Negro before."

"Neither have the rest of us." Emma knotted off her thread and bit it with her teeth. "I'm told they put food in their mouths and chew. I hope we don't stare at him when he performs that strange custom."

"Oh, Mother."

"I'm not crazy about the idea, either, but what are we going to do? At least Danny has had a little help over the past couple of weeks, but he's still worn to a nub. We may as well give the colored man a try."

"At a minimum, could we not refer to him as 'colored?' They prefer 'Negro.'"

"He's not likely to know what we call him. He can't hear a word, remember? And I expect it's your father and Danny who will have all the dealings with him. If it goes with him like it's gone with the others, he won't be here a full week anyhow. Let's hope for the best, okay?"

Two hours later, on her way into town with Milton, Rose delivered the message from her father.

Milton laughed. "Oh, I suppose I'll have to call you Miss Scarlet Rose — darling of Terra Firma."

"You'd better not, Milton Shelby. Not unless you want a swift kick in your Rhett Butler."

Chapter
Twenty

The Curse of Canaan
Coon River Rapids, Minnesota
October 1956

WILLIE FLIPPED OPEN a clean page in his notebook and wrote the following:

1. Milk cows/feed them
2. Feed calves
3. Feed steers
4. Feed pigs
5. Feed chickens/pick eggs
6. Haul manure
7. Do field work
8. Check with boss or his son before doing anything else
9. Stay away from Mrs. and little girl and other daughter except at mealtimes.

He handed the page to Emil who, with only his seventh grade education to support him, had far more of a struggle reading it than Willie had writing it.

"That's right," Emil confirmed. "Do you know how to drive a tractor and hitch up machinery?"

Willie had only limited experience with mechanized farm equipment, but he was determined to make a good showing for this job. The way Mr. Shelby had explained it, his living expenses would be furnished by his employer. Anything he was paid beyond that could all be put aside to save toward bringing his mother to live with him. He could learn anything he needed to if it meant clearing fourteen dollars a week. Willie wrote the word "Yes, sir," on his notepad and showed it to Emil.

"Good." Emil pointed toward Danny, who was standing in the doorway, and said, "My boy will show you the room in the barn where you'll sleep. After you get your things put away, he'll take you out to the machine shed and tell you anything you need to know about each implement. Some of our machinery is kind of old, but it still works. You just need to know how to coax it along. Understand?"

Willie looked Emil in the eye and dipped his head to show his comprehension.

"All right. Go on, then." Emil swept his hands away from his chest as though whisking him out of the room. Willie followed Danny out the door.

"Danny," Emil hollered, "you keep a sharp eye out. Don't leave him alone anywhere until we're sure we can trust him, hear?"

Danny doubled back past Willie to talk to his father. "Okay. Do you want me to have him drive the tractors and stuff this afternoon?"

"Might as well. If he's going to screw things up, I'd rather know it right off. If he can operate that sticky throttle on the Farmall, chances are he can drive anything."

Of course, Emil had no way to know that Willie could hear this conversation between father and son. Willie made a mental note about the tractor's uncooperative throttle and waited outside the door for Danny to show him the way to his new quarters.

About a year earlier, Emil had added on to his barn to make a bigger milking parlor for his expanded herd of Holsteins and to construct a room to house a bulk tank. He was one of the first farmers in the vicinity to install a bulk storage tank for his daily milk production. Every other day, a tanker truck came to the Schmidt farm and vacuumed up the 1,300 pounds of whole milk for transport to the dairy plant. Before that upgrade, Emil had stored his milk in a vat of cold water in ten-gallon galvanized milk cans that had to be loaded up daily and hauled to the local creamery. Now, with this bulk tank operation, Emil was considered a Grade A milk supplier, so each hundredweight of two-point-five percent butterfat milk brought him a premium price.

In the process of remodeling, Emil had also built a structure connecting the old portion of the barn to the new parlor and bulk house. He thought he might eventually need some additional calf pens there, but so far, he'd left it an open room, about fifteen feet square, perfect to become Willie Rice's living space.

When Emil and Emma had reached the conclusion that a hired hand was a necessity, Emma and the two older children had scrounged in the attic of the farm house and hauled down a metal, open-spring bed frame and a reasonably serviceable mattress. They had furnished the space with a chest of drawers, a rocking chair, a small Formica table, and two metal folding chairs. Emma provided two of her least favorite lamps—a floor lamp and a table lamp—from the things crammed in the dining room while Emil's bed occupied the living room. Willie's new quarters certainly weren't pretty, but with a picture, a mirror, and a calendar hanging on the walls and scatter rugs on the poured concrete floor, the space was functional.

Even Emil and Emma didn't have the luxury of indoor plumbing, so it never crossed their minds to worry about bathroom facilities for Willie. He'd use the outhouse or the woods or the gutters in the barn like the rest of them did. Running water, both hot and cold, was piped into the barn. The cold water lines fed the watering basins at each of the cow's stanchions and ran into the bulk house as well. A water heater sat in the bulk house to generate hot water for washing the stainless steel bulk tank and the milking machines—"milkers" as they were called—five-gallon vacuum-sealed canisters that had pulsing rubber cups that were attached to the cows' udders. Willie could avail himself of those sources for his drinking and washing water.

"This is where you'll stay," Danny stated, forming each word carefully and speaking louder than normal. "It stays real warm in here, even in the winter, because the heat from the cows carries all through the barn. Lots of times, I don't even wear a coat when I'm down here because it's pretty much like being in the house."

Not exactly, Willie thought to himself as the odors assaulted his nose. The reek of cows, manure, alfalfa, and lord only knew what all else threatened to overwhelm him. Obviously Danny had long since become completely inured to the fragrance of the farm, but Willie stifled his gag reflex and looked around the room. A pair of two-foot square windows side by side provided natural light from the mid-afternoon autumn sun. No one would ever mistake the living quarters for a luxury suite, but it wasn't all that much different from the room he rented at Able Apartments—a lot smellier, though.

Willie pulled his notebook from his shirt pocket. "Give me ten minutes to put my things away, then you can show me where everything is." He held the page out to Danny.

"Maybe I'll sit here and wait," Danny replied, remembering his father's caution about not leaving Willie alone.

Willie had expected as much and simply set about stowing his few worldly goods. Soon, he and the compact, muscular farm boy were out touring the farm and its inhabitants and looking at the various farming devices.

Emil owned three tractors: the Farmall for lightweight work like pulling wagons and mowing hay, the Allis-Chalmers for more demanding tasks like hauling rocks or pulling the corn planter, and his International diesel which was the workhorse for heavy-duty jobs, like plowing and running the corn picker and the combine/thresher. After Danny took Willie past all of the pieces of equipment, he motioned to the Farmall.

"Want to get some practice driving? We could go out to some of the fields, and I'll show you where the corn is that still needs picking."

Willie climbed into the metal seat and looked over the unfamiliar instrument cluster. Danny stood on the draw bar immediately behind him. Willie pointed to the double pedals on the right side of the passenger platform and looked over his shoulder at Danny's lips.

"Right wheel brake and left wheel brake," Danny explained. "The clutch is on the left."

With a quick, silent prayer, Willie slapped the gearshift knob to be sure the tractor was in neutral. He pulled the choke, cranked the key, and punched the starter button. The Farmall coughed to life. The top of the gearshift had a diagram depicting the gears' locations. With his right foot depressing both brake pedals, Willie stomped the clutch in with his left foot, grabbed the knob, and aimed for first. The gears ground momentarily, then the engine engaged. He grasped the throttle lever attached to the right of the steering column and edged it forward. It resisted. Aha, the temperamental throttle, Willie reasoned. He nudged it a little more until the tractor ran more smoothly.

Painstakingly, Willie released both brakes and let the clutch out. The tractor lurched forward. Danny hung behind him, his fingers grabbing the edge of the metal seat and his knees flexed so that the balls of his feet would bounce on the draw bar. Off they went, Willie strangely exhilarated at the prospect of driving a far more sophisticated machine than he'd ever been entrusted with before and Danny more than moderately impressed at how quickly Willie had mastered the uncooperative throttle. Danny pointed out over Willie's shoulder to the left as they exited the farmyard. Willie steered that direction and headed down the lane that led to Emil's fields. He shot Willie a thumb's up as he drew his hand back to hang on to the seat. Willie turned his head and grinned at the boy.

If they could have read one another's minds, they'd have seen the same message: "What do you know? This might work out all right."

GINNY HAD BEEN watching out the front window for Danny and Willie to return from their excursion around Emil's 160 acres, a hundred acres of which was arable. At long last, the tractor came lurching into her view. Excitement in her voice, she said, "Here they come, Mom!"

"Okay. Go tell them to get washed up for supper." While Ginny was delivering that instruction, Emma took Emil's supper in to him, then returned to join the others who had gathered around the big, yellow, enamel-topped table in the kitchen.

Emma sat at the head of the table, Danny and Rose were on one side, and Ginny and Willie were on the other. Sunday evening supper at the Schmidt house was usually nothing more than a quick meal of leftovers, but since this was Willie's first night, Emma had fixed a pork roast with boiled potatoes and fresh applesauce.

That wasn't the only unusual circumstance at the table that evening. First, Willie dropped his head to return thanks — silently — for the meal, which prompted Ginny to insist that the rest of them pray, too.

"All right, Ginny. Would you like to ask a blessing?"

"Rub a dub dub. Thanks for the grub. Go, God, go. Amen."

"Mother, really." Rose sighed. "If she's going to pray, can't she at least do a real prayer?"

"That is a real prayer," Ginny protested. "I heard the cook on the Roy Rogers TV show say it."

"I doubt it, Ginny," Rose said.

"Don't argue; eat," Emma directed.

The second strange thing was that the usual constant chatter around the table was missing. Tonight, an observer would have assumed the group assembled was a family of deaf mutes hosting another deaf mute. Silence. Weird, uncomfortable, make-it-hard-to-swallow silence.

Finally, Willie pulled his notebook from his pocket. "This is delicious, Mrs. Schmidt. You're a very good cook. Thank you for letting me sit at your table." He passed the page to Emma.

She blushed. She was about to take the notebook from him to write a reply, but Willie shook his head and then pointed first at his eyes and then Emma's lips.

"Oh, that's right," Emma stammered. "You can see what I'm saying."

Willie nodded.

"You're sure welcome for the supper, but anybody can put a roast in the oven and boil water with potatoes in it."

Willie wrote again. "Yes, but knowing when to take it out of the oven and when to turn off the burner is a skill. And you had to season the meat, peel the potatoes, and prepare the apples to make the sauce. Every bite is real good."

Emma didn't get many compliments, and she certainly had never gotten one from a colored man before. "Thank you. It was nothing."

Willie dropped his eyes and stared at his plate. Ginny tapped Willie on the arm. He met her inquiring gaze. She asked, "How come you can't hear or talk? Were you born that way?"

"Ginny, that's rude!" Emma scolded.

"You know what they tell Thumper in *Bambi*," Rose added. "If you can't say something nice, don't say anything at all."

Danny was secretly glad she'd asked because he'd been wondering the same thing.

Willie ignored the women chastising the little girl. Once again, he wrote in his notebook. "Tell her I had an accident when I was young that made me not hear. I used to know how to talk, so that's why I can read lips and know what the words are. Tell her I think she was brave to ask me." He gave the notebook to Emma.

"He had an accident. He used to be able to hear, but now he can't." Emma knew that telling Ginny that Willie thought her question was brave would prompt a hailstorm of follow-up queries. "He also said, 'please don't ask any more questions like that.' Now tell the man you're sorry for butting in to his personal affairs."

Ginny waited until Willie looked at her. "I'm sorry, Mister."

Willie retrieved his notebook. "Tell her to call me Willie, and she can ask me anything she wants to."

"He said his name is Willie and he forgives you—this time."

"Is there dessert tonight?" Danny asked. "I need to get down to the barn. We had two more cows come fresh today, so I'll need extra time to tend to them and their calves, and I'll probably need extra time to teach Willie how to use the milkers and all."

"Yes, we have dessert." Emma pushed back from the table. "Rose baked a chocolate cake and frosted it with chocolate icing. If you're ready for it, I'll get you a piece."

"Make it a big one, okay?"

Rose cleared the table while Emma cut the cake, then Rose took the two biggest pieces to the table for Danny and Willie. Emma came right behind with three smaller pieces for Ginny, Rose, and herself. She was about to have her first bite when she suddenly gasped. "Oh, I forgot about Emil. He'll want cake, too." She hastened back to the counter to correct her oversight. While she was out of the kitchen, Rose and Danny, still not sure what to do about making conversation with a man who couldn't talk, nosed down into their desserts.

Ginny, meanwhile, carefully peeled the layer of chocolate frosting from her cake and smeared it across her cheeks and upper lip and the over the backs of her hands. She licked the excess frosting from her fingers and then tapped Willie on the arm.

"Hey, Willie, look. Now I'm like you."

Emma came back into the kitchen at the same moment Danny and Rose looked up. They were all flabbergasted to see the youngest family member looking like Al Jolson, albeit Al Jolson at the hands of a totally inept make-up artist. Time froze. They had no idea what to expect from the stranger at their table — anger, outrage, embarrassment, retaliation.

Willie held Ginny in his gaze a moment. He used his index finger to swab a smidgen of frosting from his plate. He wiped it above his already dark upper lip. Ginny giggled in delight; a happy look spread across Willie's face.

Then, to the Schmidt family's surprise and relief, Willie laughed a deep, infectious guffaw that came from way down in his gut.

Chapter
Twenty-One

The Curse of Canaan
Coon River Rapids, Minnesota
November 1956

EMMA PULLED ON a light overcoat. "I can't take Ginny along with me, Emil. I'm going into town to get her birthday presents. She'll have to stay at home with you."

"How am I supposed to keep an eye on her? If she takes a notion to go outside or whatever, I can't exactly get up out of this bed and chase after her, now can I? Besides, what if I need something?"

"She plays by herself for hours on end every day. She's not likely to get into any trouble. I'll tell her she has to stay close by to take care of you. Now that she's six, she understands what it means to be responsible. Do you need me to give Willie any instructions before I go?"

"Yes. I want him to shell the corn he picks today. I had told him to leave it on the cob, but before Danny left for school he told me we're running low on corn to grind for hog feed, so I need to be sure Willie doesn't put the ear corn in the corn crib."

"Shouldn't I send him in here for you to tell him that? I don't want to get the instructions wrong."

"No, he'll know what I mean. We've been over the difference between shelled corn and ear corn. I think I hear him coming back with the manure spreader now."

"All right, then. I'll talk to Willie and to Ginny before I go. I need to get some groceries, too, so I'll be gone a couple of hours." She patted her hair in place and picked up her purse and the car keys. "See you around lunch time."

She went down to the cow pen where Willie was backing the manure spreader next to the barn. He switched off the tractor's engine and hopped down to meet Emma as she approached.

"Emil said to tell you he wants you to shell the corn instead of storing the cobs in the corn crib. Do you understand?"

Willie twisted his hands around an imaginary corncob to

demonstrate his comprehension. Emma did the same for emphasis. "Right, shell it." She jangled her keys in front of Willie. "I have to go into Coon River Rapids for a while. Ginny's birthday is tomorrow, so I'm going to get her presents and pick up a few groceries."

Willie pulled his notebook and pencil from the pocket of his jacket. "Mrs., would you do something in town for me?" Emma read his note.

"Go to the Woolworth's and buy a mix of Ginny's favorite kinds of candy. I want to give her a birthday present, too." He handed the notebook to Emma and dug in his pocket for a dime.

"That's very generous, Willie, but you don't need to get anything for her. Besides, I don't know what her favorite kinds of candy are. She usually goes to town with her dad."

Willie wrote: "Malted milk balls, jelly dollars, caramel drops, red licorice bites, and candy corn."

"Now, how would you know that?"

Willie scratched hurriedly: "I worked the candy counter. She was one of my best customers." He looked at Emma. "Please?" he formed silently with his lips.

"Oh, all right. That child is already so spoiled I don't suppose a little more will make much difference. Do you happen to know where Ginny is?" Emma looked around the farmyard.

Willie beckoned Emma with him into the barn and led her to his room in the connecting structure. Ginny sat in Willie's wooden rocker holding her current favorite picture book with several of her storybooks at her elbow on the little side table.

"Ginny, what in heaven's name are you doing in here?"

"Willie said I could."

"After you nagged him to the point of insanity, I suspect."

"Huh uh. I only asked him one time."

Emma glanced over her shoulder where Willie stood. "Is it okay with you for her to be in here?"

Willie lifted his notebook and jotted a line. "She likes to tell me the stories she reads—sometimes, she makes up new ones all by herself."

"Anytime she gets on your nerves or you decide you don't want her in here, please tell her to leave you alone. You might have to tell her more than once, but be firm." Emma glanced at her watch. "Oh goodness. I've let the time get away from me. Ginny, go up to the house and sit with Daddy while I'm in town. You're his nurse 'til I get back, okay?"

"I want to go to town with you."

"No, Ginny, not today."

Ginny was all set to whine until she got her way. Willie stepped around Emma and between mother and daughter. He tapped Ginny lightly on the head, then pointed in the direction of the house. He laid his finger across his lips, then pointed at Ginny.

She sighed. "Okay, Willie. Not another word out of me. I'm going." Ginny pushed past them and headed up the incline toward the house.

Emma stood slack-jawed. Willie made another entry in his notebook and passed it to Emma. "Sometimes, the best argument is no argument at all."

Emma certainly couldn't argue with that.

MILTON SHELBY DROPPED Rose back home following their usual Sunday evening outing. Rose came in to find her mother reading her Bible at the kitchen table. "Mother, you'll never guess what we talked about at the young adults' meeting at church tonight."

"No, I probably won't. Why don't you tell me?"

"Slavery."

"Seems kind of a strange topic for Reverend Van Slyke to present to the group."

"It wasn't Reverend Van Slyke's idea. Didn't I tell you that we're doing an entire series this fall on the religions of the world and how the various Christian denominations differ from each other?"

"I guess you might have, but with everything that's gone on around here the past couple of months, I'd forgotten. How is it that slavery was the subject of your meeting tonight?"

"Milton's father is one of the deacons. When he was arranging for Willie to live at the Able Apartments in town, he met those two young Mormon missionaries who are staying there, too. He's the one who suggested we invite the Mormons to talk to our group."

"And the Mormon boys picked slavery as their subject?" Emma asked, bewildered.

"The first thing they said is that everything the Mormons do is based on direct instruction from God. Don Ahrens said he had heard the Mormons don't allow Negroes in their churches and asked if that was so. The one guy, Elder Kishel, said they allow them in the church, but Negroes couldn't hold any offices or be missionaries or anything. Then Don asked how they could justify that."

"And what did the Mormons say?"

"They said the Bible decreed that the Negro should be the slave to the rest of the world."

"I don't remember reading any such thing in the Bible."

"I wrote it down." Rose dug in the side pouch of her handbag and unfolded a piece of paper. "Look in Genesis, chapter nine, verses eighteen through twenty-seven."

Emma paged to the reference and read the verses aloud. "Okay, so it says that Ham was the father of Canaan. 'Cursed be Canaan. The lowest of slaves will he be to his brothers.' I don't see a single reference to Negroes."

"I know. With everything that's in the news about what's going on in the South these days, several members of the group got real upset by what these two Mormons were saying, but the missionaries defended their church's position."

"How did they do that?"

"They explained that the parts of the earth that Ham and his descendants went forth and populated are the places where black-skinned people live. They claim that if you follow through the rest of Genesis and trace the story, the proof is there. When God cursed Canaan, he intended Negroes to be slaves to everyone else."

"And what do you think about that?"

"I think it proves that people can pull things out of the Bible and twist them any way they want to so it will seem like it supports some idea they have."

"So suppose the Mormons are right? What then?"

Rose frowned. "Do you think there's any chance they are?"

"I'm hardly an authority on the Bible or slavery and race relations, but I know that this country has spent almost a hundred years trying to figure out if and how the two races can co-exist. And I wouldn't be surprised to see it get worse before it gets better."

"What about Willie, Mother?"

"What about him?"

"Are we treating him like a slave?"

"Hardly. Why would you even say such a thing?"

"Because we make him live in the barn with the animals, and we pay him much less than we'd pay a white man to do the same work."

"Hold on a minute, miss. When we tried out those other men as hired hands, they stayed in the same room down in the barn that Willie is living in now. We're not treating him any worse than we treated the others."

"What about his salary?"

"That's good business. You always pay the least you can to get the most you can. If Willie had asked for what we paid the others, we'd have given it to him."

"I'll bet he doesn't know what we offered the others. Nobody gave him the chance to demand an equal wage."

"And nobody's going to, either. Don't you go getting any crazy ideas about telling him. What with all your father's medical bills and the poor prices they're paying for slaughter hogs and feeder cattle, it'll be all we can do to make ends meet. The last thing we need is to hand out big wages for hired help. You keep your nose out of it. Are you clear on that?"

"Yes, Mother." Rose stepped away. "The Bible tells me so," she sang, her tone somewhere between sad and sarcastic.

Emma mother closed the book in front of her and sighed. "As if I didn't have enough to worry about. Now she wants me to get involved with rights for Negroes, too."

DANNY WAS ABOUT to hook the milking machine up to the big red roan Emil called Bessie when Willie caught Danny by the arm and flashed his notebook at him.

"It's Christmas Eve. I know your family is waiting for you in the house. I'll do the milking tonight — my Christmas present to you."

"Would you? That would be great. Thanks."

In the winter, Willie's workdays were much less demanding. He often had the cream separator washed and reassembled and most of the morning milking done before Danny even got to the barn. Without the fieldwork to consume the middle of each day, Willie had time to read and rest — or nap — most afternoons, so he had no reason not to go ahead and get the milking underway. Danny Schmidt was not one to shirk his responsibilities, but having Willie do most of the morning milking and other chores meant he could sleep a little more, catch the bus and get to school on time, and not be consumed with guilt about what still needed doing on the farm. Danny tried to show his appreciation to Willie by working extra hard on the evening chores, but if Willie was willing to do the milking alone on Christmas Eve, Danny was glad to accept the offer.

Willie clapped him on the shoulder and gave him a playful push toward the door. Danny responded in kind with a light punch to Willie's upper arm, then bolted from the barn. Willie took his time with the evening milking. After disassembling all of the milkers and washing them with hot water and disinfectant liquid and hanging them to dry, Willie put on his coat and walked out of the farmyard and down the trail that led to the fields. He felt the bite of the twenty-degree air. The snow crunched underfoot. Willie liked walking in the starlit nights on the farm. The snow was still white — not all trampled and gritty like the snow on the streets of Chicago. And quiet — so profoundly quiet that it almost made Willie think he was truly deaf — or the last person on the face of the earth.

He left the trail and made his way across the pasture through the rock outcroppings to the edge of the cattle pond, a natural body of water almost a mile in circumference. Once it froze solid, at Emil's direction, Willie put a blade on the front of the little tractor and scraped the snow off an area of the pond so Ginny and Danny could use it as their skating rink. He sat down on the bank of snow that rimmed the near edge of the pond.

Overhead, the sky was like an inverted bowl with bits of sparkle dust flung all about. He thought back to hot summer nights when he and his mother had sat outside on the porch of their little house in Canaan such a long, long time ago. He recalled how she used to tell him that if he ever felt lonely, he should look up at the moon and remember that the same moon shone everywhere. "Chances are, son, the person you're most missing is looking up at the moon, too," she had said. "Think of that person sitting right next to you when you look up at the moon. Then you won't feel so all alone."

When Willie was in Chicago, he had James and Neecy to blunt the edge of his loneliness, but since he'd been in Coon River Rapids, he hadn't a true friend to his name. He knew he was entertaining a foolish dream, but right up until lunch time that day, he had let himself half hope that Emma and Emil would invite him to sit in the house with them — at least for a little while — on Christmas Eve. When Emma sent him away from the lunch table with a sack of sandwiches and a piece of pie for later, his hopes were dashed.

He had even gone into town with Emma one day and picked out gifts for everyone: new kitchen towels for Emma, a work hat for Emil, a special ink pen for Rose to use when she became a teacher, a pocket knife for Danny, and a book for Ginny. But now he wouldn't get the chance to give them the Christmas gifts. At least they were things he could use himself, and he'd slip the book in with the others that Ginny left in his room. Almost every day, Ginny sat in his big rocking chair telling and retelling the stories from her books. Like as not, she'd leave a stack behind when she tired of that and went off to find other diversions.

The cold was settling in his bones, and the chill made his toes ache. He labored to his feet and brushed the snow from the seat of his pants. He took one last long look at the moon. "Merry Christmas, Mama. Maybe next year we can spend it together."

Back in his room, Willie changed out of his overshoes and work boots and put on clean socks and dry shoes. Danny had been right about the barn staying warm from the heat of the animals. Luckily, Willie hardly noticed the stench anymore. He took his transistor radio from its hiding place and popped the earpiece in place. As he suspected, the Fargo station was broadcasting Handel's *Messiah*. He moved his rocking chair so that he could prop his feet on the end of his bed and listened to the Christmas classic.

EMMA GRIPPED HER daughter's wrist as she reached for the plate of treats. "Ginny, how many cookies have you had?"

"Some."

"More like too many, I think. I'm surprised you're not sick to your stomach from all the cookies you've eaten tonight. That's enough, understand?"

"Yes, Mom."

Tradition at the Schmidt house called for oyster stew and spare ribs right after evening milking on Christmas Eve; then everyone sat around the Christmas tree and opened presents. Emma always had trays of cookies, fudge, and divinity and other treats sitting out to snack on through the evening.

This year, they moved a few more things out of the living room to make room for a small tree. It sat atop a flare-legged, square table near the doorway to the dining room.

"If I never smell another pine tree, it will be soon enough for me," Emil groused. "After tomorrow, that's got to go."

"I didn't think it would bother you. We can drag it out of here tonight, if you want."

"No, I've lasted this long with it, but by six o'clock tomorrow night, I want it gone."

Christmas was never a big affair at their house, but with all the extra bills and expenses, Christmas 1956 was even more limited. Emma stretched out the gift opening as long as possible, but with only a few presents for each person, she couldn't make it last beyond eight o'clock. All that was left was the clutter of torn paper and empty boxes.

"Danny, if you're going to play that infernal game, go somewhere else to do it," Emil snapped. "I can't hear the TV above all that racket you're making." One of Danny's presents had been a carom board. He and Ginny were using the spring-loaded cue sticks to pop the carom rings across the veneered surface. Without a word, Danny picked up the board and retreated to the kitchen. Ginny followed.

"Want to go outside and watch for Santa?" Ginny asked.

"No. I don't think Santa is coming this year."

"Yes, he will. He always does."

Santa wasn't a major contributor to Christmas morning. He usually left one small present for each of the children and some candy and fruit for everyone. Ginny always put out milk and cookies for Santa and a plate of carrots for the reindeer. Last year, it had seemed to her that Santa's note of thanks looked suspiciously like her mother's handwriting, but she was wise enough to keep it to herself.

"I think I'm going to go out and look," Ginny said. "I'll be back in a little while." She slipped into her buckle overshoes and pulled on her coat and flap-eared hat. She reached under the table and picked up a big brown grocery bag with the top rolled down.

"What's that?" Danny pointed to the bag.

"Some scraps I saved for the dogs. They need a Christmas present, too." Ginny let herself out the door before Danny could say anything more.

The big yard light in the middle of the farmyard illuminated the pathway between the house and the barn. She trod the well-worn trail down the short hill. She lifted the latch, opened the barn door a crack, and squeezed inside. A couple of the cows strained against their stanchions to look at the familiar intruder.

Pepper and Boots got to their feet in their beds of the hay at the rear of the barn, shook themselves awake, and loped out to greet their little friend. She dug into the paper sack and pulled out a plastic bread bag full of some meaty bones she had spirited off the plate after supper and doled them out to the dogs. "Merry Christmas, guys. Don't let the sleigh bells spook you." Then she walked back through the barn, across the milking parlor, past the bulk house, and stood at the doorway to Willie's room.

Willie's chair was moved so it left him with his back to the doorway. As Ginny got there, Willie took the earpiece from his ear and pulled the jack from the radio. Faint strains of music came from the palm-sized transistor.

"Drat. The batteries are dying," Willie said, "and I don't think I have any spares."

"I knew it!" Ginny cried. "I knew you weren't really deaf. Deaf people don't listen to the radio, and they don't say 'drat.'"

The sound of the child's voice startled Willie so thoroughly that he toppled the rocking chair over as he leapt to his feet. He wheeled to face Ginny.

"I think it's great that you can hear," she babbled on. "Now we can talk to each other. You always thought I was too little to read what you wrote in your notebook, so I always had to wait 'til a grown up was around so I could ask you questions. I won't have to do that anymore."

She sounded so delighted that it took Willie a moment to respond. "Why aren't you up at the house with your mom and dad?" A full sentence spoken aloud to another person felt odd and alien to Willie. The sounds seemed to ricochet all around the room.

"I wanted to bring some bones down for the dogs so that they could have Christmas, too."

"Oh. And have you done that?"

"Uh huh."

"So why didn't you go on back to the house if you've done what you came to do?" Willie's tone was harsher than he intended.

Ginny was rolling and unrolling the top of the brown bag. "Because I wanted you to have Christmas, too."

"What?"

"I brought you a whole bunch of my mom's cookies and homemade candies." Ginny held the bag out toward Willie. "Some of them might have got broke, but they'll still taste real good."

Willie accepted the brown sack. "Thank you, Ginny."

"And I've got a present for you, too. It's in there."

Willie opened the bag and looked inside. As Ginny had said, there were several cookies and pieces of fudge and divinity jumbled in the bottom. He also spied a clumsily wrapped, smallish, soft package.

"Open your present," Ginny directed. Uninvited, she plopped herself down on the corner of Willie's bed and undid the buttons on her coat.

Willie righted the rocking chair and sat down. He undid the tape and let the paper fall away. Inside was a notebook, much like the ones he carried with him to write his responses and questions in. This one, though, had a clear plastic sleeve on the front, meant to hold a business card or a small photograph. Ginny had drawn a picture of a dark-skinned man sitting on a tractor and slipped it behind the plastic.

"I guess you maybe won't need notebooks anymore now that you can talk."

"I know you're only a little girl, but I'm going to ask you to keep a great big secret." Willie tapped the notebook against the palm of his left hand. "I don't want you to tell anybody I can talk — not your mom and dad, not Danny, not Rose, not even the dogs. Do you understand?"

"Why don't you want them to know? Talking is easier than writing everything down."

"You're right. Talking would be easier, but it's better if people think I can't hear or talk. It's too grown up a story to tell you why. You have to believe me when I tell you it's better for me not to talk."

"Is it like a game?"

"Yes, that's right," Willie said, seizing her suggestion. "I'm playing a long, long game of let's pretend. You know how to play let's pretend, don't you?"

"Sure. Sometimes I pretend my leg is broken like Daddy's leg, and that I've got a big cast on, and I drag my leg around and go up the stairs on my butt. Oh, oh. I'm not supposed to say 'butt.' I meant 'behind.'"

"Have you ever kept a secret before?"

"Lots of times."

"Like what?"

"No fair. If I tell you, then it won't be a secret anymore. I can't tell you, even if you ask." Ginny folded her arms across her chest like she'd seen grown ups do.

"That's the way," Willie beamed. "Even if someone says to you 'do you think Willie can hear or talk?' you keep the secret. Don't say yes, don't say no. Don't say anything at all. Okay?"

"Okay." Ginny let her eyes wander around Willie's room. "What are those?" She pointed to the table in the corner where the stack of presents Willie had wrapped for the Schmidt family sat.

"Santa came by earlier and left those for you and Rose and Danny."

"I see more than three presents."

"He left one each for your mom and dad, too."

"Why did Santa leave them here instead of in the house?"

"He saw you coming outside, and he didn't want you to see him, so he left them down here with me."

"He's not supposed to come 'til later. I didn't get his cookies and milk put out or get the carrots ready for the reindeer. He'll be mad."

"No, Santa doesn't get mad about things like that. Besides, he probably has to come by here on his way back to the North Pole. You should put them out anyway. I'll bet he stops on his way home."

Ginny yawned.

"You probably better get back up to the house, young lady. Won't your mom wonder where you are?"

"I told Danny I was bringing bones down for the dogs. They know where I am."

"All the same, it's time for you to get to bed." Ginny stood up and buttoned her coat. "Do you think you can carry all these presents if I put them in your bag?" Willie asked.

"Uh huh. I'll wait 'til no one is looking and then put them by the tree. I'll keep the secret about Santa leaving them down here." Willie took the cookies and fudge from the bag, shook out the crumbs, and tucked the five packages down inside.

"And what's the other secret you're going to keep?" She picked up Willie's new notebook and took a pen from the table beside the bed. She labored to form the words on the page. Willie took the notebook from her. "Wil E is def," he saw. "Perfect. Now, get on back to the house."

"Merry Christmas, Willie," Ginny said sleepily on her way to the door.

"Merry Christmas to you, too. Thank you for the cookies and for the new notebook."

"You're welcome." She walked a few paces, stopped and went back and stood directly in front of Willie. "You're welcome," she mouthed again, this time without sound.

Willie flashed his gold-capped grin. Then he laughed like a man who knew he'd found a friend.

"EMIL, 'FESS UP. You gave Rose the money and had her get these presents and put them under the tree."

"Okay, play your little game, Emma. I know you bought these extra presents. You even got one for yourself to make it look convincing, and then you put them under the tree for Christmas morning. We could hardly afford it, but the kids all seem to like what you picked, so I guess it's okay."

"For the last time, I don't have any idea where these presents came from. I got the flashlight for Ginny, and the perfume for Rose, and the work gloves with the fold back flap over the fingers for Danny, but I had nothing to do with the story book about the dogs, or the pocket knife, or the fancy pen. I didn't buy you a new hat, and I didn't buy kitchen towels for me, though heaven knows, I sure can use them."

It went on like that all morning. Emma would try to get Rose to expose her father as the perpetrator. Rose would suggest that Danny had done it as some sort of clever trick. Ginny was the only one who blithely accepted all of Santa's gifts, even if they had come in two installments, and she never planned to tell that she'd put one set under the tree while her father was dozing.

As he did every morning, Willie came to the house with Danny after the milking was done. Emma took a tray of eggs and toast in for Emil while Danny and Willie washed up, then returned to the kitchen to serve breakfast to Willie and the children.

Ginny looked Willie in the eye and asked, "What did Santa bring you?"

Emma, Rose, and Danny felt their hearts freeze. Christmas morning, and they hadn't given a moment's thought to a gift for the man who had been holding their farm together since October.

Danny pushed away from the table. "Be right back. Ma, Rose, stall for time." Rose and Emma exchanged bewildered glances. Danny was back before either of them had thought of a single stall tactic.

"Here, Willie. Santa doesn't wrap presents. He just leaves them under the tree. These are for you." Danny held out the gloves and the pocketknife that had been his Christmas morning presents and the hat that Willie (aka "Santa") had given Emil.

Willie slipped on the gloves and made a big show of folding and unfolding the flap that came forward over the fingers. He put the cap on and adjusted the bill and earflaps, cocking his head from side to side and pretending to admire himself in an imaginary mirror. He laid the gloves and hat aside and picked up the pocketknife. He opened the blades and whetted the edge against his finger. He lifted his notebook from his shirt pocket and wrote, "The gloves are a good fit. The hat is, too. It's the kind of knife I'd have picked myself. I hope Santa knows I'm grateful for these nice presents." The notebook went first to Danny who then showed it to his mother and sister.

"I know something else Santa left for Willie." Ginny jumped off her chair and raced into the living room where her Christmas treasures were heaped. She blazed back into the kitchen with her new penlight flashlight and the storybook Willie had picked for her. She unscrewed the top of the flashlight and dumped the batteries out beside Willie's plate, then carefully put them back in and fastened the top. "I bet you can use this," she stated, remembering his lament about the batteries in his radio the night before.

"And now, here's a story for you on Christmas morning." The book Willie had picked out for Ginny was called *The Three Friends*. It told a simple tale of two dogs and a cat that played together in the shade of an old apple tree. One day, a bad storm came and tipped the tree over, and the three friends were sad that their favorite place to play was ruined. The story ended, though, with the apple tree recovering. Instead of growing up straight, it grew at an angle, close to the ground. The dogs and cat liked the tree even better now, because the dogs could play tag jumping over the trunk, and the cat could climb safely out into the boughs of the tree and not have to worry about how she'd get back down. And even the apple tree was happy because it liked to be able to lie down and rest.

By breakfast time, Ginny had heard the story read to her so many times that she could recite it word for word. She acted out the entire tale, much to Willie's amusement. "And the three friends were happy again in the shade of the lazy, fall down apple tree," she said with a flourish as she closed the book.

Not wanting to be left out, Rose excused herself from the table and returned carrying the fancy pen that had shown up under the tree for her. "We almost forgot to give you this present from Santa. You can use it when you write questions and answers in your notebook."

The scene was bittersweet. If he included Ginny's enactment of the book, the three children had now returned to him four of the five presents he had selected for the family. He was delighted that his little accomplice had succeeded in getting them under the tree without anyone finding her—or him—out. They hadn't planned ahead to have so much as a token gift for him, and yet, when they recognized their oversight, they were unstinting with what was at hand.

He retrieved his notebook and penned a long missive. "Danny, I don't think it's right for me to have the hat and gloves and knife. You take two and I'll keep one. Rose, this is the sort of pen a teacher should use in her first classroom. I'd be afraid of losing it out in the barn or fields. You take it. Ginny, I think you need this little flashlight so that you can read your books under the covers at night. I want you to keep it for yourself. I like it when you tell me stories. I'd be happy to have that be my present." He offered the notebook to Emma who read his wishes aloud.

Willie took the notebook again. "Mrs., your children are generous. That must have been your gift to them." Emma felt a knot catch in her throat.

O. Henry wasn't the only one who encountered latter day magi.

Chapter
Twenty-Two

The Curse of Canaan
Coon River Rapids, Minnesota
January 1957

EARLY IN JANUARY, Emma arranged for the ambulance to come out to the farm and take Emil into town to see the doctor so that they could X-ray his legs to see how the healing was progressing. While the technicians were getting Emil situated in the back of the van, Emma fought through the bitter wind and went down to Willie's room in the barn.

"Willie, I hate to ask this of you, but would you mind keeping an eye out for Ginny? I need to follow the van into town and talk to the doctor after he's seen Emil." Ginny was hunkered in a blanket on top of Willie's bed with her back against the wall and a book on her lap.

Willie scratched a quick note. "No problem. She spends most mornings down here with me anyway."

"Thank you. I probably won't be back by lunchtime. Help yourself to leftovers in the fridge."

Willie and Ginny waved good-bye. Emma pulled her coat more snugly around herself and headed back up the hill to the car.

Ginny said, "I sure will be glad when winter is over. Won't you?"

"Yes, I will. I don't think I was meant to live in cold weather."

"Everybody has cold weather in the winter. That's what makes it winter."

"Do you know there are some places where it almost never snows and where it hardly ever gets cold?"

"You're making that up."

"No, it's true. Where I grew up, the weather was warm all year-round."

"Didn't you have to wear coats and boots and mittens?"

"Nope. Sometimes we needed jackets, but I didn't see snow until I was older than Danny."

"Oh, Willie, stop teasing."

"One time when I was a little boy, it did get real cold. We had to build a big fire to stay warm."

"That sounds like the start to a story."

Willie drew his head back. "You know what? My mama did tell me a story about that. She called it 'The Story of How the Coyote Stole Fire.'"

"Tell me, Willie. Tell me about the Coyote and the fire."

"That was a long time ago. I'm not sure I remember."

"Then make it up. The best part about stories is making stuff up if you have to. Come on, tell me."

And so he began the tale:

"When the world was new, the earth was warm all the time and never cold. Spring, summer, and fall were the only seasons.

"Coyote liked warm weather and spent all day resting in the sun, thinking about what he would catch to eat. But one day, the world began to get cooler. Soon, nights became so cold that all of the animals had to find dens and nests to hide in. Their fur coats helped them stay warm. All of the animals either learned how to keep warm or found places to sleep and hide during the winter. But man couldn't sleep or hide that long, and he didn't have any fur. Coyote decided to help man find a way to stay warm."

"What did Coyote do, Willie?"

Willie told Ginny how Coyote knew that way up in the mountains, there were three fire beings who had stolen a piece of the sun, and they kept it hidden in a secret place. Coyote decided he would find a way to bring a little bit of the fire from the sun down from the mountain for man to use.

"Coyote saw that the three fire beings took turns guarding their treasure all the time, except for a little bit of time every day, so it took three days for Coyote to figure out how to steal the fire. Early each morning, the fire being on guard would leave his post and go to wake up one of the other keepers of the fire. The one who was sleeping didn't always get up right away, so there were a few minutes when the piece of the sun was unguarded.

"Coyote convinced the other animals in the forest to help him bring fire to man so he wouldn't freeze to death. One morning, when the guard went to wake up his replacement, Coyote was waiting. For the few moments when no one was watching the fire, Coyote dashed into the fire beings' camp, snatched up a glowing piece of the fire in his mouth, and rushed down the mountainside.

"The fire beings saw Coyote running away. They ran as fast as they could, but Coyote ran faster. They tried to surround Coyote, and as they were about to catch him, Coyote tossed the piece of fire to a squirrel in a nearby tree. The fire being touched Coyote on the tip of his tail, and its white-hot flame scorched the very end of

Coyote's tail bright white, and that's why all Coyote's have white-tipped tails."

"So really, it wasn't the coyote, but the squirrel was who gave fire to man, right, Willie?"

"No, there's more to the story. Squirrel ran through the tree tops with the fire on her back. She was very brave, because the fire was very hot and burned so badly that her tail curled up and over from the pain — and squirrels' tails have been that way ever since."

"Then what happened? Tell me." Ginny tugged on Willie's sleeve.

"The fire beings were still chasing Squirrel, trying to get their fire back, but as they were closing in on her, Squirrel threw the fire to Chipmunk. She scurried along the ground, dodging and weaving, popping in and out of hiding places. The fire beings clawed at Chipmunk as she ran and almost caught her. If you look at a chipmunk, you'll see the three scorched finger marks down its back. Those are the marks that were left there as they tried to get the fire back."

"I know!" Ginny said. "I've seen those marks on the chipmunks in our woodshed."

Willie patted Ginny on top of her head. "Chipmunk was tired. She tossed the fire to frog, but that wasn't such a good idea. Frog was too slow to stay ahead of the fire beings. One of them caught frog by the tail. They were about to crush frog for helping steal fire when frog's tail broke off, and he hopped away. That's why grown up frogs don't have tails. Frog managed to throw the fire to Wood. Wood took the fire down deep inside of itself and stood very still." Willie sat silently for a moment.

"That's a dumb place for the story to end." Ginny made a face at Willie.

"I still have one last part to tell you. Do you think Wood ran away?"

"That's so silly. Wood can't run."

"That's right. So, the fire beings caught Wood right away, but Wood refused to give the fire back. The fire beings kicked at Wood, and hit Wood, and dug at it with their knives, but Wood never let go of the fire down inside. Coyote had seen everything that happened. He showed man how to get the fire out of wood by rubbing two sticks together so that the fire inside would come out and burn. And that's how Coyote taught man about fire so that he wouldn't have to be cold in the winter."

"Oh, what a good story. Tell it again."

Willie knew she'd get her way, so he told the saga anew. He was astounded at how much of the story Ginny could already tell by herself despite having only heard it once. On the third time, through, he sat back and watched in awe as the child enacted the whole thing, complete with voices for all of the characters. He only stepped in occasionally to add a detail or make a bridge to the next segment.

"All this story telling makes me hungry." Willie tousled the child's hair. "How about you?"

"Uh huh."

They pulled on their coats and hats and left the warmth of the barn. The bitter wind made the walk to the house seem extra long. Once inside, Willie and Ginny hung their coats on the hooks behind the door and left their boots on the newspaper below. Willie stoked the flat-topped cooking range that sat in the middle of the kitchen.

"Good thing Coyote got that fire away from the fire beings," Ginny said. "I like being warm better than I like being cold."

Willie opened the refrigerator and pulled out several containers of leftovers for lunch. They spent a long time eating and laughing and retelling favorite parts of the story. They were having such a good time that they didn't notice Emma had come back from town. Instead of coming through the kitchen door, she came in through the porch door to make sure the path would be clear for the ambulance attendants to wheel Emil back to his bed in the living room at the rear of the house.

"Who else is here?" Emma demanded as she came through the doorway from the dining room to the kitchen.

"No one, Mom. Just me and Willie," Ginny assured her, wide-eyed.

"I heard someone else's voice a minute ago. What's going on here?"

"I was telling Willie a story. I had to make myself sound mean like the fire beings." Ginny used her deepest, growling voice to demonstrate. "You bad Coyote. We'll get you for stealing our fire."

Emma wasn't convinced, but what other explanation could there be? No one else was in the house, and it certainly couldn't have been Willie's voice she heard.

"All right then. Finish up your lunch and take your dishes to the sink. They'll be along soon with your father, and I need to get his sheets changed before they get here." Emma shed her coat and went back to the living room to complete preparations for Emil's return.

"No more talking in the house," Ginny whispered. "From now on, we only talk when we're in the barn."

Willie was again amazed at the child's quick thinking. Many times lately, he wished that when he'd arrived in Coon River Rapids he'd dropped his subterfuge of being deaf, but now that he'd used the ploy for over a year, he didn't see how he could end it. No longer did he worry that he'd be found out and sent back to Mississippi to face bogus murder charges, but that he'd be fired from his job and have to leave Coon River Rapids and find somewhere else to call home. Surely he could move on and start over in another new town, but he remembered his early experiences fleeing Holly Springs and roaming from town to town. He was happier with a fixed place and a routine. Better to leave by choice than by force. Willie slipped into his coat and boots and headed out to do the afternoon chores.

Emma came back to the kitchen after tending to Emil's bed linens.

"I'd better toss another shovel of coal on here. It's supposed to be way below zero again tonight." Emma lifted one of the circular lids from the range and scooped a flat ladle of anthracite from the bucket behind the range.

"Let me tell you how man got fire in the first place," Ginny offered as she watched her mother. She recapped the highlights of the newest legend in her repertoire. The medical van pulled into the farmyard as she concluded.

Emma looked long and hard at her youngest child. "You are a wonder. I never know what you'll come up with next." Then she hastened off to help the men bring her husband back into the house.

"LOUSY WORTHLESS BASTARD," Emil said, then snorted in disgust. "All this time wasted. That jackass better hope to God I never meet up with him alone in a dark alley."

The X-rays had shown that Emil's right leg was healing fine, but apparently the traction hadn't pulled his left leg back into proper alignment. The bone couldn't knit back together because the gap was too big. Emil would have to be readmitted to the hospital, have another surgery to adjust the traction pins, and then start the healing process all over again.

Emma looked at her husband, concern written all over her face. "It's not the doctor's fault. He did the best he could. How was he to know the bone would pull apart?"

"I'll be damned if I'm going to pay him for any of this. He already robbed us blind the first time. I should make *him* come out here and get my fields ready for spring planting. Crooks. That's what they are. Every damn doctor I've ever dealt with has been nothing but a money-grubbing crackpot."

Emma rearranged the pillows behind Emil's bed. "Don't get yourself all worked up again. Willie and Danny are doing fine taking care of the farm. Dr. Ross said that as fast as your right leg seems to be healing, once they get the left one set properly, it should come along real fast, too." Emma fussed with the covers on the bed. "They should be able to take the cast off your right leg when they do the surgery on your left one. Won't that feel good?"

"It would feel a damn sight better to get them both off. And if that quack hadn't messed it up, I could have."

"We can go 'round and 'round about this. I'm sorry there's been this little setback, but blaming the doctor and yelling at me isn't going to change anything. Do you need me to do anything for you before I go make supper?"

"No," he said curtly. "Go."

Emma busied herself with supper preparations. She was no happier than Emil was at this turn of events. The doctor had told her that the muscle atrophy in Emil's legs appeared to be extensive. Weeks of physical therapy would no doubt be necessary for him to regain full use of the limbs. Angry as Emil was about the miscue on setting his left leg, there certainly was no point in telling him about the elongated treatment program needed once the break healed.

Supper was a patchwork of bits and bites Emma pulled from the refrigerator. Emil was too agitated to have an appetite, and Emma was only hungry for life to return to normal. Danny, Rose, Ginny, and Willie gathered around the enamel-topped table in the kitchen and ate with abandon.

"Oh," Rose said as they finished eating. "I almost forgot that today Dad saw the doctor. What happened?"

Emma toyed with giving a fictitious report of good news, but opted for the truth. "One of his legs hasn't healed right. They'll have to operate on him next week to reset the bone." The children sat silently, mulling the consequence of this revelation.

Willie pulled his notebook from his shirt pocket, wrote something, and handed the notebook to Emma. "Mrs. I'm sorry about Mr.'s troubles. Please tell him that I'll stay on here as long as you need me to help out. If you need to cut back some on my wages, I'd understand."

Emma read Willie's note aloud. "Thank you. We count on you. As for your pay, we made an agreement with you, and we'll keep it." Then she appended silently, *Though where the money will come from, God only knows.*

Emma rose from the table. "Rose, you and Ginny do the dishes. I'm going in to sit with your father for a while." Danny and Willie folded themselves into heavy coats and boots and set off for the barn for evening milking while Ginny and Rose cleared the table.

Emma stepped into the room where Emil was slouched in the bed. "Are you sure you don't want some supper? I could still bring you a plate."

"Not hungry."

"Willie said to tell you he's happy to stay on here as long as we need him."

"Might as well give him the damn farm," Emil growled. "I'll

never be able to work it again."

"Why do you say that?"

"Because my goddamn leg is busted all to hell and will never heal, that's why."

"That's not true. Dr. Ross said that your leg will heal fine once the bones get lined up right."

"If this is the best he can do in getting the bones set, it's going to be a long damn time in the coming, isn't it?"

"It's going to be all right. But it's going to take a little longer than we thought."

"For chrissakes, it's already been four months — now it's going to be at least another four months. I can't stand it. I'm not meant to lie around like this. I stare at the walls, thinking about everything that needs doing around here, and I feel like I'm going to explode. I can't do this anymore. I can't."

Neither Emma nor Emil were educated people. She had finished high school, but Emil hadn't even officially completed grade school before he dropped out to work full-time on his parents' farm. She didn't know much about clinical depression and knew even less about psychology. She did know that her husband was about at the end of his ability to cope with his confinement and his fears — real and exaggerated — about what was likely to be his long-term fate. Her repository of tools both for helping him and for helping herself was less than well stocked. She picked up one of the only ones she saw.

"Then I guess you'll have to quit," she said evenly.

Emil's dark mood made him wonder how he could drag himself to the shotgun's hiding place, load a shell in the chamber, and remove himself far enough from the house to put a slug in his brain without someone interfering and stopping him before he could accomplish it. His wife's comment stunned him.

"Quit?"

"Yes. You're sick of being in that bed, and God's truth is, I'm sick of your being there, too. So quit. Get your sorry ass up off that mattress and quit being such a lazy cuss. My mother warned me that you'd never amount to anything. Turns out she was right. You've let a little thing like two broken legs keep you in bed for months and now, because one of them hasn't healed up right, you're talking about staying there for another who knows how long. Quit being such a faker." Emma let a coy look play across her face. "You never take me anywhere. You lay there in the bed acting like it's the only thing you have to do. Well, I'm sick and tired of it, mister. You quit, right this minute, and get up and put on your good shirt. I'm not much for dancing, but tonight, doggone it, I want you to take me out and show me a good time."

For emphasis, Emma rose from the chair she'd been sitting on and waltzed clumsily around the room, holding the edge of her skirt between her thumb and forefinger and twirling like a tipsy and somewhat demented Loretta Young. Under the best of circumstances, Emma was anything but lithe and graceful. Her eastern European heritage gave her big bones, large feet, and an ample padding around her hips and mid-section. Running the household left her little time for anything as frivolous as make-up or manicures.

Slack-jawed, Emil watched his usually staid wife.

"So, are you going to quit hiding in that bed, Emil Schmidt? Seems to me if you had a choice, you'd rather be out here dancing with me." Emma continued her pirouettes and curtsies.

"Hell, the way you're throwing yourself around, if I was to dance with you, you'd probably break my only good leg. I think I'd better stay right here." He paused and rubbed the stubble on his chin. "Guess I'm being a damned fool, huh?"

Emma perched lightly on the side of the bed near her husband. "No. You're a man who's been laid up for months who got some hard news today. I don't blame you for being upset." She leaned over and kissed him lightly. Emil wrapped his arms around her and pulled her to him.

"I don't know about dancing, but I sure know something I'm going to do with you as soon as my legs will let me."

"Emil," Emma chided. "The children."

"How do you think we got them?"

Emma breathed a sigh of relief. If Emil was thinking about that, she had hope after all.

TO EVERYONE'S RELIEF, after that one setback, Emil's recovery proceeded smoothly. He provided daily instructions from his bed, and Danny and Willie were able to get the crops in right on schedule that spring. Emil was even strong enough to take a brief tour of the fields riding in the bed of his pick-up truck, propped up on enough blankets and pillows to cushion any jolts from the field roads. In early May, he began rehabilitation on his right leg even though the left one was still in a cast.

When Rose graduated from her teacher training program right before Memorial Day, Emil was able to attend the commencement with the aid of a wheelchair Emma rented from the medical supply house in town. He fumed about the indignity of, as he put it, "riding around like some old cripple," but he forgot about that embarrassment when his daughter was honored at the ceremony for having achieved a perfect score on the final written examination for her certification.

Emma had always thought she would have liked to go into teaching, too, but a handsome young farmer named Emil Schmidt had persuaded her to pursue the occupation of housewife and mother instead. Emma made no attempt to hide her pride — or her tears — that night. She couldn't have, even if she'd wanted to.

Following the graduation exercises, Milton took Rose out for a congratulatory dinner at the best restaurant in Coon River Rapids. When Milton brought Rose back to the farm that night, Rose was not only a newly-certified rural school instructor, she was also an engaged woman. With a year of employment under his belt at the office supply store in town, Milton's finances were stable. In addition, he had been offered the position of director of music at the Coon River Rapids First Presbyterian Church. With his two jobs, and Rose sure to be hired by a rural school district in the vicinity, neither saw a reason to wait any longer to begin their life as husband and wife.

Thanks to Willie's help on the farm, Danny had been able to have a fairly normal school year. Emil and Emma were sure that any day he'd take an interest in a local girl and either buy a farm of his own or farm in partnership with his father. If he had a little book learning to go with his life on the farm, all the better.

As for Ginny, as long as someone would read her a story or watch her re-enact one she'd committed to memory, she was happy. When summer was over, she looked forward to going to school with the big kids — something she had been asking to do for at least two years. With all the time that Rose and Danny spent reading to her and all the books she and Willie looked at time and again in his little room in the barn, by the time she cleared the door for first grade, she had a vocabulary bigger than that of most fifth-graders.

Other than the one slip up when Emma almost caught her and Willie speaking to one another, she was flawless in keeping Willie's secret. Whenever they were absolutely certain no one would hear Willie talking, he would tell her more tales that he remembered (or concocted) from his childhood in Mississippi. Had anyone outside the Schmidt household given it any thought, no doubt they would have thought it strange to the point of unnatural for a twenty-six-year-old black man and a six-year-old white girl to be such good friends. But farm life in Minnesota in 1957 was an insular business, so it passed without remark.

Although no one told Willie anything directly about Emil's recuperation and the likely scenario of him regaining sufficient use of his legs to resume his farming duties, Willie surmised his days as the hired hand on the Schmidt farm were numbered. He decided that enough time had passed that it would be safe for him to venture back

South — maybe even all the way to Canaan to see his mother. As soon as Emil and Emma no longer needed him — maybe as soon as the coming fall — he'd be on his way home.

The prospect of actually seeing his mother again filled him with such joy that he wanted to sing out loud, but of course he never did. And the only thing he would miss about northern Minnesota was a little sprout of a storyteller who had wrapped herself around his heart.

Chapter
Twenty-Three

The Curse of Canaan
Coon River Rapids, Minnesota
August 1957

WITH BB GUNS and a sack full of empty tin cans, Danny and his cousin, Robbie, walked through the fenced lot for the feeder cattle on their way out to the open field behind the homestead. In the distance, Danny saw Willie driving the Farmall on his way back to the yard after shoring up some of the fence posts around the big pasture. Robbie spotted him as he bounced across the stubble of the hay field. "Who the deuce is that?"

"That's Willie," Danny said. "He's helping out here while Dad's laid up."

"I can't believe you've got a jigga-boo working here."

"Jigga-boo?"

"Yeah, you know—spook, monkey-man, seed-spitter." Robbie imitated eating a watermelon and ejecting the seeds through his teeth.

"He's just Willie." Danny wanted to offer a stronger defense of the man, but he knew Robbie would make fun of him, so he held his tongue.

Robbie was the youngest child of Emil's older brother, Rolf. Rolf had fled Coon River Rapids at his earliest opportunity to seek his fortune in the big city of Milwaukee, Wisconsin. Late in the summer of each year, Rolf and his wife loaded up whichever of the kids were still at home and made a week-long visit back to Minnesota.

"My dad says if he hadn't left the armpit you call your home town, I'd be out here flinging cow dung like you." Robbie used the butt of his BB gun to point to a recent offering from the steers grazing in the lot they were passing through. "Never looks to me like it's all that much work to run a farm."

"That's because when you're here, we ease back on things a little."

"The only reason you're saying that is because you know

farming is nothing but going to camp. You're jealous because I've got a million things to do in Milwaukee, and all you've got is cow shit and target practice."

Robbie and Danny were nearly the same age, but other than sharing a last name, they had virtually nothing in common. Robbie had already been in so much trouble in high school that his parents had enrolled him in a vocational/technical institute in Muskego, a neighboring suburb to their south Milwaukee community.

Robbie cocked the pump handle on his BB gun and raised it to his shoulder. He pivoted so he was facing Willie on the tractor, a good two hundred yards away. He pulled the trigger and the BB exited the barrel in a burst of air.

"What the hell are you doing?" Danny slapped the gun down from Robbie's shoulder.

"Getting some target practice, Cuz."

The old Daisy air rifle was not nearly powerful enough to have launched the BB anywhere near Willie, but Danny was appalled that his cousin would even consider doing something so reckless as aiming a loaded weapon—even a BB gun—at another human being.

"You know the rules about handling guns. Never, ever point a gun at anyone, even if you think it's not loaded."

"Hell, what's the use in pointing a gun at a spade if it's *not* loaded? We knock 'em off a dime-a-dozen back home."

"I don't give a hang what goes on in Milwaukee. Willie's done the work of six men around here for most of the past year. We never would've made it without him."

"I'm glad to hear it. The best use for a colored is doing hard work for a white man. Does he do a little shuck and jive dance for you after he's hauled the shit out of the barn?"

Danny seethed, but past experience had taught him not to try to win an argument with Robbie. "Do you want to shoot these cans or not?" Danny shook the gunny sack, and the cans rattled inside.

"Might as well. If you're going to go all girly on me when I try to shoot at Toby's hind end—" he arced his head in Willie's direction— "I guess I can make do hitting cans."

And so it went all week. At every opportunity, Robbie pulled some stunt to embarrass or intimidate Willie. He found Willie napping under a tree down by the corn crib and dipped his fingers in a pan of warm water in the misbegotten hope that Willie would wet himself. He short-sheeted Willie's bed. Willie kept a bottle of sugar in his room to use in his coffee; Robbie replaced it with salt. He scooped an ant hill into a bucket and deposited it in Willie's dresser drawer, then stacked empty milk cans behind the door into Willie's room so when Willie pushed the door open, they tumbled over and clattered about on the concrete floor. He caught garter snakes and dropped them down the back of Willie's shirt. The fact that Robbie thought Willie couldn't yell at him or hear the various epithets Robbie used to insult him with only sweetened the deal. "Like shooting fish in a barrel," he kept saying, and then he'd hurl racial slurs and denigrating comments at Willie's retreating back.

Danny tried to run interference, but he had all his usual chores to do, so he couldn't always keep an eye on Robbie. Besides, he tired of Robbie's meanness and made excuses not to have to spend time with him in hopes of sparing himself witnessing yet another of Robbie's unkind actions. He repeatedly apologized to Willie on his cousin's behalf, but Willie would simply point to the note he'd written in his notebook on the first day Robbie was there: "Not your fault. Be patient. He'll go home soon."

Toward the end of Robbie's week on the farm, Danny even enlisted his father's help. Robbie had tripped Willie at the head of the stairs in the second floor of the granary causing Willie to take a nasty tumble. Fearing that one of Robbie's stunts would get out of hand, Danny asked Emil to talk to Rolf about Robbie's behavior. When Emil suggested to Rolf that he rein in his son, Rolf's reply cleared up any doubts about why Robbie acted as he did.

"As much crap as we put up with from the nigger brothers back home, who can blame the boy for wanting to get even a little?" Rolf blustered. "Besides, what with the Hebes and the Kikes and the Spics taking over Milwaukee, pretty soon places like this will be as bad as St. Paul. We should have locked all the borders into this country a long damn time ago."

When Robbie got wind of Danny's tattling—or "rat finking" in Robbie's vernacular—he vowed one final volley to teach both Willie and Danny exactly who held the upper hand. It took him nearly a whole day to scheme it through and to work out the logistics, but he was convinced it would settle the score once and for all.

"I WAS BEGINNING to think you'd never come in for breakfast." Emma said to her son as she wiped her hands on her apron. She set the bowl of scrambled eggs down on the table in front of Danny. "What's taking Willie so long to get here?"

The previous afternoon, Uncle Rolf had gathered up his family and headed back for Milwaukee. Danny was so fed up with Robbie's treatment of Willie that he barely made an effort to wave good-bye. The car pulled out of the yard, and Robbie rolled down the back window and spat a parting shot at Danny under his breath. "Coon lover. You'll both get what's coming to you."

Emma moved to the counter and waited for her son to answer. When he didn't, she asked again. "Danny, where's Willie? Am I supposed to hold breakfast for him or not?"

Danny looked dazed and overwrought. He struggled to put words together. "No," he finally managed to say. "Willie's gone. He won't be coming for breakfast."

"Gone? Gone where?" Emma wheeled from the counter with a plate of toast in her hand.

"I . . . I don't know," Danny stammered. "He's not down in the barn. I did the milking by myself." He looked out the window. "That's why I'm so late."

"Where could he be? It's not like he's got anyplace to go or any way to get there."

Danny sat mutely.

"Are you going to eat, son?"

"I'm not very hungry."

"Do you feel okay?" Emma made a move to put her hand on his forehand. Danny pushed it away.

"I'm all right. I'm tired from having Robbie around all week and from doing all the chores alone this morning." He pushed back from the table. "I'm going to clean the barn now, and then I need to move some of the steers out to the other pasture."

Emma could sympathize with her son's state. The relatives' week-long visit—more like a siege—had worn everyone out. They had been constantly underfoot at Emil and Emma's house. She had been glad to see their taillights disappear down the driveway yesterday.

She poured two cups of coffee to take into the living room to Emil, still camped in his hospital bed. "Danny says Willie wasn't in the barn when he went down there this morning. Did he say anything to you about not being here today?"

"Good lord, the man has been here for months now. You know darn well he can't talk, so how could he tell me anything?"

"You know what I mean. Did he write you a note to say he had something else to do?"

"No. Far as I know, today should be like any other day."

"Seems strange that he'd up and disappear. He's been as reliable as sunrise." Emma gulped her coffee. "I'm going down to the barn to look around his room to see if he left a note there. I'll be back in a little while to get you ready to go to your doctor's appointment."

When Emma got to the barn, Danny was scooping manure out of the gutters with a vengeance. "Slow down, Danny. You'll hurt yourself."

"I've got a lot to do today. With Willie gone, it'll be all I can do to finish by dark."

"Oh, he'll probably show up by lunch time. It's not like Willie not to let us know where he is. Maybe he's out in the pasture helping a cow with a calf or something."

Danny didn't pause in his labors or respond to his mother. Emma let herself into Willie's little room off the milking parlor and looked around. It looked exactly as it always did. All of Willie's possessions were right where they'd always been. She was more convinced than ever that some emergency on the farm had drawn him away, and any minute he'd amble in and smile his wide grin while jotting a note of explanation for her in his pocket notebook. She didn't have time to linger and ponder. Emil was due at the doctor's office in less than two hours.

GINNY WAS SITTING in the rocking chair in Willie's room, her picture books in her lap. Every day for the past ten days, Ginny had camped there, recalling every moment of her time with her good friend. If Emma had let her, Ginny would have slept there, in case Willie dropped by in the night to claim his things — or better yet, to tell her he was back to stay. "Mom, do you think he's ever coming back?"

"It doesn't look like it, honey."

"But why would he go away? He liked it here. I know he did. And even if he had to go away, why would he leave without telling me good-bye?"

Emma hated to acknowledge that she was plagued by the same questions her little girl posed. She hated even more to acknowledge that she had no answers to offer. She and Emil had talked about the situation several times. The most likely explanation was that Robbie had somehow managed to do something so degrading or annoying that Willie had simply up and run off. They couldn't imagine what that might be, but it seemed as plausible an explanation as they could muster. They had both asked Danny if he had any insights to offer, but each time he shrugged his shoulders and walked away.

School started a few weeks later, and Ginny got caught up in the world of formal education. Her visits to Willie's room tapered off, and by Thanksgiving, when Emma cleared all of Willie's clothing out of his room and took it to the church rummage sale, Ginny had just about stopped talking about him.

As they hoped, by the time the first hard frost fell, Emil's legs had healed enough that he was able to resume some of his farming chores. Things settled back into a routine much like it had been before the accident. Danny worked harder than any two fifteen-year-olds combined and never complained or asked for compensation. He had always been a quiet child, but now no one could get more than a few words out of him.

Rose was busy with her teaching duties and planning her

wedding, which would take place right after spring planting in the coming year, 1958.

Once in a while, one of them would mention Willie. "Remember when. . ." someone would venture, and they'd recall some incident involving the industrious dark-skinned man who had been with them for a while. But soon, even those passing references stopped altogether.

As mysteriously and inexplicably as he had appeared in Coon River Rapids, Coon Willie vanished from the friendliest town in Minnesota.

Chapter
Twenty-Four

Columbus, Georgia
September 2006

ELIZABETH REREAD THE last sentence in the manuscript for the fourth time. "As mysteriously and inexplicably as he had appeared in Coon River Rapids, Coon Willie had vanished from the friendliest town in Minnesota." She flipped the final page over, somehow expecting that the story might continue on the backside.

"This can't be how she meant to end this book," Elizabeth mused. "She must have been in such a hurry to bring this over that she forgot the final chapters."

She dropped the manuscript on the floor beside her chair and checked her watch. For nearly two hours, she'd sat spellbound by the last part of the tale Colleen had woven. She groaned as she stood up. Every muscle in her body was cramped and tight from being in one position too long.

She checked her watch again and did a quick calculation. *It's not too late. Colleen dropped in unannounced on me earlier. Why not return the favor? And besides, we need to resolve things between us once and for all.*

She made a quick dash through the bathroom to wash her face and brush her hair, changed into khakis and sweater, then stuffed some cash, her driver's license, and a credit card into her back pocket. After grabbing the manuscript, she claimed her keys from the table by the back door and headed for LaGrange. On her way, she swung through the drive-thru at "slow death on a bun" as she referred to the fast food joint, and ordered a chicken sandwich and a chocolate shake.

Less than an hour later, Elizabeth pulled up in front of Colleen's house. Muggins and Buster were in the backyard and heard her approach. Elizabeth saw Colleen pull back the curtain in the front room to see what had caused the dogs to set up their commotion.

Colleen met Elizabeth at the door. "Long time no see. What brings you to LaGrange—as if I don't know." She stared at the package in Elizabeth's hands.

"I was wondering if the author Colleen McCrady is at home?"

"She is. May I say who's calling?"

"Her publisher," Elizabeth replied, then lowered her voice and added in almost a whisper, "and someone who is very sorry for the way things have been going between us lately."

"Come in. I'm glad to see you. I've been thinking about you all day." Colleen closed the door behind her.

"Me, too." She set the manuscript on the small table inside the door, then accepted Colleen's soulful embrace. "I truly am sorry, Collie."

"So am I. Maybe we can talk a little more civilly to each other this time."

"I hope so. I'd like that." Elizabeth clung to her another minute.

"Have you eaten?" Colleen asked as they stepped apart.

"Yes, I picked up something on my way out of Columbus."

"Nutritious and delicious, I'm sure," Colleen said lightly. "Would you like something to drink? Some wine maybe, or a soft drink?"

"A glass of water would be good."

"I'll get it. Sit down. Let me go assure the dogs that I'm not being taken prisoner against my will, and I'll be back in a minute."

Colleen disappeared into the kitchen, and Elizabeth faintly heard Colleen's voice as she talked to the dogs in the back yard. She claimed a spot on the sofa. In a few minutes, Colleen was back in the living room with two tall glasses of water. She handed one to Elizabeth, then dropped onto the sofa beside her. "So?"

Elizabeth faced Colleen. She opened her mouth to speak but suddenly felt at a loss for words.

"I told you you'd hate the book." She avoided looking directly at Elizabeth.

"No, I don't hate it." Elizabeth set her water glass on the end table and summoned her courage. "Like all of your other books, it's a captivating, engrossing plot, but—"

"It's not the sort of book I can build lesbian love scenes into."

"I'd have to agree with you there." Elizabeth glanced across the room then brought her gaze back to Colleen's face. "I wouldn't dream of suggesting you put any in it, but that's not my concern. The book quit in the middle of nowhere. It didn't have a conclusion, or a dramatic last scene, or a triumphant tying up of loose ends. It ran out of steam and died before it got to the finish line. That's not your style."

She waited for Colleen to respond, but she didn't. Elizabeth didn't know what to say, and Colleen's expression was unreadable. Why wouldn't Colleen open up and talk about this book? The silence stretched on so long that she feared Colleen would never answer her, and something inside told Elizabeth that whatever Colleen was holding back mattered — and mattered a great deal. She tried again.

"You've maintained all along that you know the novel isn't typical Sappho's Shadow material. When we were at the restaurant this morning, you said you didn't care if I read the rest of *The Curse of Canaan* or not. That can't be true. Obviously, you wanted me to read it, or you wouldn't have told me about it in the first place when I was here with you at Christmas. And you wouldn't have driven up to Columbus to deliver more chapters for me to read in the spring. And today, you brought me what you said was the whole manuscript. What's so important about getting me to read this book?"

Time stopped again, and when Colleen finally spoke, her voice sounded conciliatory. "You're a smart woman. I bet you can guess."

Elizabeth frowned. "No, I can't. Not tonight and not in a million years." Elizabeth felt like she was watching calendar pages fall while waiting for Colleen to speak.

Finally, she did, in a shaky voice. "Because I decided if you and I are ever going to be together — be a real couple — I needed to tell you what you're getting into. Putting it in a book was the only way I could make myself do it." Colleen drew in a noisy breath. "What you read tonight is my autobiography."

Elizabeth pondered Colleen's remark. She was all set to say something flip along the lines of, "You used to be a deaf, black farmhand?" but the look of consternation on Colleen's face made it clear that this was hardly the time for levity. "How can that be? No one in that story could possibly be you. The only one who comes close is little Ginny, but you told me you're an only child."

"I am." Colleen cleared her throat. "I wasn't, but I am now."

"As Spock used to say on *Star Trek*, this is not logical, captain. Either you are an only child or you're not. Which is it?"

"I should have told you the whole story right away — or at least after we'd been together for a few months." Colleen sighed. "It's so bizarre that, if I hadn't lived it myself, I'd never believe it actually happened." She grabbed one of the throw pillows and hugged it to her chest, then rose from the sofa and walked around the living room clinging to the pillow as though it might save her from drowning in the sea of memories she was drifting in.

"You mean the part about a strange black man working as a farm hand in northern Minnesota in the late fifties?"

"Odd as it may seem, that may be the least difficult part to explain."

"Okay, for the moment, let's accept that as a given. What's the hard part?"

"The parts about my sister and brother."

"Danny and Rose?" Elizabeth asked.

"Yes, but like they used to say on the cheesy TV programs, the names have been changed to protect the innocent."

"So you have an older sister and brother?"

"*Had,*" Colleen said, but her voice faltered before she could go on.

Elizabeth got up and took hold of Colleen's upper arms to stop her from meandering around the room. "Wouldn't this be easier if we sat down and talked it through?"

"It might take a while, and I'm not sure we've got time to get into it tonight. Don't you need to get back to Columbus?"

"We've got nothing but time." Elizabeth's voice was gentle. "If it's all right with you, I'll sleep here tonight and get an early start for the office in the morning. If it has to, Triple S can function an hour or two without my guiding hand tomorrow."

Colleen studied Elizabeth's face before venturing a reply. "Of course you can stay here. You know I love it when you spend the night with me. The way things have been going between us for the past couple of months, I've been worried that we're not going to make it."

"I know. I've had some doubts myself." Elizabeth put both hands on Colleen's face. "First, we'll talk about this book. Then we'll talk about us, okay?"

"Okay. I still wish we didn't always have to be together only under cover of darkness, though." Colleen freed herself from Elizabeth's hands and walked over to the small window overlooking the back yard. "I should bring the kids in. The dew will be settling soon, and these September nights can get chilly."

"Sure," Elizabeth said. "I'll be right here." She gestured toward the sofa.

Elizabeth picked up Colleen's manuscript and read a few passages in it again while she waited for Colleen and the dogs to return.

She heard the back door slam, and the dogs bounded into the living room to greet her. She delivered an ear rub for each and helped them get the last of the rowdies out of their systems.

Colleen sat down next to Elizabeth. "Where should we start?"

"Wherever you wish. It's your story, after all." Elizabeth tried to look relaxed and interested, not like an inquisitor on a mission.

Colleen's face was serious, and Elizabeth could almost see her searching for a place to begin. At last, she shook her head resolutely and said, "My sister's name was Anna, not Rose, and she was fourteen years older than I — like it says in the book."

"Where is she now?"

"Dead." Colleen could barely choke the word out.

"What happened?"

Hoping for inspiration, Colleen stared at the magazines on the table by the sofa. "I wish there were a Reader's Digest version of this, but there isn't."

"Start at the beginning and tell me what you think I need to know."

"Much of what's in the book is accurate. She did teach in the country schools in the county where we lived. She did marry a local boy, but his name was Michael, not Milton. He wasn't the music director at our church; he was the guy in charge of the Sunday School programs for all of the kids. About two years after they got married, she had a little boy. They named him Mickey—well, Michael, Junior, but we called him Mickey."

"So you have a brother-in-law and a nephew."

"Had," Colleen corrected. "Give me a minute and I'll get to that."

"Sorry to interrupt. Go on."

"In 1967, the church sponsored a trip to Israel. I still remember the flyer in the church bulletin announcing it. 'Walk the paths of Jesus' it said across the top. 'Visit the Holy Lands and hear the ancient hills speak to you.'"

"Did you go?" Elizabeth asked.

"No, I was a rebellious teenager by then. My crowd was already making noises about 'God is dead' and that sort of thing." Colleen offered a wry smirk. "But my sister and her husband were among the first to sign up. They decided Mickey was old enough to go, too, and so they pinched and saved and came up with the registration money for the three of them." Colleen squeezed her lips together tightly and willed herself not to cry. "They'd sit for hours poring over maps of the Middle East talking about what they'd see—Bethlehem, Golgotha, Mount Sinai, the Dead Sea."

"And did they?"

"They went in the spring, the last day of May, in fact. They had only been there for a couple of days. The whole tour group was at an outdoor café in Jerusalem having lunch. Anna, Michael and Mickey were sitting right next to the street. My guess for why they picked that table is because Mickey always wanted to examine every car and bus and truck that he ever encountered. Some… some…" Colleen labored to select the right word, "…some *zealot* picked that precise moment to explode a car bomb. Fifty people from our church saw my sister and her family ripped to sheds. No one else suffered anything worse than superficial cuts from flying glass and metal."

Elizabeth listened in horror as Colleen continued. "Thanks to the benefit of hindsight, we know now that bombing was part of what became known as the six-day war. You remember—Golan Heights, Gaza Strip, closing the Gulf of Aqaba, Sinai Peninsula, Suez Canal, West Bank—all that crap." She drew in a breath. "Of course, it's gone on so long now that we're all half-numb to it, but I can assure you, in 1967, the Presbyterian Church in Coon River Rapids was anything but numb to the idiocy that has been bloodying the Fertile Crescent for who knows how long."

"Oh, Colleen. I don't know what to say."

"Neither do I. It's been close to forty years, and I still don't have words to wrap around it." Colleen stared at her hands for a long time before saying anything more. "We decided not to have a funeral for them. In fact, they never even recovered enough of the bodies to ship them home. The tour group cut the trip short and came right back to the States. We held a memorial service a week after it happened."

"That must have been hard for you and your family."

"I only remember two things from that day. One was the minister saying something stupid like 'How favored they must have been in God's sight to have been called home to heaven from such hallowed ground' or some such pandering, and the other was my mother looking like she'd been beaten senseless by someone swinging a two-by-four against her head for a day."

"Of course she would be upset."

"'Upset' doesn't begin to describe it." Colleen's despair was palpable. "She couldn't handle it. We kept thinking she'd come around, that the grief would pass, but it broke her spirit."

"What do you mean?"

"We ended up having to put her in a state mental institution. She never got out. I'd go to see her, and she'd call me Anna and ask how her grandson was." Tears rolled down Colleen's cheeks. "At times, I thought I might as well take a room adjoining hers."

"I'm so sorry, love. I can see now why my remark today at the restaurant about not knowing if you were an escapee from a mental institution was like a dagger in your heart."

"You didn't know about my mom, LJ. And you were right. You didn't know anything about me, because I was too ashamed of my past to tell you about it." Colleen angrily wiped the tears away. "I was pretty young when I figured out it's a screwed up world. Innocent people die every day because some asshole thinks his cause is more righteous than someone else's."

Even though words were Elizabeth's business, she didn't know of any that could contradict what Colleen had said. She took Colleen's hand in hers and held it, waiting to see what the next chapter would reveal.

"She was decent person. She deserved better."

To Elizabeth, the look on Colleen's face was heartbreaking. "I'm sure that's true." Elizabeth didn't know if Colleen's reference was to her sister or her mother, but what difference? Either one was a tragic tale. "What happened to your dad?"

"He shrunk down to a shadow of himself. What choice did he have? Minerva — that was Mother's name, not Emma — was his reason for being. It probably would have been better if she had died, too. He tried to be a good husband. He'd sign her out of the mental ward and bring her home to the farm, but after a couple of hours of her nonsensical ramblings, Dad couldn't stand it any longer and would take her back to the hospital. Each time he came home after handing her over to the keepers, as he called them, another bit of life went out of him."

"How long did she stay there?"

"Mom was a little over fifty when she was committed. She lived — if you can call it that — eleven years in her own personal hell."

"I know you told me you've been without both of your parents for a long time."

Colleen studied the ceiling while she answered. "Mom died in seventy-eight. I had hoped that once she was gone, maybe Dad would rally, but that's not the way it went. He died in eighty-three, a very old man at the very young age of sixty-two." She made a sound somewhere deep in her throat. "I guess that means I've been an orphan of sorts for about twenty-three years."

"What did your dad die of?"

"Loneliness. Bitterness. Maybe a mild case of remorse or regret. Probably a little self-pity, too, for good measure."

Elizabeth reached out and drew Colleen towards her. "I can understand the loneliness, but why bitterness or regret?"

"My sister was his angel child. He thought the sun rose and set on her. She was his perfect child — his delight and his pride. He wasn't all that keen on Michael — thought Anna deserved someone with higher aspirations who wasn't such a town boy. I think if he could have arranged it, he would have gladly gone as crazy as Mother did, so he'd never have to remember how his baby girl died."

Elizabeth waited for Colleen to go on with her narrative, hoping that the last segment of Colleen's family's story — the part about Danny or whatever his name was — could be free of further heart-wrenching twists.

"That leaves my brother, Sean."

"Or Danny as you called him in the book."

"Sean Daniel McCrady." Colleen pulled her knees up to her chest and twisted around on the sofa so that she was facing Elizabeth's profile. Elizabeth followed suit so they sat toe to toe.

"Tell me about him," Elizabeth urged.

For the first time in her recap of her immediate family's history,

Colleen broke down and wept uncontrollably. Without knowing exactly why, Elizabeth joined her. They fell into one another's arms and sobbed, Colleen for the lifetime of hurts she had run from for so long, Elizabeth for the agony so painfully evident from Colleen's wails.

"Sorry," Colleen said. "I didn't expect the waterworks to kick in like that." She grabbed a box of tissues from the end table and placed it on the couch, then blew her nose and brushed the back of her hand across her cheek. "You'd think I'd have been cried out years ago."

"Why is that?" Elizabeth pulled a tissue from the box and dabbed at her eyes.

"Twelve years is a long time to cry."

"Danny — I mean Sean — has been dead twelve years?"

"As of next month, yes."

Elizabeth knew that if she could be patient for a minute or two, Colleen would find her voice and tell her the details.

"He was such a strange mixture of characteristics," Colleen said. "Even when he was young, he was the hardest-working person on earth. He'd have most of the milking done before Dad got up in the morning. He'd come home from school, tackle the evening chores, and then study late into the night in his room. In the summer, he practically ran the farm all by himself."

"Even when your dad wasn't laid up with broken legs?" Elizabeth asked. "Or was that something you made up for the book?"

"No, that did happen. It's how Willie came to live with us."

"So Willie is a real person."

"Uh huh. I need to finish telling you about Sean, and then there's the whole Willie legend." Colleen checked her watch. "Are you sure you're up to it? It's getting late."

"As if I could sleep. Unless all of this is too much for you?"

"I'm fine." Colleen's words were edged with sorrow. "All of this is comfortable shoes and old clothes for me. I've worn it for so long I can't remember it ever being any other way. I'm not used to talking about it, that's all."

"So, tell me about Sean."

"You'd think someone who was as driven as he was might be kind of dour and humorless, but Sean was totally the opposite. He never missed a chance to pull a practical joke or make someone laugh. His jokes weren't mean like our cousin Robbie's, though."

"Robbie was a real person, too?"

"Yes, if you want to call someone that cruel a *real* person." Utter disgust registered on Colleen's face. "I don't want to talk about him any more right now, okay?"

"Agreed," Elizabeth said, and was happy to see that Colleen took it as her cue to continue.

"When Anna and Michael were dating, Sean would do things like sneak out of the house and wait for them to come home from the movies or wherever. He'd hide in the bushes near the house and creep up behind Michael's car. Then, at precisely the moment when Michael would make his move to plant a kiss on Anna, Sean would grab the bumper and rock the car. Or at Christmas time when we'd have bowls of nuts out on the table, Sean would take the walnuts, carefully crack the shells open, and take the nutmeats out. Then he'd put little slips of paper inside with screwed up Chinese fortunes and glue the shells back together. His tricks never hurt or upset anyone; he only wanted to make people laugh." Colleen reached back in her memory bank. "He'd bring home boxes from the grocery stores in town and build elaborate play houses for the cats. He'd make street signs that would say things like Mewlon Rouge or CleoCatra Boulevard. Then he'd take the clothes from Anna's old dolls and dress up the cats and put on skits for me with the cats as the actors in his dramas."

"Sounds like quite a guy."

"He was. I still miss him."

"Do you want to tell me what happened?"

"You'd think with the awful way Anna and Michael and Mickey died and the toll it took on my mom that would have been enough for one family to go through, but the Fates weren't done with the McCradys."

Colleen shook her head as if to take herself back to the moment. "After Dad died, the farm passed to Sean and me. What use did I have for half of a hundred and sixty acres in the far reaches of Minnesota? Sean had never done anything other than work that land with Dad. As best I know, he didn't so much as date a girl, let alone ever think of getting married.

"I was already long out of college by the time Mom died. I was so relieved to shake the remnants of snow off my boots and get gone that I think I made it back to Minnesota exactly twice after Mom's funeral before I needed to be back there to help plan Dad's. Sean was well on his way to becoming a reclusive bachelor farmer by then. We didn't do anything about legally putting the farm in his name only, but he knew I'd never give him a minute's problem over it, so we left it jointly titled with rights of survivorship."

"But something happened?"

"Yes. Things went along pretty well for about a dozen years. I was living in Atlanta and working as a high school English teacher. On a beautiful October day the principal came into my classroom and said he needed me to come to the office with him. Of course, paranoid little me assumed they'd figured out I was a lesbian—albeit one who hadn't had a lover in ages—and that I'd be tarred and feathered by sunset. Instead, he told me I had an urgent phone call.

"I picked up the receiver. Sean was on the other end of the line, but it hardly sounded like him. His voice was so weak I could hardly make out what he was saying. All I knew for sure was he wanted me to come home." Elizabeth saw tears rimming Colleen's eyes, but Colleen forged on.

"I didn't get to the Coon River Rapids hospital until late that night. Visiting hours were long over, but because Sean was in such critical condition, they let me in to see him."

"Did he recognize you?"

"Yes, but he was running a high fever and was half out of his mind from the drugs they were giving him."

"What was wrong with him?"

"I didn't know it at the time, but he was dying of uremia."

"Kidney failure?"

"What I eventually pieced together is that about a week earlier, he'd been out in one of the pastures cutting down dead trees. He stumbled backwards and fell against a pointed tree stump. The force of the fall was enough to slightly rupture one of his kidneys. Of course, as tough an old bird as he was, he figured the pain in his back was nothing more than his bad luck from being so clumsy. A couple of days later, he was passing blood in his urine and was as weak as a kitten. Finally, he decided he needed to let a doctor look at him, but by then, the damage was done."

"Couldn't they have done dialysis or found a donor for a transplant?"

"Maybe if he had gone to the doctor right away, but the ruptured kidney failed altogether and the toxins it pumped into his body were so strong that his other kidney was overwhelmed in a matter of days. By the time I got there, the best they could do was keep the pain under control."

"Oh, Collie, I..." but Elizabeth had nothing with which to complete the sentence.

"He hung on three more days. Right after they'd give him his pain shot, he'd be pretty lucid for an hour or so, but then he'd fall asleep, and when he'd wake up, the pain would be back so strong that he'd beg me to smother him with the pillow. At least we got to have some time together before he died."

Elizabeth could tell from the tone in Colleen's voice that she had tried many times over the intervening years to convince herself that their little bit of time was enough, but it rang as hollow this time as it had on all her previous attempts.

"So there I was, a middle-aged woman with no parents, no siblings, and the proud owner of a farm that needed tending."

"What did you do?"

"I had a pretty easy time finding neighbors who wanted to buy the livestock. I held an auction to sell off the machinery and most of the tools. I gave nearly all of the furniture to the charities in town. By the time the first snow fell, next to nothing was left to suggest the McCrady family ever lived there.

"Next to nothing?"

"I couldn't bring myself to deal with Sean's personal effects. They're still in his room in the old farm house." Colleen laughed half-heartedly. "I never could decide if it was the sweetest thing in the world or a sign that he wasn't quite right in the head, but even after our parents died, he didn't move into the main part of the house. He still slept in the same little bedroom he'd always had. Our old house has a room on the second floor over the kitchen, but to get to it, you have to go through the narrow attic space that's right under the eaves."

"So you haven't been back to take care of it?"

"No, at first I was afraid there were too many ghosts there. Now I wonder if they'd even recognize me."

"The farm and the house are sitting there abandoned?"

"Not exactly. A year or two after Sean died, I converted about half of the farm into what they call the soil bank."

"I don't think I've ever heard of a soil bank."

"I'm sure it had some other fancy name that I never can remember, but everybody back home called it the soil bank. Some time in the fifties, I think, the government figured out that the way agricultural exports were expanding, the United States was growing too many crops. Not only that, but erosion was getting worse every year, and prices for farm products were sinking like stones. To stabilize the prices, cut back on excess production, and help with the soil erosion, they came up with this program where they'd pay farmers *not* to work the land. Then along about the early nineties, some scientists figured out that plowing up the land releases huge amounts of carbon dioxide into the atmosphere, so they modified the soil bank program to include keeping land untilled in hopes of reducing the amount of carbon dioxide in the air. The long and short of it is the federal government's Department of Agriculture actually pays me to let the land lie there unused."

"How about that? Where but in the good old USA, huh?"

"On top of that, I heard about a reforestation program administered by the Department of Natural Resources. I filled out all the paperwork, and darned if they didn't accept the application. They provided me with six thousand trees, which I had planted on twenty-five acres. Every year, they pay me a fee for letting the trees grow. I don't know what genius in Washington came up with these ideas, but they sure have worked out well for me.

"And the house?"

"Dad modernized it in the early sixties—installed central heat and indoor plumbing in the main part. It's old, but it was built to withstand anything that the ravages of Minnesota's winter might throw its way, so it's in pretty good shape. I put a couple of heavy-duty padlocks on the door to Sean's unheated room on the second floor. The rest of the place is rented out to kids attending the junior college in town. One of the real estate offices in town handles everything for me. I pay them a percentage of the rent, and they have all the headaches."

"Are you ever going to do anything with your brother's clothes and other things?"

"More than once, I've tried to convince myself I should, but I've never managed to get it done."

"The ghosts you mentioned earlier?" Elizabeth asked softly.

Colleen hesitated a long time before deciding to answer. "Not exactly." She paused, obviously anguished. When Colleen spoke again, Elizabeth had to strain to comprehend the words. "I'm afraid I'll find out I was an accomplice to murder."

For a fleeting second, Elizabeth thought Colleen must be making a lame attempt at totally inappropriate humor, but Colleen's ashen face told her the statement had been sincere.

"Do you want to elaborate?" Elizabeth wasn't sure she wanted to know, but in for a dime, in for a dollar.

"It must be pretty obvious by now."

"Obvious to you maybe, but not to me."

"You know what happened to my parents. You know how my sister died. You know that Sean died from kidney failure. Who's the only person unaccounted for?"

Elizabeth struggled for a moment and then the light dawned. "Willie!" she exclaimed.

"Exactly."

"Willie was murdered?"

"Probably."

"As I reminded you much earlier in this conversation, Spock would tell us that's not logical. Either he was or he wasn't. Which is it?"

"I honestly don't know."

"Maybe you should tell me what you *do* know."

"Everything about Willie in the book is the truth."

"How could you possibly know that? I thought you made all of that up as a vehicle for your story."

"Think back over the story line. Who spent the most time with Willie?"

"Ginny. . .who was, in actuality, you, I guess."

"Try again. In the book, Willie and Danny worked side by side, day in and day out. If Ginny managed to stumble on to the fact that Willie was pretending to be a deaf mute, wouldn't it stand to reason that Danny might have figured it out, too?"

"Sure, now that you point it out." Elizabeth considered the possibility. "So Danny—I mean Sean—knew Willie's life story." Elizabeth's comment was half question, half statement.

"Right."

"And he told you."

"Right again."

"When?"

"The day of my dad's funeral. That night after all the assorted relatives and neighbors had gone home, Sean and I were sitting in the old farmhouse, talking about life and all its crappy turns. He'd had quite a few beers and was in a mood to say a lot more than he usually volunteered. We were talking about how strange it seemed for Dad to die so young, since he had never been sick a day in his life. That led to a discussion of when Dad broke his legs, and that, of course, segued into my saying 'I wonder what ever happened to Willie.'"

"What *did* happen to him?"

"I wish I knew." Colleen threw her hands up in the air in exasperation. "You could have knocked me over with a feather when I learned Sean had known longer than I that Willie could talk and hear. In my egocentric way, I always thought I was the only one who had been let in to Willie's inner circle. But like he did with me, he swore Sean to secrecy. The difference was Sean figured he was helping keep Willie's neck out of a noose."

"Okay, your brother and this secretive black man worked together on the farm, and he told your brother how he came to be in Coon River Rapids."

"Right," Colleen said.

"He had to flee Mississippi for his life because they thought he killed a white woman?"

"According to what Sean told me, yes."

"But that still leaves two huge questions." Elizabeth stood up and shook herself like a dog needing a stretch, then reclaimed her seat next to Colleen. "What happened to Willie? And why would you think you were somehow involved in a murder?"

"I can't answer the first question, and I can only speculate on the second one." Colleen was again on the verge of tears. "I badgered Sean for hours that night trying to get him to tell me what else he knew, but all he would say was I was better off not knowing—that what I didn't know couldn't hurt me."

"That hardly sounds like implication in a murder."

"No, but when I knew Sean was dying and I went back to Minnesota to be with him, I figured it was my last chance to ever find out the truth." Colleen wrapped her arms tightly around her chest. "It's what he told me then that made my blood run cold."

"What did he tell you?" Elizabeth shivered from the hairs on the back of her neck rising.

"Remember, he was in excruciating pain and doped up with painkillers. I thought if I told him stories about our childhood, it might somehow distract him and give him some happy memories to take with him." The catch in her voice made Colleen stop and swallow hard before continuing.

Elizabeth pulled Colleen's arms out of her self-embrace and took both of Colleen's hands in her own.

"Tell me the rest of it, sweetheart. It will be easier for you once you've shared it with someone."

"Without thinking about what I was saying, I told Sean that it sure would be nice to see Willie one more time and find out how his life had panned out. Sean got all agitated and angry and tried to get out of bed. I finally got him sort of calmed down, but I had to ask the nurse to give him something to stop him from hurting himself with all the thrashing around he was doing. Right before he slipped under from the tranquilizer, he looked me square in the eye and said, 'Willie's dead. You never should have given Robbie that alarm clock.'"

Elizabeth dropped Colleen's hands. "Now I'm officially confused. What does that mean?"

"Once again, my only answer is I don't know."

"*Did* you give your cousin an alarm clock?"

Colleen was trembling. "Any time Robbie was around, he was always bribing me in some way. He'd convince me to do something that would help him with one of his nasty hoaxes, or he'd give me a dime and tell me get lost so he could show Sean the dirty magazines he'd brought along. I do have this dim memory of Robbie telling me he'd pay me a dollar to steal the wind-up alarm clock from my parents' bedroom, but I don't know if I did, or if I only imagined doing it. And if I did, was it during the trip that Uncle Rolf's family made to the farm right before Willie disappeared? I don't know."

"That was most likely the pain and the drugs talking. Sean probably didn't know anything more about what happened to Willie than you do."

Colleen pursed her lips and shook her head. "No. Every time Sean talked to me between that conversation and the night he died, he'd ramble incoherently that an awful thing happened to Willie. I'm sure he knew the whole story." She sucked in her breath. "And I'm sure I was at least partly responsible."

BOTH ELIZABETH AND Colleen were exhausted, Colleen from the telling, Elizabeth from striving to comprehend what Colleen had told her. Sleep, however, eluded them. Shortly after midnight, Colleen gave the dogs one more opportunity to visit the back yard, and then she and Elizabeth flopped down in the bed.

They made and then broke one agreement after another not to discuss things any further until morning. A thought would occur to one of them and be voiced aloud, and soon they were immersed in chasing another thread of possibility.

At five a.m. they gave up the charade and went back to the living room. Colleen brewed a pot of strong coffee and made them each two slices of peanut butter toast.

As the sun slanted over the eastern horizon, Elizabeth asked, "Isn't there anyone back in Minnesota who might be able to clear all this up?"

"I can't imagine who. Sean didn't have many friends, and even if he did, I'm sure he wouldn't have talked to just anyone about something like this."

They chased it from every angle for another two hours and finally decided they were too brain dead to have any hope of making headway.

"I'm going to run through the shower and then get going," Elizabeth said. "Why don't you come back to Columbus with me? We could talk on the drive."

"No, I don't think so, but thanks for the offer." Colleen curled up in a corner of the sofa, Muggins at her feet and Buster beside her on the floor. "Grab clean towels from the closet behind the bathroom door," she called as Elizabeth retreated down the hall.

Ten minutes later, Elizabeth was back in the living room, a towel around her head and another wrapped around her torso. "What are you doing next week?"

"I dunno," Colleen murmured. "Why?"

"Let's go to Minnesota."

"Lack of sleep does strange things to you, dearest." Colleen looked intently at Elizabeth. "Why on earth would you want to go there?"

"I'll bet you anything there's something in Danny's—oops, sorry, I mean Sean's—room that will help us figure this out."

"Oh, I doubt it."

"It's our best shot, Collie." The shower had given Elizabeth a new surge of energy. "And if it doesn't, maybe being there will give us an inspiration about some other source of information."

"Sean's been dead for twelve years. And if what he told me is true, Willie's been dead for, let's see—what?" Colleen did the calculation in her head. "About forty-eight years. This isn't like those

TV programs where someone pulls a box off the shelf and sifts through old files and miraculously solves some long-forgotten crime."

"Where do you think the writers get the ideas for those shows?" Elizabeth edged onto the sofa, Muggins still between her and Colleen. "We've got to at least try, babe."

Colleen pondered Elizabeth's suggestion. "I suppose, but I'll have to give the renters a day's notice before we can get in. That's part of the rental contract."

"We've got more than enough time to do that. You work on plane reservations and rental cars and whatever other logistics need to be arranged. I'll go back to Columbus and tie down as many loose ends as I can. I'll call you late this afternoon, and we can talk about the particulars."

Elizabeth leaned across the dog and gave Colleen a deep, lingering kiss. She made a move to get up, but Colleen held her in place. "What if we find out that I'm at fault?"

Elizabeth shooed Muggins off the sofa and moved in close to Colleen. "First, I can't imagine that'll be what we find out. I mean, for heaven's sake, you were a little girl. How could you possibly be responsible for the death of a man you didn't even know was dead? Second, I repeat, you were a little girl. No one would hold you accountable even if you *were* somehow involved. Third, I love you. Nothing, I repeat, nothing is going to change that."

"You're sure?"

"As sure as I'm in this room with you. I don't know why I've fought it so hard."

"Maybe because I'm not very lovable." Colleen looked away.

Elizabeth rubbed the pulse point on Colleen's wrist below the hem of Colleen's sleeve. "Or maybe because I was too scared to admit to myself what you mean to me, and my being scared made you scared, too."

"You love me in spite of everything I've told you?"

"In spite of, because of, before, after. I'm so glad you finally told me about your past." They kissed, then studied one another's eyes.

This time, when Elizabeth made a move to rise from the sofa, Colleen released her grip and let her go.

"You're taking quite a chance, Elizabeth Albright." She looked lovingly at the woman whom she was so glad to have back in her life.

"That's what life is for."

Colleen kept her seat and watched as Elizabeth headed back to the bedroom to get dressed. Absent-mindedly, she bent down to pet the dogs around her feet. "Okay, Pepper and Boots, maybe we're finally going to get to write the last chapter."

When it dawned on Colleen that she had called her dogs by the names of her long-gone childhood pets, it flipped a switch somewhere deep inside. Telling Elizabeth about her family had taken a huge burden off her soul. Never before had she dared tell anyone anything but the most cursory of details, for fear they'd flee in abhorrence. But Elizabeth hadn't fled upon learning about Colleen's unfathomable past. In fact, Elizabeth was offering to help, to finally find out what facts belonged in the closing chapter. Perhaps — at long last — healing would be within her reach.

Chapter
Twenty-Five

Coon River Rapids, Minnesota
September 2006

"WELL, THEY WON'T win any good housekeeping awards," Colleen observed dryly as she and Elizabeth worked their way through the clutter on the main level of Colleen's childhood home. They had flown from Atlanta into Minneapolis on the last Wednesday of September and rented a car for the two-hundred-mile drive to Coon River Rapids. Elizabeth was glad that Colleen had insisted she bring a warm jacket. Minnesota was at least thirty degrees cooler than Georgia.

They'd picked up a key for the house at the real estate agent's office in town, then stopped at the Lazy Loon Motel to book a room for the next couple of nights. Now, at long last, Elizabeth was surveying Colleen's childhood home.

"How many students are living here?" Elizabeth asked as she surveyed the odd assortment of furniture and general disarray that lay before them.

"I don't know. I leave all of that to the rental agent, and now that I've seen what the place looks like, I'm perfectly happy *not* to know what goes on here. Given the condition of this house, my mother is probably rolling over in her grave." Colleen led the way to the stairs that would take them to the off-limits room above the kitchen. "Come on, Sean's room is up here."

They passed through the attic that occupied the sloped area above the eaves. Colleen fished a ring of keys out of her pocket and worked the padlocks open. She steeled herself as she laid her hand on the doorknob and pushed the door open.

In contrast to the frenzy of the floor below, the small bedroom was neat and tidy, though covered with dust. Seeing her brother's things — laid out as though he might walk in any minute and pick up where his life had left off — hit Colleen like a punch in the stomach.

"I'm not sure I can do this," she said softly.

"We don't have to do anything right this minute," Elizabeth

assured her. "Maybe we should sit here for a little while." She pulled a straight-backed wooden chair out from under a table that obviously had doubled as Sean's desk. She took a tissue from her jacket pocket and wiped the top layers of dust from the seat.

Colleen went over to the windows that looked out the front of the house and pulled the cord to raise the Venetian blinds. One tug on the rotted cord, and the entire assembly fell off the window frame in a heap at her feet, causing a swirl of dust to encircle her. "I was hoping to let in a little light." She laughed nervously. "I guess I've succeeded."

Colleen roamed through the room tenderly touching and caressing various articles of clothing and other worldly possessions once used by her brother. Colleen picked up his pocket knife and opened and shut the blade. She read the inscription from his 4-H trophy that he won for raising the champion steer sold at the Junior Livestock show in South St. Paul. She ran her fingertips over Sean's name in gold letters on the front of the Bible the First Presbyterian Church had given him when he was in second grade. She picked up a framed photograph—taken at Anna's wedding—showing the McCrady family together, happy, whole.

Colleen saw the look that registered on Elizabeth's face. She knew Elizabeth had seen that picture before—when it fell from a stack as Colleen pulled *The Curse of Canaan* out of its hiding place in the box in her closet back in LaGrange. Colleen remembered her lie. She had told Elizabeth that the bride and young man were her cousins.

"This is your sister and brother, Anna and Sean, isn't it?" Elizabeth stared at the photograph. "I'm starting to understand why you didn't want to tell me much about your past."

"I wanted to, but I couldn't." Colleen swept the room with a glance. "I know we came here to figure out what happened to Willie," Colleen said as she blinked back her tears, "but I think I've had all I can handle for today. Besides, the renters will be back soon, and I'd rather not have to make conversation with strangers."

"Sure, sweetheart. I can see where this is heavy-duty emotional stuff." Elizabeth slipped her arm around Colleen's shoulder. "We're both tired from the trip. Let's go find something to eat and get some sleep."

Colleen secured the padlocks, and they wended their way downstairs and back outside to their rental car.

"I thought we came from this way." Elizabeth pointed to her right as Colleen pulled out of the driveway steering the car to the left.

"We did, but I thought you might want to see one of the ten thousand lakes this state is famous for. We've still got some daylight."

"Okay. Will it take us long to get there?"

Colleen tossed her head back and laughed. "You can't go ten miles in any direction without hitting at least three lakes up here. And I don't mean those silly little man-made mud holes that Georgia pretends are lakes, either."

Colleen commenced a listing of the lakes in the immediate vicinity. "Long Lake, Lightning Lake, Dead Lake, Stalker Lake, Battle Lake, Pelican Lake, Swan Lake, Cormorant Lake, Star Lake, Rush Lake, Wall Lake."

Elizabeth let her go on with her avoidance activity so that Colleen wouldn't have to think about the real reason for their trip. "That only leaves you nine thousand nine hundred and eighty-nine to go," Elizabeth said.

"The good news is that lots of the names are used over and over. I bet there's more than a hundred Long Lakes in the state. But still, wouldn't you be surprised if I could name them all?"

"Not in the least. You've got a writer's mind. You notice all the details. It's what makes your books so much fun to read."

Colleen reached across the seat and gave Elizabeth's upper leg an affectionate pat. "Flattery will get you everywhere, you smooth-talking vixen."

They lapsed into a mutual silence while the car rolled down the road. Soon they were at the public access beach at Jewett Lake. They walked along the shore line and talked of many things, none of which was about Sean McCrady's room or what they might find when they returned there the next day.

They sat side by side on the dock and watched the sun fall behind the far horizon. "Breathtaking," Elizabeth sighed.

"Imagine what it must have been like before all these cabins and resorts were crammed in here." Colleen gestured widely. "No wonder the early settlers had to run the Native Americans off. They couldn't possibly have appreciated it."

Dusk had faded to total darkness by the time they got back into the car for the drive into Coon River Rapids. "Hungry?" Colleen asked as they passed the city limit sign.

"A little. How about you?"

"No, but I know I'll feel terrible in the morning if I don't eat tonight."

"Maybe we could pick something up and eat in our hotel room."

"Good idea." Colleen said as she turned down a street a few blocks before the hotel. "Is Chinese okay?"

LESS THAN AN hour later, with the remnants of their selections from Tommy Chou's restaurant deposited in the garbage, Elizabeth and Colleen curled together on the queen-sized bed.

Colleen said, "Sorry I wimped out on you at the house this afternoon."

From her position behind Colleen, Elizabeth massaged her shoulders. "No apology needed. I've never seen a user's guide for how to go about something like this. It's hard for *me*, and I never even knew your brother or the rest of your family. Just walking through the door of the farmhouse must have taken every bit of courage in you."

Colleen pressed back closer against Elizabeth. "I've let myself hide from it for so long. If not for you, I probably never would've dared come back here at all."

Elizabeth kissed the back of Colleen's hair and wrapped her arms tightly around Colleen. "Do you think you'll be ready to go back to the house tomorrow?"

"Uh huh. No point putting it off any longer."

Elizabeth freed one hand and resumed kneading the tight muscles in Colleen's upper back.

"That's delicious," Colleen groaned as Elizabeth convinced some of the knots between Colleen's shoulder blades to loosen. "You're hired."

"Can't hire me. I only work for free."

"At least let me offer a gesture of appreciation." Colleen rolled over to face Elizabeth. She kissed her and was surprised at the blaze of arousal that ripped through her. Colleen whispered huskily, "I bet you've never made love in the land of sky-reflected waters."

"I bet you're right, but I'm not opposed to seeing what it's like."

"You definitely should try it." Colleen raised herself up onto her knees and pulled her sweatshirt off over her head.

Elizabeth touched Colleen's inviting breasts. "Only if you'll show me the right way to do it."

Colleen helped Elizabeth disrobe and then finished removing her own clothing. She lay back down on top of Elizabeth. Ever so slowly, ever so slightly, she pulsed against Elizabeth to an unheard but universal rhythm.

Elizabeth moaned. "You Minnesota girls are nothing but big teases."

"Give it a minute. You might surprise yourself."

Colleen intensified the pace and the intensity of her movements. Suddenly, Elizabeth was on the verge of orgasm, and before she could alert Colleen, the peak was upon her, lifting her toward the heavens.

"Oh...my...god... " Elizabeth finally managed to groan. "Where did that come from?"

"From the most beautiful woman on the planet," Colleen whispered in her ear. "Was it nice?"

"If I could bottle and sell it, I'd be a millionaire."

Colleen looked down at Elizabeth's face as she spoke. "Good. I'm glad." She lowered her face so she could reach Elizabeth's lips. "I'm probably crushing you."

"If this is what it feels like to be crushed, I hope it goes on for a lifetime."

They lay together happily for a while. "Seems to me we're only halfway home." Elizabeth put her hands beneath Colleen's shoulders and rolled her onto her back. "Where would you like to go?"

"Anywhere you want to take me," Colleen replied.

"Then let's get started." Elizabeth leaned in and kissed Colleen's lips and teased Colleen's tongue with her own. "Lie back and relax, my love. I'll drive you home."

Elizabeth moved low on Colleen's body and gently wedged her face into the rich, damp place between Colleen's legs.

For once, Colleen refrained from commenting on her "one-trick pony" characteristic and surrendered to the moment, letting Elizabeth do as she pleased.

"Oh, LJ." Colleen knew she was hearing her own voice, but she wasn't sure she was speaking. "That's magic."

Elizabeth didn't lose a beat but continued her measured stroking with lips and tongue. When Colleen's climax hit, both could feel its intensity. In the instant it took for Elizabeth to move up so that she could hold Colleen in her arms, Colleen had dissolved into rivers of tears.

Wordlessly, Elizabeth enfolded her beloved angel and rocked her until blessed sleep freed them both from the thoughts that had plagued them all day.

COLLEEN AND ELIZABETH arrived at the farmhouse shortly after eight o'clock the next morning, and for the next five hours they painstakingly combed through everything in Sean's room. Elizabeth was in charge of the dressers and the closet where Sean's dusty shirts and trousers still hung. She went through every pocket and felt every seam in case there might be something important tucked inside a vest slit or sewn in a garment. Those items of clothing still serviceable she sorted aside to give to one of the charities in Coon River Rapids. The badly worn things—which far outnumbered the serviceable ones—would be dropped at the dump on the edge of town.

As she emptied each drawer, she pulled out the newspaper that lined the bottom and made sure nothing was in the folds and creases. She even scanned the pages to see if one of the articles or advertisements had been highlighted or notated in any way that might give them a lead.

While Elizabeth worked through the clothing, Colleen leafed through the books on the bookcase beside Sean's makeshift desk. She sifted through every file folder in the three-drawer cabinet beside the table, and before long, she could tell you what Sean had spent for artificial insemination for the milk herd, how many gallons of fuel he had bought for the farm tractors, and what his adjusted gross income had been for each of the years he worked the land. But she couldn't tell one thing more about Willie and the fate that befell him than she already knew.

Like Elizabeth, she had made decisions about the disposition of each object and piece of paper that she handled. As a memento, she kept Sean's Future Farmers of America patch that was supposed to have been sewn onto one of his jackets more than four decades ago. She also took his high school diploma and the certificate of baptism dated February 20, 1941. Most everything else, though, was nothing but trash. She and Elizabeth had agreed that they'd build a small fire in the clearing out behind the house before leaving at day's end to burn anything with Sean's name or social security number on it and anything else that wasn't worth the effort of hauling back to Georgia to run through the shredder.

"It looks like this was a colossal waste of time." Colleen made no attempt to hide her disappointment. "I was afraid that would be the case." She tied a knot in the top of the thirty-gallon plastic bag she was holding and deposited it next to the others heaped by the door to Sean's room.

"What do you have left to look through, sweet girl?" Elizabeth asked Colleen as she made her way back from the stack of bags edging into the room.

"Only these things on top of Sean's desk." Colleen waved her hand over a small stack of letters and other papers still littering the surface. "If you'll strip the sheets off the bed and check under the cushion of that upholstered chair over there, I think we can call it done." Colleen plunked down on the straight-backed chair and assessed the final remnants of Sean McCrady's life.

The letters in the flimsy plastic holder had postmarks of October 1994. "He must have already been too sick to deal with these," Colleen remarked as she opened the first one. "Sean never let a piece of mail sit unopened. These came in the day before he was admitted to the hospital, October ninth, 1994." Some of what she discovered were unpaid bills, now a full dozen years overdue. "Maybe I'll run by the electric company office when we go back into town later. I'm sure they've long since written this off as uncollectible, but I hate for them to have a black mark next to Sean's name."

She opened a file folder containing a copy of the bulletin the funeral home had prepared for Sean's funeral and, with it, several notarized copies of his death certificate and three copies of his one-page will that named her as his sole beneficiary and appointed her his executrix. After burying Sean, she remembered feeling too overwhelmed to do anything more than drop the folder on this desk and screw the padlocks into the doorframe before returning home to Atlanta. Now she put the documents with the Future Farmers Emblem and the other keepsakes.

Elizabeth made a careful inspection of the stuffed chair in the corner of the room. She even went so far as to tip it on its side and make sure nothing was taped to the bottom. Satisfied that the chair would offer up no secrets, she focused her attention on the bed. The sheets were dank and musty from having been in a closed, airless room for so long. Without consulting Colleen, she made the decision to stuff them in a trash bag and add them to the mountain designated for the dump. She was all set to do the same with the pillows without even taking them out of the pillow cases, but as she squished one of them to poke it in the bag, something crinkled beneath her fingers. She reached inside the pillow slip and groped about.

Elizabeth wanted to shout, "This is it!" but instead, she walked the few paces across the room and tapped Colleen on the shoulder. "Special delivery for Colleen McCrady," she said, her voice wavering. She handed an envelope to Colleen.

"What's this?" Colleen gingerly took the envelope from Elizabeth's shaking hand. Colleen instantly recognized Sean's rangy handwriting. The upper right corner bore a notation of October 9, 1994, and it was addressed: *For my sister, Colleen McCrady. Private and personal. Please destroy if not delivered to Colleen McCrady.*

Colleen turned the envelope over and over in her hands. She brought it to her chest and hugged it to her heart. She laid it against her face and then pressed it against her cheek.

"Open it," Elizabeth urged. "Open it!"

Colleen willed her inert fingers to pull the flap.

"Dear Collie....," Colleen read. She paused and looked up from the single sheet she held and met Elizabeth's gaze. "You and Sean are the only ones I ever let get away with calling me that."

"I can tell I'm in good company," Elizabeth said warmly. "Go on. Read what he had to say."

Colleen looked down again and continued reading aloud. "I haven't been feeling so good the past couple of days. I don't think it's any big deal, but if things go to hell somehow, I figured I owed it to you to be sure you knew some things. You and I are all that's left now."

Elizabeth watched as Colleen caught a tear as it escaped the corner of her eye.

"I've left something for you where 'your three best friends used to play.' It will tell you about some stuff that happened a long time ago. If you figure out the clues, it will take you on a treasure hunt for gold. Chances are, if you're reading this, I'm dead, so let me tell you one other thing here I probably should have said a long time ago. I'm glad you were my sister." Colleen's voice caught in her throat, and she handed the page to Elizabeth.

Elizabeth read the last line. "We never were much for mushy stuff, but I love you, Collie."

Sean had signed his full name and written the date below it.

Elizabeth waited while Colleen pulled herself back together. She folded the page and handed it to Colleen who reopened it and read it again silently.

"Why do you suppose he put that one phrase in quotes?" Elizabeth asked when she felt the time was right to speak.

"He didn't want someone else to find whatever he left for me."

"What exactly was it he said?"

Colleen read the line again, " — where your three best friends used to play."

"A school yard? Somewhere here on the farm?" Elizabeth guessed. "What does he mean?"

"I don't think I know. Maybe if I'd found this twelve years ago when he meant for me to have it, it would have made more sense."

"Where your three best friends used to play," Elizabeth said each word slowly, deliberately. Then she repeated it three more times. "Why does that sound so familiar? It's like I've heard that expression somewhere else recently."

"We both *want* it to mean something, LJ. We've come more than a thousand miles to solve a puzzle that can't be solved. We're grasping at straws and looking for meaning where none exists. Sean was most likely already eaten up with fever when he wrote this. It probably doesn't mean anything at all."

Elizabeth sighed in exasperation. She glanced up at the shelves above the table where Colleen was sitting. A stack of children's books stood on the bottom shelf. The title of the top book caught her eye.

"And then again, maybe it *does* mean something." Elizabeth grabbed a book and pushed it in front of Colleen's downcast face.

"*The Three Friends.*" Colleen spoke each word like she was dragging it out of the deepest corner of her memories. "This was my favorite one."

"And you used it in your story about Willie." Elizabeth pumped her fist in the air. "I knew I had come across that phrase somewhere else!"

"I started writing *The Curse of Canaan* so long ago I'd forgotten I put that bit about this story in it." Colleen paged rapidly through the slim, well-worn volume. Once in her hands, she felt as though she were six years old again. Every word on every page played one more time in her mind's ear. "My favorite Christmas present," she whispered.

Colleen lifted the book so that the illustration was right in front of Elizabeth's eyes. "And the three friends played in the lazy fall down apple tree, and they were happy again."

Colleen dashed across the room. "Come on," she yelled over her shoulder as she headed for the stairs. Elizabeth was right on her heels.

From the house, Colleen led them between two of the outbuildings to a badly overgrown trail. In two minutes, they were standing in what remained of a small apple orchard. "Whatever Sean left me has to be down here," Colleen said. "He knew I'd remember that book and how the dogs and cat in it always played under the apple tree." She stomped quickly around the base of each tree. "I'm going to get a shovel and something to cut the grass back." Colleen sprinted off leaving Elizabeth alone in the grove.

When she returned, she said, "Here, poke this down into the ground while I use this hand scythe to get some of the tallest grass out of the way." She handed Elizabeth a three-foot iron crowbar and dropped a pointed spade a few feet away.

For an hour, the two worked like women possessed.

"Where did he put it? Why can't we find it?" Tears of frustration stung the backs of Colleen's eyelids. She flung the shovel to the ground in disgust.

Elizabeth took Colleen in her arms and tried to calm her. "Maybe what he left was another letter or something else that didn't survive the elements all this time," Elizabeth suggested. "You said yourself that you maybe should have done this twelve years ago—"

"No!" Colleen's voice was strident. "He said it would take me on a treasure hunt. He knew he'd have to use something that would hold up 'til I found it. I'm not giving up."

Colleen resumed her search around each of the trees. Elizabeth couldn't bear to see her laboring alone, so she started digging again. They probed and dug and cursed and dug some more until the sunlight failed.

"We'll try again tomorrow," Elizabeth consoled as she took Colleen's hand for the walk back up to the yard.

"And come up empty again," Colleen predicted. "We might as well go back to Georgia."

"You're tired. Things will look brighter in the morning." The optimism in Elizabeth's tone was fake, and they both knew it, but neither had the energy to say anything more.

"LJ, WAKE UP!" Colleen was shaking Elizabeth so hard that her teeth rattled in her head.

"What? What is it?" Elizabeth said as she came awake.

"We've got to get back to the farm."

Elizabeth looked toward the window in the Lazy Loon Motel and saw the dimmest shade of gray-green dawn beyond the crack in the curtain. "Sure. We said we were going back to keep looking under the apple trees."

"We were looking in the wrong place."

"There's another apple orchard out there?"

"Sort of." Colleen was so animated Elizabeth feared she might hurt herself as she bounded around the room. "Hurry up. Get dressed." Elizabeth didn't argue. She pulled on her jeans and a clean sweatshirt and put on her shoes as quickly as she could.

They raced to the rental car. Colleen sped out of town and out to the farm. The car skidded to a halt in the farm yard.

"Isn't it awfully early?" Elizabeth asked as they exited the car. "Won't we be waking the renters?"

"Maybe. Don't care. The key I got from the real estate agent will fit the back door, too. If we go in that way, we can go right upstairs. They'll never even know we're here."

Again, Elizabeth could tell Colleen would not be swayed from her planned course of action. Quietly, they let themselves into the house and went up the narrow steps that led to the attic bedroom.

The sun had rallied well above the horizon and was streaming through the naked window where Colleen had inadvertently yanked the Venetian blind off the frame. Streams of light played off the glass of the only picture hanging in the bedroom.

"*That* apple orchard," Colleen said with a flourish as she pointed to the picture.

Elizabeth walked over and inspected the print. What she saw was a lithograph of three apple trees.

"Take it off the wall," Colleen directed.

Elizabeth did, and Colleen took the picture out of Elizabeth's hands and set it on the table. She bent the metal wedges that held the backing in place and lifted the cardboard from the frame.

"I'll be damned!" Elizabeth was thunderstruck.

Taped to the back of the matting was a single silver key. Colleen peeled the cracked tape and cradled the key in both hands, then offered it to Elizabeth.

"How did you know?" Elizabeth accepted the key from Colleen's out-stretched fingers.

"Sean was too weak to go to the orchard and bury something under one of the trees. I lay awake all night thinking about everything I could remember from those last few days with him. I remembered how frail he was when I got to the hospital. The date on the envelope told me he didn't think about leaving a letter for me until right before he took himself in to be admitted. He would have had to leave whatever he wanted me to have somewhere he could get to without exhausting himself."

"Brilliant," Elizabeth beamed. "Simply brilliant."

"He was, wasn't he?" Elizabeth had meant that Colleen was brilliant for having figured Sean's hiding place out, but she was content for the little sister to share the moment with her only brother.

"Now all that's left is to find out what this key fits," Elizabeth mused.

"Way ahead of you, amateur," Colleen said as she took the key back from Elizabeth. "I'm pretty sure it fits a safe deposit box at the only financial institution the McCradys ever patronized."

IT HAD BEEN years since Colleen had set foot in The First National Bank of Coon River Rapids. Of course, it had long since been bought out and merged—twice or three times, at least—with other larger institutions, but the gray granite building still sat on the corner of Mill and Court Streets.

She and Elizabeth walked over to the desk that had a Safety Deposit Boxes sign posted behind it.

"Hello," she said to the young woman behind the desk. "My name is Colleen McCrady. My brother passed away several years ago, but I think he had a safe deposit box here. I've got his key."

Colleen handed the woman a couple of papers. "Here's a copy of his death certificate and his will showing me as his executrix."

The woman took the papers from Colleen and looked them over. "Okay, let's see what we've got here." The woman thumbed through the card file behind her. "How about that? He rented this box for the longest term we offer—ninety-nine years—and paid the full rent back in 1957. He's still got fifty years on the agreement." She offered the registration card to Colleen so she could see the dates.

The last signature on the card was dated August 15, 1994. Seeing his handwriting looking so young and strong in contrast to his writing on the note from the pillow case made Colleen comprehend how terribly ill her brother was in his final days. She hurriedly signed her name on the card and returned it to the bank employee.

"This way, please," the attendant said as she rose from her chair. She led Colleen and Elizabeth to the entry to the vault and punched in the cipher code to open the steel mesh door. They stepped inside, and the door swung shut behind them. "Over here."

Colleen and Elizabeth followed her to the wall of double-locked boxes. Each of them inserted her key into the slots on Box Number 1023. The woman pulled the tray from the rack.

"I'll show you to a private room where you can sit and look through the contents." Carrying the tray, she ushered Colleen and Elizabeth into a cubbyhole with a polished wooden table and two small chairs with cushions. She slid the box onto the tabletop. "Press this button on the wall when you're finished, and I'll come get you to let you out through the security door."

"Thank you." Elizabeth slid into one chair and Colleen dropped into the other. The attendant left, closing the door to the tiny room behind her.

Colleen's hands trembled as she lifted the hinged lid on the box. She peered inside. She saw three things in the twelve-by-eight inch compartment: a savings account passbook, an envelope that felt like it contained several folded pages, and a small spiral notebook with a faded picture behind the cover of a yellowed plastic sleeve. Drawn in a child's scrawl, the sketch showed a man on a tractor.

She picked up the passbook. The inside cover gave the account number and listed Sean as the owner and her name as beneficiary. The first deposit had been made in August 1957. She was dumbfounded by the princely sum with which her brother had opened the account: $1,406.73. That was only the beginning, though. Every year from 1958 through 1994, another deposit of at least a thousand dollars had been made to the account. The last deposit, dated February 28, 1994, showed the balance, with interest accruals, to be slightly over $90,000.

She laid the passbook aside and took the envelope out of the box. It slipped from her hands and fell to the floor. As she picked it up, she noticed a note on the back flap. "Read notebook first." Once again, the sight of her brother's handwriting brought a lump to her throat. She set the envelope aside and claimed the notebook from the container.

Colleen stared at the primitive picture on the cover. "Gosh, that looks familiar," she said as she wagged her head. She peeled the cover back. "Wil E is def." The words jumped off the page at her. "I gave this to Willie the only Christmas that he was with us," she explained as she showed it to Elizabeth.

Colleen went to the next page, dated Christmas 1956. A masculine, disciplined hand had written,

> My name is Wilbur Rice. I was born on April 20, 1931. I am employed by a family named McCrady to do farm work while Mister's legs heal following an accident. This notebook was a Christmas present to me from their little girl, Colleen. She was six years old on her last birthday.

I left Mississippi in May 1949. I had trouble there that's best not written about. I worked my way to Chicago by December of that year. While I was in Chicago, I worked on an underground railroad—not the kind that moved slaves from place to place, but a real one with tracks that delivered supplies to businesses. I lived with Dr. James Rice and his wife Neecy until December of 1955, when I came to Coon River Rapids. Dr. Rice and his wife both passed on of natural causes.

As far as I know, I am the only colored man in these parts. I have not seen someone who looks like me since leaving the rail yards in Minneapolis on my way to Coon River Rapids from Chicago.

I am the youngest child of Edwin and Eunice Rice. My father died in 1946. I pray that my mother is still alive, but the last time I talked to her was when I left Canaan, Mississippi, so I don't know if she is living or dead. I've written down the names of my brothers and sisters at the back of this book. Because of the trouble that happened in my life when I was young, I didn't dare contact any of my family for fear of what might happen to them if someone thought they knew where to find me.

Again for reasons best not written down, everyone believes I'm deaf and mute. The only people in Coon River Rapids who know that I can hear and talk is the little girl who gave me this notebook and her brother, Sean, who works with me on this farm.

I've decided that I will use this notebook to write down what happens in my life. No one here knows me or knows anything about where I came from. I don't know if my own family remembers me any more. If I should die, I would hope that someone would be good enough to tell my mother that her son Wilbur thought of her every day of his life and begs her to forgive him for any pain he caused to her.

The narrative for Christmas Day ended there. Colleen folded back the next page and Elizabeth read over her shoulder.

New Year's Day, 1957. I hope this is the year that I can send for my mama and maybe get to see some of my other family. It's cold. Sean, the fifteen-year-old boy here on the farm, says it's thirty below. Good thing I've got the heat from the cows to warm my room.

> February 10, 1957. More snow. Almost two feet. Winter lasts a long time here.

And on it went, day by day. Nothing profound or unusual — nothing more than the daily journal of a lonely man hoping to one day put his life back together.

The last entry was August 14, 1957.

> Mister's relatives are here visiting from Milwaukee. The boy is mean to me. He's made lots of problems for me while they've been here. I'll be glad when they go home.

Colleen closed the notebook and laid it on the table.

Elizabeth said, "That confirms most of the details you put in your book, but there's nothing in there about the white girl he supposedly killed or why he faked being deaf."

"No, but he told Sean, and Sean told me. I'm pretty sure I've got the facts of the Willie Rice story recorded accurately." Colleen gave a disparaging chuckle. "Of course, I *may* have embellished a detail or two or made up some conversations to make the plot flow more smoothly."

"But we still don't know what ultimately happened to him."

"We will when we open this." Colleen picked up the sealed envelope she had placed on the table earlier. She exhaled loudly. "Ready?" she asked more of herself than of Elizabeth. She crossed her fingers and shook them twice for Elizabeth to see. Then in one motion, she ripped the end off the envelope.

> My name is Sean Daniel McCrady. Something happened on our farm a couple of weeks ago that needs to be recorded in case anybody ever wants to know the truth.
>
> A man named Willie Rice was working for us because my dad was laid up with two broken legs. Willie was a Negro man from Mississippi. I've included a notebook with this letter that tells more about him.
>
> Someone was visiting our farm and they did something that caused a terrible accident. I wasn't there exactly when it happened, but I talked to the person who might have known everything that went on, and I think this will explain most of it.
>
> This person set up a timer using an alarm clock so that a wire would carry an electric current from a piece of equipment — a milk separating machine that was used to spin the cream out of whole milk — to a metal bed frame that was in Willie's room in the barn. The alarm clock was set to

go off real early in the morning. The way the person had rigged it, when the clock tripped, it would kick on the milk separator. A string of fence wire came off the coil of the separator motor and attached to the bed frame.

The idea was that the clock would start the motor and the electricity would run down the wire and into the bed frame. It was supposed to be a practical joke.

But that's not what happened. First of all, that part of the barn was wired with 220 volt line to handle the bulk tank. I'm pretty sure the person who did this thought he was hooking up to something that was only 110 volt, but it was 220. If Willie had still been in bed, the shock would have been awfully strong, but the mattress might have insulated him enough. The thing is Willie was already out of the bed when the clock went off. He had filled the metal bowl on the separator with hot water and disinfectant so he could wash it before we did the morning milking. The clock tripped the motor on. Because of the way the person had run the wire from the motor, the current ran up through the metal legs of the separator. Willie was standing there with his hands in the water in the metal bowl. Between the water and the 220 volts, it electrocuted him, and he died right away.

I know I should have called the sheriff, but I was pretty sure I knew who the person was who had arranged the wires and clock and everything, and I wasn't sure what to do about that. All I could think was to get Willie's body out of the milking parlor before my little sister saw him. She liked him a lot, and I was afraid what it might do to her if she saw him dead.

I took Willie out and buried him in one of his favorite places.

A couple of days later I talked to the person I was pretty sure was to blame for this, and he told me that it would only be my word against his, and that if I knew what was good for me, I'd never tell anybody what he did. I had already hid the wire and taken the alarm clock out of the housing of the milk separator, so I couldn't prove it.

Willie had been saving his wages. His money was wrapped in a box in the top drawer of his dresser. I took his money to the bank and opened an account. I'm going to put some more with it every year, and one day when I'm older, I'm going to take it to his mother. His notebook tells about her and where she is.

Whoever reads this, I swear it's the truth as best I know

it. I'm real sorry I wasn't able to help Willie or to keep this
other person from hurting him.
Sean Daniel McCrady
September 29, 1957

Elizabeth and Colleen passed the pages back and forth between
them and reread them many times.

"Robbie?" Elizabeth finally said, rancorously.

"I can't imagine anyone else who'd have done that," Colleen
replied.

"Where is he by now?"

"A shining example of the consequences of divine retribution. I
heard through the family grapevine he was convicted and jailed for
selling cocaine. He smarted off with a racial epithet one too many
times and ended up on the wrong end of a shiv at the Wisconsin
prison. He bled to death in the corner of the exercise yard. " Her
loathing was patently evident. "I suppose the cretin learned just
enough about electrical circuitry in that vocational school he
attended to think he could pull off a stunt like that."

Elizabeth let the storm clouds fade from Colleen's face before
probing for her reactions to Sean's letter.

"How do you feel, Collie?"

"Overwhelmed, mostly. And relieved to finally know what
happened to Willie." She thought a moment. "Sad." Her face showed
the intensity of her words. "Sadder than I can say."

Elizabeth gathered up the few things they'd pulled from Sean's
safe deposit box and pushed her chair away from the table. "Let's get
some air, okay?" She offered her free hand to Colleen.

The September day was bright and crisp. How ironic that exactly
forty-nine years earlier — to the day — Sean had written his
explanation of Willie's demise. Even though Elizabeth had no
familiarity with Coon River Rapids, she instinctively knew that
wandering the streets of Colleen's childhood home town would be
like a medicine for her.

They walked in silence for a while, but soon Colleen was
pointing to buildings and offering her recollections. "There's where
the old pool hall used to be where my dad brought me all the time."
Then she pointed to the other side of the street. "The Woolworth's
was there. I owe these hips to the habits I developed at their candy
counter." Another few blocks passed. "If you keep going this way to
the edge of town, that's where all of the implement dealers had their
lots. My dad could spend a whole day kicking tires and talking about
the width of the tine feeders. Here's where he bought his corn and
wheat. " As they passed the farmer's co-op with all its stacks of feed
and seed, Colleen gestured toward the door. "Let's stop in. I want to

buy some work gloves. I think we'll need them after while."

An hour later, Elizabeth managed to lead them back to the bank parking lot where their rental car was parked.

"Thanks for the tour, sweetheart," Colleen said as she let herself in the passenger door. "If I didn't know better, I'd think this was *your* home town." She cleared her throat. "We need to make two more stops before we go back to Georgia."

"Okay, name them."

"I need to go back to the farm one more time."

"Of course, sweetie. What else?"

Colleen finished her thought. "And then I think a swing through Mississippi is in order."

"WOW, I CAN'T believe how big some of these trees have gotten." Colleen and Elizabeth were walking down what used to be the road leading to the fields Colleen's father and brother had tended. The prairie grass had encroached, making it more like a footpath than a tractor lane. Colleen carried a small, canvas tote bag over her shoulder.

"Where are we going?" Elizabeth asked.

"You'll see in a minute."

They crested a small knoll, and Elizabeth felt her heart skip a beat. "Oh, this must be what paradise looks like."

"We always thought so."

From their vantage point, the large body of natural water that the McCradys had used as their cattle pond was visible in the background. Off to one side, paper birch trees, their white bark starkly contrasted with the perfect blue of the sky, shimmered their golden leaves in the light breeze. On the other side, oaks and maples, boxwoods and elms in every possible hue of orange, red, and yellow made a picture postcard backdrop for the open meadow of grass — now more brown than green — that stretched in front of them. Birds flew overhead and chirped their annoyance at the human intruders.

Elizabeth said, "I thought scenes like this were faked in a studio somewhere for the September pictures on calendars that merchants hand out every year at Christmas."

"Nope. This is the real deal. Willie used to tell me that if he couldn't get home to die in Mississippi, he hoped he could be buried here. If he told me, he must have told Sean, too." Colleen heard the hollow sound in her own voice and wondered if she'd actually be able to carry through with what she had come to do. She led them a little further, around a small grove of trees to the far side, until they came to a large pile of rocks standing three feet high in some places and spreading in a ten-foot circle.

"Are you up to a little physical labor?" From the front pouch of her hooded sweatshirt Colleen pulled out the two pair of work gloves she'd bought earlier.

"Tell me what to do," Elizabeth replied as she put on the gloves.

"Help me move some of these rocks." Colleen went to the edge of the rock pile, picked up a stone the size of cantaloupe, and tossed it to the side.

"Are we doing this for the heck of it?" Elizabeth asked as she grabbed a rock and pitched it.

"No. I'm pretty sure we'll find the final piece of the puzzle somewhere nearby."

"How did this mountain of rocks get here anyhow?" Elizabeth asked.

"The frost heaved them out every winter, and every spring, we'd have to drive through the fields and pick them up so that Dad could plant his crops."

"Ohmigosh! A snake!" Elizabeth jumped back. A yellow and black fellow about eighteen inches long slithered off into the grass.

"He's harmless—nothing but an old garter snake. We'll probably find lots of them in here before we're done. They like to hide in the rocks."

Elizabeth willed her heart back into her chest and resumed heaving rocks off the pile. She could sense that Colleen wasn't in the mood for conversation, so the only sounds were the birds, the breeze in the trees, and the thunk and clunk of the rocks as they landed. Several times, they paused to relieve the muscles in their aching backs and to drink from the water bottles that Colleen had brought along in the canvas tote bag.

Late in the afternoon, Colleen stood and indicated that Elizabeth should stop moving rocks. "I think we've found him," Colleen said reverently. She pointed to a pile of bleached bones now visible.

With the care of seasoned archeologists, they cautiously moved the next rocks until the full form of a man was visible. The skull faced away from them. Colleen summoned every shred of courage still left in her and reached down to rotate the head so they could see it clearly.

"Look."

Elizabeth followed the line of Colleen's finger.

What she saw, weathered by time and nature, was a solitary gold cap lodged in a tooth in the upper jaw line. "Sean's letter said we'd find gold at the end of our hunt." Elizabeth's voice was little more than a whisper.

"He was right. We did."

Colleen picked up the tote bag and pulled out *The Three Friends* storybook—her only gift from Willie in the guise of Santa. She hugged the book to her and wiped the tears that formed on her lashes. She bent down and laid it on top of the bones below her.

"Good bye, Willie. I'll never forget you and all the stories we shared. Thank you for being my friend."

Then one by one, they replaced the rocks.

"What a strange looking squirrel," Elizabeth commented as they neared the end of their task. A small creature scampered out of sight behind a rotting tree on the floor of the grove.

"That's not a squirrel. It's a chipmunk."

"I thought I saw stripes on his back."

"You know," Colleen said, "the chipmunk got his stripes because he helped Coyote steal fire."

"So I've recently learned. Why don't you remind me of how the story goes?"

She waited until she was sure she could trust her voice. "This is a story about how Coyote stole fire so that man could stay warm in the winter. When the world was new, the earth was warm all the time and never cold. Spring, summer, and fall were the only seasons—"

Colleen finished telling the tale that Willie had taught her so long ago. She could only hope it would serve as a fitting eulogy and, though long overdue, carry his soul to a peaceful rest.

Chapter
Twenty-Six

COLLEEN AND ELIZABETH stayed one more day in Coon River Rapids. They cleaned out the last of Sean's things from the old farm house. Colleen made the rounds of places she thought her brother might have left unfinished business or unpaid bills so she could zero out the books. She renewed her arrangements with the real estate office to continue managing the house as rental property. The next day, they drove to Minneapolis and boarded a plane.

"I've never been to Memphis, have you?" Elizabeth asked as they touched down.

"No, and I never thought I'd be using it as a jumping off point for what we've come to do."

"Any ideas for how we should go about this?"

"We know Willie was the youngest child in his family and that he was born in the early 1930's. Even if his mother was fairly young when he was born, she's probably been dead for ten years or more. I wondered if we can find the cemetery where Willie's parents are buried. It might be a way to track down some of his other family members."

"That sounds like a good plan, sweetheart."

They rented a car at the Memphis airport and drove south on U.S. Route 72 across the Mississippi state line to Canaan. They found two cemeteries on the far side of the little town. They were no longer labeled as such, but clearly, one had been for whites and the other for blacks.

They located Eunice Rice's headstone in the black cemetery next to her husband, Edwin's.

"Isn't that something?" Colleen traced the date carved in the granite with her finger. "Willie's mother died on August 17, 1957. That's only two days after Willie was electrocuted."

"According to her date of birth, she was sixty-nine."

"So, since Willie was twenty-six when he was killed, we know he was a late-in-life baby for her. I hope that doesn't mean his siblings are all gone, too." Colleen felt her heart sink.

"Don't lose hope yet," Elizabeth said as she wrapped an arm

around Colleen's shoulder. "We might still be able to find someone."
Elizabeth waited a moment before continuing. "Isn't it strange that
she died so close to the same day that Willie did?"

Colleen caressed the rounded crest of the grave marker.
"Remember what he wrote in his notebook? He wanted someone to
tell his mother he thought of her every day of his life. She must have
somehow drawn strength from his thoughts of her, and when they
stopped coming, she lost her will to live."

"Do you think that's possible?"

"I knew Willie Rice. I was only a little girl, but he was one of the
sweetest, gentlest human beings I've ever met. Because he pretended
to be deaf, he was always so quiet—but even when he spoke, his
voice was soft and hushed. And I always knew I could trust him. I
felt so safe whenever he was around." Colleen rubbed the headstone
again. "I spent almost fifty years wondering what happened to him.
My connection to him was that of a child who loved to hear him tell
stories, but I felt an ache for him for a long, long time after he was
gone. I can only imagine what it must have been like for his
mother—never knowing where he was or if he was even still alive.
Think of how she must have dreamed about seeing him again—
picturing in her mind what he looked like. But she knew if he ever
came home to Mississippi, he would probably be hanged." She
shivered despite the warm October sun.

Memories carried Colleen to a place and time she had feared for
most of her life. What a relief to find that the ghosts no longer
taunted her soul.

Elizabeth stood quietly by Colleen's side. When she felt the time
was right, she spoke. "Ready to go, love?"

"I suppose we should."

They drove slowly through Canaan.

"Let's stop here, okay?" Colleen asked as she pulled up next to a
small brick church.

"Why?"

"I'm not sure. I just have a feeling."

They walked toward the main door of the church. As they did
so, a diminutive, elderly black man wearing dark trousers and a
Tennessee Titans football jersey emerged from the side door.

"How do, ladies? I didn't hear y'all drive up." He shuffled
nearer to where the women were standing. "I was having a little rest
after lunch and shut my hearing aid off so's to block out the noise
from cars driving by. Can I help you?"

Colleen extended her hand. "Hello. My name is Colleen
McCrady and this is my friend, Elizabeth Albright. Do you work
here?"

"As best the Lord lets me. I'm the church janitor and as close to a handyman as they've got."

"Have you lived around Canaan long?"

"All my seventy-eight years."

"Would you mind if I asked you some questions, Mr. — uh — ?"

"Call me 'Touchdown.' Everybody does."

"Maybe we could sit on the steps for a few minutes. Would that be all right, Touchdown?"

"Be all right with me. I'm better at sitting than standing."

Touchdown eased onto the second step and braced his back against the post of the hand rail. Colleen sat down a foot away from him while Elizabeth stood nearby.

"We've been out to the cemetery on the road toward Walnut and saw some graves for people we have a connection to."

"Now why would two skinny young white girls have any reason to visit an old colored folks' bone yard?"

"It's a very long story, but I'm pretty sure I knew the son of some people who are buried there."

"I can tell from the way you talk, you ain't from around here. How'd you come to know anybody from Canaan, Mississippi?"

Colleen decided candor was her best bet. "I used to know a young man named Willie Rice. We saw the markers for his mother and father, Edwin and Eunice."

Touchdown opened his eyes as wide as they'd go. "You wouldn't be pulling an old man's leg would you?" He lifted his left leg and did his best to give it a vigorous shake.

"No, it's the truth." Colleen placed her hand on the step next to where she was sitting. "I swear on this sacred place."

"Me and Willie went to school together way back when. Willie Rice. Umh, umh. He was bound for bigger things, I can tell you that."

Colleen had to keep herself from throwing herself around the old man and hugging the air out of him. "You knew Willie?"

"I did. Sure as I'm sitting here with you this minute. Funny thing about Willie. One day he was here talking smart, dressing smart, helping his mama. The next day," Touchdown shook his head, "like he never made a footprint in this part of Mississippi. I heard lots of crazy talk about Willie killing some white girl, but anybody who knew him for more than a minute never believed a word of that. Willie was real quiet, real respectful of folks, especially white folks." Touchdown looked Colleen in the eye, then continued. "And you could trust him with your best friend and your last dollar. He didn't have a bad bone in him. As far as I know, nobody in Canaan ever knew where he went."

"Do you remember when he left?" Elizabeth moved in a little closer.

"Oh, honey, you asking old Touchdown to dig way back now."

He squinted his eyes in concentration. "It was around 1950. I remember because when I got sent to Korea in 1951 he was already gone and half forgot by some folks 'round here."

Colleen exchanged a knowing glance with Elizabeth. The timeline matched perfectly with what they knew of Willie's past.

"Do you know if any of Willie's brothers and sisters are still alive?" Colleen tried to sound casual, conversational.

"Willie was tail end of the bunch. And his daddy and mama been dead and gone for I don't know how long."

"About fifty years, according to the dates on their graves," Elizabeth said.

"See? That's damn near a lifetime. Forgive my cussing while we're at the Lord's house."

"That's okay, Touchdown." Colleen smiled at the man. "We don't mind, and I'm sure the Lord will overlook it this time. But think for a minute and see if you can remember anything about any of Willie's family."

It took Touchdown a few minutes, but then the recollection hit him.

"The sister next up the line from Willie was named Pearl." He smiled self-consciously. "Pearl, Pearl, Pearl. Such a pretty county girl." Touchdown sang the words in a surprisingly strong voice. "She married a boy from right here in Canaan. He was one of the Crowder boys. We always called him 'Chowder — like the soup, you know?"

Once again, Colleen had to will herself to stay calm, lest she scare the old man with her exuberance.

"Is Pearl Crowder still in Canaan?"

"Mercy, no. They moved to somewheres up around Memphis right after they got married. I remember Pearl came back for their mama's funeral, but I don't know as I've seen her since."

Once again, Colleen stole a look at Elizabeth. She was sure Sean had told her Willie had gotten help from his sister in Memphis when he fled Mississippi. She had included that detail in *The Curse of Canaan*. Elizabeth gave her a quick wink to indicate she remembered it, too.

Colleen focused on Touchdown. "One last question, and then we'll be on our way."

"Don't hurry off on my account."

"You don't happen to remember Pearl's husband's first name, do you?"

"You came to town for the sole purpose of breaking what's left of my mind, didn't you, child?" Touchdown scratched his ear lobe. "Let's see — Crowder — Chowder — ." Then he tilted his head back and hooted till he coughed. "It was Glen. Get it? Glen Crowder — Clam Chowder. His real name was Glen Crowder, but we called him

Clam Chowder. Don't that beat all?"

Colleen grasped Touchdown's hand in both of hers. "Your mind works real well, Touchdown. Thank you for spending time with us this afternoon."

"You're welcome, missy. You come on back and talk to old Touchdown any time."

"IT WILL TAKE us days to call all these people." Elizabeth drew her hand down the page in an open phone book. "If I'd brought my laptop with me, we could've culled the field using the internet."

After their conversation with Touchdown at the church in Canaan, they backtracked to Memphis in hopes of finding Pearl Rice Crowder. They took a hotel room near the airport and were scanning listings for Crowders in the greater Memphis area. They were staggered and dismayed to see forty-three entries, none of them for a Glen or Pearl Crowder, however.

"I doubt that using a people search feature off the web would have helped much," Colleen said as she closed the book. "We'll have to take it name by name and see if one of these Crowders knows Pearl or Glen, or if we get really lucky, Willie."

"And if they do, if they're willing to talk to us." Elizabeth flopped onto the bed. "Not everyone is as willing to part with information as your new best friend, Touchdown, was." Elizabeth laced her fingers behind her head and stretched her neck. "I still don't know how you lucked up on finding someone who knew Willie at the very first place you stopped to ask."

"Luck? More like angel wings. Willie's mother's spirit met us in that cemetery. She knows we've come to lay all those old heartaches to rest. She took us into town and led us to Willie's boyhood friend."

"Do you really think so, Collie?"

"It's the best explanation I've got." She lay down next to Elizabeth. "And God's truth, I don't want another one."

"You've never said much about religion before."

"With all that happened with Anna and Michael, and then my mom and Sean — I didn't figure God and I were on very good terms."

"And now?" Elizabeth rubbed Colleen's forearm.

"Now I think there's a lot that goes on in this life that can only be described as metaphysical. Ever since we — you — found the letter Sean left for me, I feel like hallowed guides have been keeping their hands on our shoulders, helping us find exactly what we need to take us to the next right place." She waited for a reaction from Elizabeth, but none was forthcoming. "Too much psycho-babble woo-woo tripe for you?"

"No, not at all. I suppose the same could be said for you and me.

I mean, if Toni hadn't arranged the appointment between us to go over your first draft of *Scrapbook* a year and a half ago, none of what's transpired in the past week would have ever come about—at least not with me by your side."

"I don't believe in predestination."

"I don't either."

"I'm not even sure I believe in coincidence." Colleen laid her head on Elizabeth's shoulder. "More like divine synchronicity."

"That has a nice ring to it." Elizabeth stoked Colleen's curls. "Do you think there's enough divine synchronicity for us to find Pearl?"

"Absolutely." A tear slipped down her cheek. "Willie's almost home."

COLLEEN'S PROPHECY ABOUT finding Pearl proved out. Their eighth call the next morning located her in Colliersville, to the east of Memphis. When Colleen was able to give Willie's birth date, middle name, and the names of all of the siblings (thanks to what they read her from Willie's notebook), Pearl agreed to meet with Colleen and Elizabeth.

"He's dead, isn't he?" Pearl pressed before they hung up.

"Yes, I'm sorry to tell you he is, but I'd still like to talk with you if I could."

Pearl gave them directions to her home.

When the stooped woman answered the door of the barely-standing cracker box house, Colleen said, "Mrs. Crowder, thank you for agreeing to meet with us. I'm Colleen McCrady and this is Elizabeth Albright."

"Y'all call me Pearl." She pushed the door open wide. "I'm the one should be thanking you if you've come to tell me what happened to my baby brother. When so much time passed without any of us hearing from him, we all knew he wasn't ever coming home again." Pearl used a cane to steady herself. "Come in, come in. Sit down and tell me everything you know."

Elizabeth and Colleen took seats on the faded floral sofa. With effort, Pearl sat on a straight-backed chair. "Now, how is it you know my brother?"

"I think this will be easier if I tell you right away that I know he had to leave Mississippi because some people thought he killed a woman." Colleen saw Pearl draw back. "I also know that he was innocent, but the fear of what would happen to him—or to his family—kept him from ever trying to contact you."

Pearl seemed reassured. "Willie had too good a heart to ever hurt anybody. Nobody who knew him ever believed that pack of lies about him killing that white girl."

"After Willie left Canaan, he spent a few years in Chicago."

"Did he?" Pearl's eyes lit up. "I was the last of the family to see him, and he told me that's where he wanted to go. I can't picture my country boy brother in a big city like that."

"That's probably why he left — to get back to a place that suited him better. While he was in Chicago, he stayed with a nice dentist and his wife. He took care of the wife after the dentist died."

"That sounds like Willie. It about put Mama in the ground when he had to go away. She pined for him every day of her life." Pearl sniffed and wiped at her eyes. "But that still doesn't tell me how you knew him."

"When he left Chicago, he came to my home town in Minnesota — a little farming community called Coon River Rapids. My father was laid up with two broken legs for several months, and Willie lived with us and helped my brother take care of our farm while our dad was recovering."

"When was this?"

"I was five — almost six — years old. Willie came to our farm in the fall of 1956."

"Did he stay a long time?"

"I wish he had." Colleen got up from her seat and went over to Pearl. "He was a wonderful friend to me. He made up stories to tell me, and he read to me. He told me about living on a farm with his mother."

"Why didn't he stay?" Pearl reached out and touched Colleen's hand.

"There was an accident — a bad accident involving electricity."

"Oh, Lord! Did he suffer?"

"No, it was very quick. I'm told he died instantly."

"You were told?"

"At the time it happened, I was very young. My family didn't think I would understand."

"Why didn't someone tell us sooner? If he was already dead, they couldn't haul him back to Mississippi and put a rope around his neck."

"It wasn't until last week that I knew how to find Willie's family."

Colleen saw the anguish on Pearl's face. "Why did it have to be you? Someone else could have told us." Pearl pounded the tip of her cane on the floor.

"Colleen's brother was the only person who knew what had happened to Willie." Elizabeth leaned forward from her seat. "And he got sick and died a long time ago. Colleen didn't know he had left a letter for her telling her about Willie's accident. We found that letter last week and have been trying to find Willie's family ever since."

"Tell me exactly when he died." Pearl's deep brown eyes bored into Colleen's.

"August fifteenth, 1957." Colleen's voice gave way as she spoke.

"Not but two days before Mama went to be with Jesus." Pearl looked heavenward. "She always said she'd know if her baby was gone."

"I'm sorry, Pearl. Sorry for your loss and sorry it took nearly fifty years for someone to tell you what happened to Willie." Colleen moved nearer so that she could drape an arm protectively around Pearl's frail form. "Do you have family? Are any of your siblings still alive?"

"My sister DeeDee's down in Tupelo. We're all that's left of those who knew him—those who will remember him. Soon, there won't be anyone."

Colleen tightened her grip around Pearl. "You're wrong about that, Pearl. I remember him. I always will. And I saved his notebook for you. It's a sort of journal Willie kept during the last part of his life, and I hope you'll find some comfort in the way he mentions his family and especially his mama on nearly every page." She held out the weathered old notebook, and Pearl took it with shaky hands.

"This his own writing," she said, wonder in her voice.

"Yes, ma'am. He was quite a storyteller, and I'd be happy to sit with you a while and talk about some of the stories he and I shared."

They stayed with Pearl for more than an hour until Colleen ran out of memories and Pearl looked too out worn to continue. Colleen left her address and phone number, and the tiny old woman hugged both of them as they left.

Back at the motel later, Colleen said, "I've been thinking about what Pearl said."

"What, specifically?"

"She said there's almost no one who would remember Willie."

"He's been gone from Mississippi for a long time, Collie."

"I know, but I've got an idea. He still deserves to be remembered. I think I'll call Pearl and talk to her one more time before we leave."

THE FOLLOWING DAY, Elizabeth and Colleen drove to Holly Springs, Mississippi. They stopped at the Williams Brothers' Funeral Home and spoke to Mr. Rey Williams. With Pearl's consent, Colleen arranged for the funeral home to order a bronze plaque to be placed at the Canaan cemetery at Edwin and Eunice Rice's graves. It bore the inscription:

Wilbur Alphonse Rice
Beloved Son of Edwin and Eunice
April 20, 1931 – August 15, 1957

In quietness and in trust shall be your strength.
Isaiah 30:15

Elizabeth squeezed Colleen's hand as they left the funeral home. "You picked a nice tribute for your friend, Colleen."

"At least there'll be something to remember him by in years to come."

They got in the rental car and made their way to Rust College where they strolled around the grounds.

Elizabeth indicated a group of wooden benches around the clock tower in the center of campus. "If this were a movie, right about now the camera would cut away to a 1940's image of a handsome young black man and a beautiful Jewess sitting over there."

"I know what you mean. I keep getting the feeling that I'm watching myself do this through someone else's eyes." Colleen slipped her hand over Elizabeth's arm. "More of those ghosts and angel guides, I guess."

"You've done your best by him, sweetie. Willie's soul should have an easy time of it now."

"And Willie's girlfriend and his mother, too, I hope." Colleen fought back the tears. "Let's finish what we came to do, okay?"

They walked arm and arm for a ways, finally stopping at an information kiosk near the administration building. A laminated fact sheet posted there told them Rust was the oldest Historically Black College or University affiliated with the Methodist Church still in operation. Rust was proud to be one of only five HBCU's that had remained open continuously since 1867.

They made their way to the Office of the Vice President for Development and explained why they had come. Much to the surprise of the administrator, Colleen used the funds from Sean's passbook account—and a little extra from her own savings—and wrote a check for ninety-five thousand dollars to open the Wilbur A. Rice Endowment Chair for Race Relations in the Twenty-First Century. They said their good-byes to the Vice President and walked out into the blazing sunshine of an early October afternoon.

Colleen lingered on the top step and looked out over the campus. Briefly, she laid her head on Elizabeth's shoulder. "Thank you, LJ. I never could have done this without you."

"Thank you for letting me be part of it. It's been quite an odyssey." Elizabeth took Colleen's arm.

"It has, hasn't it?"

"Anything more we need to do?"

"No. I'm ready now. Let's go home."

THAT EVENING, ELIZABETH and Colleen caught a flight from Memphis back to Atlanta and then drove to Columbus. They arrived at Elizabeth's house close to midnight.

"It's so late, Colleen. Can you spend the night here instead of going to LaGrange?"

"Yeah, I'd like to do that."

"Will the dogs be okay?"

"When we were in Memphis, I called Robin, my dog sitter, and told her I wasn't sure when I'd be back. She'll take care of Buster and Muggins 'til she knows I'm home."

"Good." Elizabeth dropped her suitcase onto the bedroom floor. "Now that I'm back in my own house, it almost feels like the whole thing was some outrageous dream. I always knew you were a fascinating woman, but never in my wildest imaginings would I have envisioned the sorts of things the past week brought to light."

"Are you sorry we went to Minnesota?"

Elizabeth hugged Colleen. "Not for a minute. It will take me a while to put all of the details in place," Elizabeth tapped her temple, "but here—" she laid her hand over her heart, "everything is clear as can be."

Colleen clutched Elizabeth tightly and they rocked back and forth in one another's embrace. She loosened her grip and took Elizabeth by the hand. "Come lie with me," she said as she led her to the bed. They pulled the covers down and lay next to one another on their backs, fingers interlocked but otherwise not touching. They talked for a long time, revisiting everything they had experienced.

"I've been thinking about something else," Elizabeth ventured somewhere in the wee hours of the morning.

Colleen checked the small clock on the nightstand; it said four-ten a.m. "Tell me what."

"It's definitely time you and I brought our relationship out of the shadows and let the world know that we're a couple."

Colleen felt her heart quicken. "What about the other writers under contract with you?"

"What about them? They'll either adjust or bail out. Either is fine with me." Elizabeth rolled on her side and draped her arm across Colleen. "And I've had another idea, too."

"What's that?"

"I want to launch a new imprint at Sappho's Shadow—one where the books aren't strictly lesbian romances. If they have lesbian characters, great, but they wouldn't have to. They could be more journey of life books — books like *The Curse of Canaan."*

"Oh, LJ, I don't think that would work." Colleen sighed deeply. "I started writing that book years ago to find a way to deal with all of my old demons. I didn't mean it to be a real book. I finished writing it because I couldn't think of any other way to tell you about my past."

Elizabeth pulled Colleen near. "Not real? It's one of the most real books I've ever read. All you have to do is rework it a little and add the last chapters to tell the whole story. I bet it would be a blockbuster."

"Maybe. I guess if it did sell a few copies, I could donate my royalties to Willie's endowment fund at Rust College."

"And I could match it with the profits that Triple S earns from it."

"That would be a good way for us to keep honoring Willie's memory." Colleen lay silent for a moment. "But it seems like an awful lot of chances for you to take all at once. I mean, telling everyone we're together, launching a whole new line of books, donating profits to the college, risking losing some of your authors." Colleen squinted, trying to see Elizabeth more clearly in the dimly lit room. "Shouldn't you think this through some more?"

"I told you before we went to Minnesota that taking chances is what life is all about. Given what we've learned in the past several days, I believe that more than ever." Elizabeth rubbed her leg against Colleen. "Hey, wanna take a chance on a blanket?"

The inflection in Elizabeth's voice caught Colleen off guard, but it only took her a moment to determine that the offer was sincere.

Their lovemaking was slow and deliberate, almost like a religious rite. Their climaxes, which came nearly simultaneously, were measured and emanated from a place somewhere sacred and deep within the core of their beings. Exhaustion and contentment led them to welcome sleep.

"HI, BEAUTIFUL." ELIZABETH'S face was beaming as she watched Colleen awaken. "I've got an idea for what to call the new division of Sappho's Shadow." Elizabeth swung out of bed and padded over to the window to pull the curtains back. Bright mid-morning light poured into the room.

"So tell me already." Colleen stretched and yawned and moved to the edge of the bed.

Elizabeth went back and sat beside Colleen. "Remember how I told you last night I wanted to bring our relationship out of the shadows?"

"I remember. It's what I've always wanted for us."

"That must have reminded me of Oscar Hammerstein's lyrics for 'We Kiss in a Shadow' from *The King and I,* because I had it running through my head when I work up this morning." She kissed Colleen and then kissed her again. "Like us." Elizabeth paused to relish the anticipatory joy of shouting her feelings for Colleen out loud. "I think the new line of books should be called 'Standing in Broad Daylight.'"

Colleen reflected on Elizabeth's suggestion for a moment. "I'm not sure I understand."

"Thanks to you and all we went through in Coon River Rapids, I'm starting to see that everything I've done with Triple S Publishing has been half-hidden in the shadows. Even the name I picked for my company implied that the books I published should be kept in the dark — that they didn't deserve to be out in the open."

"It's not like we old lesbian broads are welcomed with open arms out in the big, wide universe, sweetie."

"No, we're not, and that's precisely my point. Our love is as real as any other love, and it deserves to flourish in the light of day. Think about what happened to Willie and Lila. Their love had to be kept secret, too, and even then, it was stolen from them."

"What was it about the song you mentioned that gave you the idea for the new division at Triple S?"

Elizabeth softly sang the exact phrase about kissing in the sunlight.

"So you want us to lock lips out there right in front of God and everybody?" Colleen spread her arms expansively.

"Yeah, I do, but I want us not only to kiss in the sunlight, but to live every aspect of our lives in the bright light of day."

"Just like real people, huh?"

"Exactly. It's time to claim our right to love one another and to prove that anything anyone else does — in the sunshine or anywhere else — lesbians do, too. From here on out, we're going to be standing in broad daylight."

"Standing in Broad Daylight, a division of Standing in Sappho's Shadow," Colleen said. "I like the way that sounds."

"Me too. I can't wait to show the world what standing in broad daylight really means."

Other Jane Vollbrecht titles coming soon

Close Enough

A historical romance in three parts, Close Enough demonstrates the ineffaceable bonds of the heart. Part I, set in 1941, tells the story of Hilda Stenkiewicz, an eighteen-year-old girl who gives her illegitimate baby away to virtual strangers. To try to put her life back together, Hilda moves away from her hometown and finds herself falling in love with the landlady at her boarding house. Part II recounts the life of the child Hilda surrendered. Frannie Brewster, like the birth mother she never knew, finds herself drawn to love women. Unlike her mother, however, heartbreak seems to be her constant fate. Part III picks up Hilda Stenkiewicz's story more than forty years after she gave her baby away. Hilda has never abandoned her dream of one day finding her child. With almost no clues to guide them, Hilda's niece and nephew go in search of their cousin. They draw ever closer to finding Hilda's offspring, but can they get close enough?

Available August 2007

Second Verse

Gail Larsen lives in the Tennessee woods and edits lesbian fiction for Outrageous Press. Good thing her professional life is satisfying, because she has not had much luck with her love life. Her first lover left her to pursue a different path; her next died in an accident. It has been two years since Gail has dated, and she is seeing a therapist, hoping to put her life back on track.

A special editing assignment throws Gail together with Connie Martin, one of the leading ladies of lesbian fiction. Gail is at first amused by Connie's pit-bull personality in a Pekinese body, but amusement turns to attraction, and attraction to heart-wrenching anxiety that leaves Gail anguished and unsettled.

After an intense month working with Connie on her book, Gail's lifelong friend Penny invites Gail back to Plainfield, Minnesota. Gail has always harbored an unanswered longing for Penny. Many old ghosts re-emerge, and they are forced to confront them. To Gail's annoyance and amazement, Connie tracks her down while she is in Plainfield, and now she fears she is trapped between two women, one she will never have and one she does not want. All she has ever wanted is a lifemate she could dance with for the rest of her life. Can she find someone who will last through the second verse?

Available February 2008

Reiko's Garden
by Brenda Adcock

Hatred...like love...knows no boundaries.

How much impact can one person have on a life?

When sixty-five-old Callie Owen returns to her rural child-hood home in Eastern Tennessee to attend the funeral of a woman she hasn't seen in twenty years, she's forced to face the fears, heartache, and turbulent events that scarred both her body and her mind. Drawing strength from Jean, her partner of thirty years, and from their two grown children, Callie stays in the valley longer than she had anticipated and relives the years that changed her life forever.

In 1949, Japanese war bride Reiko Sanders came to Frost Valley, Tennessee with her soldier husband and infant son. Callie Owen was an inquisitive ten year old whose curiosity about the stranger drove her to disobey her father for just one peek at the woman who had become the subject of so much speculation. Despite Callie's fears, she soon finds that the exotic looking woman is kind and caring, and the two forge a tentative, but secret friendship.

When Callie and her five brothers and sisters were left orphaned, Reiko provided emotional support to Callie. The bond between them continued to grow stronger until Callie left Frost Valley as a teenager, emotionally and physically scarred, vowing never to return and never to forgive.

It is not until Callie goes "home" that she allows herself to remember how Reiko influenced her life. Once and for all, can she face the terrible events of her past? Or will they come back to destroy all that she loves?

Coming May 2007

Devil's Bridge
by Greg Lilly

Two friends, Myra and Topher, deal with their twisting lives. Her husband beats her, his lover ignores him, and their friendship must bend with changes of its own.

Dealing with their own problems, Myra's increasingly violent husband and Topher's unrequited love for his partner Alex, they don't realize how much their lives parallel each other.

Myra's husband Gil controls her actions with his violence. Doubts finally creep into Myra's reluctant mind. Her dream of a happy family is slipping out of her reach. Although Topher helps her build self-esteem and is the stable influence in her life, he is in a crisis over where he fits in the gay community - too old for the club life, but not in a stable committed relationship. He allows Alex to manipulate him with the future possibility of love.

Finding strength to leave their relationships, Myra and Topher decide to escape from their life and start over - together. But, Myra's husband craves revenge. At a place called DEVIL'S BRIDGE, vengeance is redeemed.

Coming May 2007

About the Author:

Jane's first novel, *Picture Perfect,* was a finalist in the "Debut Author" category for the 2005 Golden Crown Literary Society Awards. *Heart Trouble,* her second novel, was released by Regal Crest Enterprises in August, 2006. Jane's short story, "Samhain" was included in *Call of the Dark* (Bella Books, July, 2005,) an anthology of supernatural tales; her short story, "My Favorite Mechanic," appeared in the *Romance for LIFE anthology* (Intaglio Publications, February, 2006.)

Jane was born and raised in a farming community in northwestern Minnesota, where she received her elementary education in a one-room country schoolhouse (obviously, more than just a few years ago.) She holds a Bachelors' degree from St. Cloud (Minnesota) State University and is a member of Lambda Iota Tau, an international literature honors society. In late 2005, she retired from Federal civil service after more than three decades with the same agency. She is now gleefully pursuing her new career as an author and editor.

She lives in the foothills of the north Georgia mountains with her many cats. In addition to spending time at the computer writing and editing books, Jane enjoys tending her gardens, feeding the wildlife on her property, and playing the piano. She encourages you to visit her via her website at www.janevollbrecht.com.

VISIT US ONLINE AT

www.regalcrest.biz

At the Regal Crest Website You'll Find

- The latest news about forthcoming titles and new releases

- Our complete backlist of romance, mystery, thriller and adventure titles

- Information about your favorite authors

- Current bestsellers

- Media tearsheets to print and take with you when you shop

Regal Crest titles are available from all progressive booksellers and online at StarCrossed Productions, (www.scp-inc.biz), or at www.amazon.com, www.bamm.com, www.barnesandnoble.com, and many others.

Printed in the United States
120812LV00008B/30/A